D0065521

HIGH HEAT

HIGH HEAT

by Carl Deuker

Houghton Mifflin Company
Boston 2003

The text of this book is set in Stone Serif.

Library of Congress Cataloging-in-Publication Data

Deuker, Carl.
High heat / Carl Deuker.
p. cm.
Summary: When sophomore Shane Hunter's father is arrested for money
laundering at his Lexus dealership, the star pitcher's life of affluence
and private school begins to fall apart.
ISBN 0-618-31117-3
[1. Fathers—Fiction. 2. Family problems—Fiction. 3.
Baseball—Fiction. 4. High schools—Fiction. 5. Schools—Fiction. 6.
Suicide—Fiction.] I. Title.
PZ7.D493 Hi 2003
[Fic]—dc21
2002015324

Manufactured in the United States of America
QUM 10 9 8 7 6 5 4 3 2

For Anne and Marian, who helped with all of it.

*I would like to thank Ann Rider, the editor of this book,
for her help and encouragement.*

PART ONE

CHAPTER 1 I'm a closer, so I can't live and die on every pitch, especially in the early innings of a game. I watch, of course. I want to know which batters swing at which pitches. But I watch with half an eye, filing things away. I've got to stay loose and relaxed, because my time comes later.

Things had been going well for me and for Shorelake, my high school team. We were 5–0 on the season, and I had three saves, which means there'd been three times when everybody had surrounded me on the mound to shake my hand and tell me what a fantastic job I'd done. There's no better feeling in the world.

We were playing on our home field. It's the best baseball diamond in Seattle, with lush outfield grass, a perfectly smooth infield, and great dugouts. You'd expect that, since Shorelake Academy is the most expensive school in Seattle. Greg Taylor, my best friend, had just smacked a leadoff home run to put us ahead of Cedarcrest by a run. I high-fived him when he returned to the bench. Greg and Cody Miller and I were the only sophomores on the team, and the three of us were the team clowns, too. We pulled practical jokes all the time, like tying guys' shoes together or putting worms in their water bottles. Stupid stuff, but it was fun, so why not do it? I got that from my dad. He was always pulling jokes on people, making them look silly.

Greg stuffed his mouth with sunflower seeds. I grabbed some out of his bag, and Cody did the same. The three of us sat there spitting shells at guys' feet as Ted Hearn, our catcher, stepped up to the plate to take his cuts.

It was Greg who spotted the bald eagle. He pointed to it as it came out of the woods east of the baseball diamond. The bird was huge, and it glided effortlessly across the sky before disappearing over a tall stand of trees directly behind the parking lot. I watched the spot where I'd last seen it for a while, hoping it would return.

When I lowered my eyes, I noticed a big American car, a Ford or Chrysler, pull into the parking lot. That struck me as strange. The game had been going for nearly an hour. Who'd be coming now?

Two men got out, one of them a little guy who was nearly bald and the other much bigger and younger, built like a professional football player. He wore dark sunglasses and had a dark beard. Both of them wore coats and ties. Cody noticed them too. "Who are those guys?" he asked.

"Beats me," Greg answered, "but the little guy looks just like Mrs. Judd." Mrs. Judd was our social studies teacher. Cody laughed, and then their eyes went back to the game.

I didn't laugh, and my eyes didn't go back to the game. I knew the short guy. His name was Rausch. He'd been by our house a couple of times to talk to my father. I didn't know what he did or whether he had anything to do with my dad's Lexus dealership, but I knew my dad hated him.

I heard a bat make solid contact and looked back to the game. Hearn had smacked a single into left center. Our fans rose and cheered, and I did too. But when I sat back down, my eyes returned to Rausch. He was standing behind my dad's car, writing something in a notepad.

I looked into the bleachers to where Dad was sitting. He was right in the middle of all the parents, where he always sat. But he was quiet, which wasn't like him. The other parents' eyes were riveted on the game, but his eyes were on Rausch and his partner.

Rausch and the bearded man were crossing the parking lot, heading toward the bleachers. They walked fast—the way people at an airport walk when they're late for a plane. Cody was telling some long, drawn-out joke, and there was a bunch of talk up and down the bench and in the stands. When Rausch finally reached the bleachers, he didn't speak loudly, but I heard every word. "Mr. Hunter, would you please step out of the bleachers?"

I wasn't the only one who had heard. The parents—Mr. Miller, Mrs. Hearn—all of them turned their eyes toward my dad.

My dad looked down at Rausch. "It's Saturday afternoon. I'm watching my son's game. If you want to talk to me, call the dealership and make an appointment with my secretary."

"Strike three!" the umpire yelled. I glanced toward home plate to see Brian Coombs heading back to the bench, his bat dragging.

Cody stopped telling his joke. Greg nudged me. "What's going on, Shane?"

I didn't answer. My heart was pounding the way it does when I'm pitching with the game on the line. Things flashed through my mind: the phone calls in the middle of the night, the strange packages at our door, the jumpy way Mom had been acting.

"Don't make this difficult, Mr. Hunter," Rausch said calmly, and now everyone in the stands and half the players on the bench were watching. "Just step down out of the bleachers."

"I told you. If you want to talk to me, call my secretary."

"Have it your way," Rausch said. He reached into his back pocket, pulled out his wallet, opened it, and showed it to the parents sitting in the bleachers. "Police business," he called out. "I'd like you to move away. Now."

My dad didn't budge, but all around him was motion. The bleachers emptied, men and women scurrying off as if some sewer rat had just crawled up their pant leg. Within seconds it was just Rausch, the bearded man, and my dad.

"Mr. Hunter," Rausch said in a ringing voice, "you are under arrest. Put your hands on top of your head and come down out of the bleachers."

Dad smiled a crooked smile. "You're being ridiculous."

"Put your hands on your head," Rausch repeated, "and come down now."

The smile disappeared from my father's face. "I'll have your job for this."

"Come down out of the stands, Mr. Hunter."

Dad's eyes went steely. "Come get me."

Rausch looked at his partner, then the two of them started up the bleachers. When the bearded man grabbed his elbow, my dad twisted away.

My dad is big—he played first base and batted cleanup at Washington State—but Rausch's partner was both bigger and younger. He grabbed my father, pulling him forward and causing him to lose his balance and fall. In a flash the big man and Rausch were both on him, pushing his face down onto the metal bleacher. Then the bearded man yanked his arms up behind him, and Rausch snapped handcuffs on him. Next, Rausch planted his knee in my dad's back and kept him pinned while he patted down his pockets. Finally they yanked him to his feet.

Rausch took out a card and started reading. "You have the right to remain silent. You have the right to . . ." As he spoke, the two of them were half pushing, half walking my father toward the parking lot.

Dad turned back to me. "Shane," he called, "don't worry. This is all a mistake. Do you hear me? I'll be home before you are."

I stared after him, watching as the bearded man pushed him into the back seat of what I now knew to be an unmarked police car, watching it pull out of the parking lot, tires squealing. I stared until the car was completely out of sight.

That's when I looked around. The game had come to a

halt. Everyone on my team, everyone on the other team, the umpires, the parents—everyone was staring at me.

In the movies the heroes take on the crowds. "What are you looking at?" they shout, and the people look away. But I slumped down onto the bench, pulled my cap over my eyes, and kept them glued to the ground. The umpire yelled, "Batter up!" I guess somebody stepped to the plate, but I didn't watch.

It was the fourth inning when they took my dad away. I kept my head down for the rest of the game. Somehow I didn't feel real, if that makes any sense. It was as if I had no weight, no substance—as if I wasn't really there.

I knew the innings were moving by only because I could feel Greg and Cody sitting next to me, then leave to go to their positions, then return. I didn't look up until there were two outs in the last inning. Somehow I could just sense that the game was ending. Scott Parino, our pitcher, threw a strike, then a ball, then the Cedarcrest batter hit a little pop-up to first. We'd won, but there was only the barest applause from the parents behind us. Players on both teams shook hands quickly, packed up their gear, and headed to the parking lot. Some peeked over at me. Most didn't.

It wasn't until nearly everyone was gone that Greg's dad came over. "I'll give you a ride home, Shane."

Greg's house was in Sound Ridge, down the road from mine.

"That's okay, Mr. Taylor," I answered. "I can get home."

"How? You're five miles away. That's too far to walk. Come with me."

He was trying to be nice, but I couldn't bear the thought of sitting with him.

"I'll call my mom."

Coach Levine came over. "I'll give Shane a ride."

I looked to Greg's dad. "I'll go with Coach," I said.

He nodded. "Sure, Shane. Whatever you want."

CHAPTER 2 In the car Coach Levine didn't say anything to me. He drove along 130th until we reached Greenwood. From there I gave him directions to Sound Ridge, which isn't the kind of neighborhood a teacher could afford.

When we reached the gated entrance, Simon Chang, the security guard, stepped out of his small brick guardhouse and approached Levine's car. "Can I help you?" he asked, his voice courteous but remote.

I leaned across toward him. "It's me, Simon. Shane Hunter."

Simon always asked how my pitching was going. But that day he only nodded, then pushed the button. The gate opened and Levine drove through.

I directed Levine through the winding streets to my house. When we could finally see it, I understood why Simon had been so quiet. Three police cars were parked in front. Uniformed officers were walking down our driveway carrying away boxes filled with file folders.

Levine hadn't come to a complete stop, but I grabbed my equipment, opened the door, and jumped out of his car. "Wait a second, Shane," he called out, but I didn't wait. I ran up the long walkway and threw open my front door.

Rausch was sitting on the sofa looking at a clipboard. Mom

was across from him; she had a dazed look on her face. Rausch stood up. "I'm sorry about today, son," he said, "but your—"

"What's he doing here?" I said, turning to my mom. "Tell him to get out."

"He'll be leaving soon," Mom said, her voice not much more than a whisper.

"Tell him to get out now. This is our house."

"Shane, that's enough," Mom said, snapping out of her apathy. "These men have work to do. When they're done, they'll leave. Now let them do it."

My mother's words stung, making me feel childish, but I couldn't let Rausch know that. I glared at him before heading upstairs to my room.

It took a while to reach it. That house was huge—the garage alone was probably bigger than the little duplex we live in now. We had an exercise room, a computer room, an entertainment room, and other rooms I can't remember anymore. It seemed as if a police officer was in every one of them.

I wanted to be alone, but when I reached my room, my sister, Marian, was sitting at my desk, a plateful of Oreos and a glass of milk in front of her. She hadn't touched either. "Shane, what's happening?" she asked, her eyes watery.

Marian is five years younger than me, but she's smart, so I couldn't bluff her. "I don't know for sure," I said. "Dad's in some kind of trouble, though."

"Is he in jail?"

"He'll be back tonight, or tomorrow at the latest."

She sat there looking at me. "He is in jail, isn't he?"

"Yes, he's in jail." I waited a minute. "You want to watch a movie?"

"No," she said.

"Come on, Marian. You might as well. I'll watch with you."

"What do you want to watch?"

"I don't know. You pick."

She went to her room and got part one of *The Lord of the Rings*. I popped it into my DVD player, and turned the volume up. We sat on my bed, watching Frodo Baggins escape one danger after another. All the time, we could hear men and women talking as they opened and closed file cabinets and moved up and down the stairs.

CHAPTER 3 They didn't leave until eight. As soon as they were gone, Mom came up. "Let's go eat," she said.

"I'm not hungry," I answered.

"Neither am I," Marian said.

"Well, I am," she said, "so we're going."

We went to the Red Mill on Greenwood, not a place we usually go. I didn't think I'd be able to eat, but once I smelled the food, I was suddenly starving. I felt guilty ordering a hamburger and even more guilty eating it, but I finished the whole thing. Marian ate everything on her plate, too. It was Mom who pushed her food around.

Back home there was a message on the answering machine. Mom turned the volume down, but I recognized the voice. It was Mr. Anderson, Dad's lawyer. I thought Mom would call him right back, but instead she had Marian shower and brush her teeth. Then she walked her up to her bedroom and sat with her, staying longer than usual. When she finally left Marian's room, she went straight to Dad's office and closed the door.

I left my own door open so I'd hear her when she headed back downstairs. Fifteen minutes passed, then another fifteen, then another. She stayed on the phone for over an hour before she finally hung up.

I stepped out of my room. "Mom," I said as she came toward me.

She put her finger to her lips. "Shhh." Then she nodded toward Marian's room.

I followed her downstairs. She went to the kitchen and poured herself a glass of wine. That wasn't so unusual; she drank wine lots of times. But after sitting down at the breakfast table in the now-dark sunroom, she reached into her purse, pulled out a pack of cigarettes, and lit one.

"What are you doing?" I said. "You don't smoke."

"I started smoking when I was your age," she said in a matter-of-fact tone. "And I didn't stop until I became pregnant with you. It was very hard for me to stop, and I don't plan on starting up again. But right now I need a cigarette. So don't say anything more, okay?"

I didn't. Instead I pulled back the chair and sat across from her. "What did Dad's lawyer say?" I asked. She looked at me, surprised. "That's who you were talking to, wasn't it?"

"He explained to me why your dad was arrested."

I waited, but she didn't say anything. "So what did they charge him with?"

She sucked on her cigarette and blew out a long, thin cloud of whitish smoke. "Money laundering."

I'd heard that expression before, but I didn't know what it meant. "What's that?"

She shook her head. "It's too complicated to explain. All you need to know is that your father is innocent."

"Mom. I'm not a little kid. Tell me what it means."

She looked at me long and hard. "Okay. Let's say somebody gets money from illegal things."

"Like from selling drugs?"

Her eyebrows went up. "Yeah, like from drugs. So they can't put a whole bunch of cash into the bank without raising questions."

"Why not?"

"They just can't. Banks have rules. They have to report any person who brings in a large amount of cash. Drug dealers use ordinary businesses to make the money look like it's from something legitimate. Businesses like your dad's."

"What do they say Dad did?"

She sucked on her cigarette again, turned her face away from me, and exhaled. "The police say that drug dealers bought cars from your dad, paying cash for them. They say your dad put the cash in the bank, then turned around and bought the cars back at a lower price a couple of months later, paying with a check. Once the drug dealers had a check, they could deposit the money because it came from a real business." She stopped. "Are you following this?"

"Sort of. What does Dad say?"

She sipped her wine, took another drag of her cigarette, then looked out the window. "The truth. That he didn't know he was involved with drug dealers. That he was only buying and selling cars, just like he does with everyone."

"But they can't keep Dad in jail once they see he's innocent, can they? They'll have to let him go."

"It's not that simple, Shane."

I thought about Rausch, his clipboard, and all the men taking files out to the cars in front of our house. There were so many people against him.

"What do we do now?"

Mom stubbed out her cigarette. "The first thing is to get your dad out of jail. Mr. Anderson is working with a bail bondsman, so that should happen soon."

"How much is bail?" I asked.

"You don't have to worry about that, Shane."

"Do we have enough money?"

She lit another cigarette. "Yes, we do."

CHAPTER 4 Dad didn't come home on Sunday morning or Sunday afternoon. It wasn't until after dinner that we heard a car pull up and the door slam shut. I went to the window and looked out. He was whistling as he came up the walkway.

Marian raced to him and hugged him as soon as he stepped in the doorway. "Come on," he said, "can't you do better than that? How about a monster hug?"

That was one of their jokes. She jumped into his arms and squeezed as hard as she could. He puffed and groaned. "You're so strong. You're going to crush me to death." He put her down and turned to me. "How about you, Shane? Are you too old to give your dad a hug?"

"No," I said. I stepped toward him, and he gave me a long hug.

Then he looked at Mom. I could tell he wanted to hug her too, but she only smiled, went to the love seat by the window, lit what seemed like her fiftieth cigarette of the day, pulled her legs up onto the sofa, and looked out the window.

He took a deep breath, exhaled, then looked from me to Marian, from Marian to me. "All right, let's get a couple of things straight around here. The next few months aren't going to be easy, and there is no sense in pretending they will be. You're going to hear a lot of things about me. But no matter what you read in the paper or what your friends might say at school, I want you to know that I've done nothing wrong. Do you understand? Nothing. If we stick together, we'll get through this, and we'll be stronger for it. Okay?"

Marian nodded, and so did I.

Dad turned to Mom, but she was still looking out the window. He watched her for a moment, then swung back to Marian and me. "How about a game of Monopoly? Just the three of us. What do you say?"

Marian had just discovered Monopoly and always wanted to play, but usually she couldn't get anyone to play with her. Her eyes brightened at his suggestion. I didn't feel like playing, but I knew Dad was trying to cheer her up, so I went along.

I set up the board, passed out the money and pieces. On his first turn Dad rolled a four—income tax. "That's perfect!" he roared as he moved the little dog forward. "Absolutely perfect."

Throughout the game he kept losing track of his turn, of his playing piece, of his properties. I wasn't much better. When Marian finally won, he put his hands on the table and looked her in the eye. "You're going to be the tycoon in this family, little lady. But now it's time you went to bed. Way past time, in fact."

Marian smiled and kissed Dad good night, but he hadn't fooled her. Just like me, she'd noticed that Mom had spent the whole evening drinking wine, smoking cigarettes, and looking out the window. And she knew that his big smile and loud laughter were fake.

I put all the Monopoly stuff back in the box, then said good night myself. Upstairs, I stuck a Lauryn Hill CD into my sound system and put my earphones on so I wouldn't disturb anyone, but after about two minutes her music seemed stupid, so I turned it off. Below me I could hear my parents talking, their voices low and serious. I opened my door and listened; I could pick up only a word here and there—nothing I could make any sense of.

CHAPTER 5 Neither Marian nor I went to school on Monday. I didn't want to go on Tuesday either, but Dad wasn't having any of that. "I pay big bucks for Shorelake," he said, still smiling too much. "You get yourself dressed, Shane. I'll drive you. You too, Marian."

As he drove us to school, Dad listened to a seventies station and sang along with the songs. The more he sang, the sicker I felt. When I stepped out of the car, it was all I could do to stand. "Bye, Dad!" Marian called back to him. She was better at play-acting than me.

There's a long set of stairs that leads up to the Shorelake campus. My legs kept wanting to give out from under me. Marian was silent. At the first pathway, she broke off from me and headed toward the lower campus. "See ya, Shane," she said, her voice small.

"Yeah. See ya."

I hadn't even reached the flagpole when Greg came rushing over. "You okay?"

"Yeah. Sure," I said, my throat tight. "Why wouldn't I be?"

"I was worried about you. We all were. You know, with what happened to your dad, and you not being here yesterday."

I shrugged. "That? That was just some police screwup. They don't know what they're doing. My dad drove me to school this morning. Everything's fine."

Greg nodded. "My mom and dad told me to tell you that if you need anything, or if your mom does, you should call us. My dad's a trial lawyer, you know."

The blood rushed to my face. I could hear them talking about us at dinner. "I just told you it was a screwup, Greg. We don't need a lawyer."

"If you do, though, later on. My dad said—"

"We won't, Greg. Okay? How many times do I have to say it?"

He stepped back. "Sorry. I was just trying to help."

"Look," I said, "I've got to go to the library to look some stuff up. I'll see you around."

Before I'd gone twenty feet, he called out. "Shane, you're going to be at practice, aren't you?"

"Why wouldn't I?"

He waved me off. "No reason. I was just checking."

In the hundred-year history of Shorelake, my dad was probably the first parent who'd ever been arrested. In every class that day the kids were polite to me, the teachers kind. It was as if I had some horrible skin disease, but they were going to show their good manners by pretending not to notice.

During lunchtime, I stayed behind in Mrs. Goure's biology class and ate there. I couldn't bear going to the cafeteria and facing a roomful of sympathetic faces. When school ended, I headed off to practice without waiting for Greg and Cody by the fountain as usual. I dressed in a corner of the locker room and then headed to the field.

Crossing from the outfield grass to the infield dirt, I saw Scott Parino and Terry Clarke, our two starting pitchers, standing together at the mound, whispering behind their gloves, grinning away.

"What's so funny?" I said.

"What?" Parino said, looking at me as if he didn't know who I was.

"You heard me, Parino. I want to know what you're laughing at."

"None of your business, Hunter," Parino answered.

I took a step toward him, squaring up with him. He was a little bigger than me, but not much. Besides, there was a softness to his face, to his belly, and I felt like cold steel inside. "It *is* my business," I said.

Clarke stepped between us. "He told you it was none of

your business, so get yourself away from here and leave us alone."

"I'm not leaving him alone and I'm not leaving you alone until you tell me what you were laughing at."

Clarke's face hardened. "It wasn't your jailbird father, if that's what you're thinking."

In an instant I'd charged him, knocking him to the ground. A second later I was on top of him, smacking him in the face. Left and right and left and right. If he hadn't had his arms up, and if Parino weren't grabbing at me to pull me off, I would have broken his nose and blackened both eyes. Still, I hit him hard enough to make his nose bleed, but he didn't hit me at all. Then I felt another pair of hands grab hold of me.

It was Coach Levine. He yanked me to my feet and held me by the shoulders to keep me from going after Clarke and Parino. "What's this all about?" he demanded.

"He started it," Clarke said, wiping the blood from his nose and pointing at me. "The guy's crazy. We were just telling jokes over there, and he comes sticking his nose in, thinking we're making fun of his old man, all ready to fight."

"Were you making fun of his father?" Levine asked.

"Hell, no," Clarke said. "What do I care about his father?"

Levine looked to Parino. "We weren't, Coach. We were talking about something that happened in history class. Mickey West had his . . ."

I don't know what he said after that. Some stupid story. All I know is that it was obvious he was telling the truth, just as it was obvious I'd made a fool of myself. My body went limp. Levine felt me relax and let me go.

"All right," he said. "Enough of this. Let's get to practice."

"That's it?" Clarke said, wiping his nose. "The little jerk hits me and you're not going to suspend him from the team?"

"You trying to tell me how to run the team?"

Clarke stared at Levine for a second, then turned and headed to the mound.

Levine walked me to the outfield. His voice was low, so low I could barely hear it. "You had it in you, Shane. To hit somebody, I mean. Now you've done it, and it's over. Any more fights and I will suspend you, from the team and from school. You understand?"

I nodded.

"All right then. Get out there and stretch."

I found an empty spot in center field. I could feel the eyes of every player on the team watching me. Again. I made a vow to myself. I'd cracked once, but I wasn't going to crack again. From that moment on, everything was going to stay inside.

CHAPTER 6 We had a game against Sammamish High on Thursday. Sammamish is a long way from Sound Ridge, and I wasn't sure how I was going to get there. Dad was busy with his lawyer all the time, and I didn't want him to drive me anyway. Marian wouldn't go see her friends, so Mom had to look after her. I didn't want to ask Greg or Cody. Then, after Wednesday's practice, Coach Levine pulled me aside. "If you need a ride tomorrow, meet me by the gym after school. I could use some help with the gear."

When I got home that night, dinner was over. Mom was

in the kitchen, loading the dishwasher; Dad was upstairs in his office, his head bent over a stack of papers, a glass of Scotch on his desk. I peeked into Marian's room. She was at her desk drawing, the pencil tight in her hand. One of her pet rats was perched on her shoulder. I went to my room, emptied my backpack, and flicked on the television. Mom brought me a sandwich, and as I ate, I half watched the Atlanta Braves get demolished by the Giants.

At breakfast the next morning Mom made toast for Marian and me, but she didn't eat anything herself. Just before she was going to take us to school, Dad came down. "I'll drive them," he said.

He was hung over. I could see it in his eyes and in the way the skin on his face sagged. For most of the ride he didn't say anything. When we were about ten blocks from Shorelake, he looked at me. "You've got a game today, right? Against Sammamish."

"Yeah," I said.

"Okay then. I'll pick you up right after school." He turned to the back seat and looked at Marian. "You don't mind going to Shane's game today, do you?"

Her whole face dropped, but he didn't seem to notice. "No, I'll go," she said.

"That's my girl."

A cold wave washed over me. "You don't have to take me, Dad," I said, keeping my voice casual. "Coach Levine is giving me a ride. I've already talked to him."

His eyes fixed on me. "Are you ashamed of me, Shane? Is that it?"

"No," I protested. "That's not it at all."

"Then why don't you want me at your game?"

"It's not that I don't want you at the game. It's only that I know you're busy. Besides, Marian doesn't want to go to my game."

"Maybe Mom could pick me up," Marian said.

"Sure she can," Dad said as he pulled up in front of the school. "All right then, it's settled. Your mom will pick you up, Marian. And Shane, I'll meet you right here at three-ten."

He was late. For twenty minutes I stood in front of the school, wondering if he was coming at all. Finally the Lexus pulled up. I hustled down the stairs and slid in. Right away I could smell the whiskey.

The Sammamish plateau is about thirty minutes from Seattle. Usually when Dad's been drinking, he talks a lot and in a loud voice. That day he didn't say anything, but when a lady in an old green Plymouth Valiant was poking along in front of him, he laid on the horn, then drove onto the shoulder and passed her on the right, nearly cutting her off.

I was the last player to arrive. I rushed out to where the pitchers and catchers were warming up, but I'd hardly had a chance to loosen up before Coach Levine motioned to us to head to the dugout.

As I ran in, I looked up into the bleachers and spotted my dad. He'd found a place in the very top row, sitting right above our bench. No parent was within five feet of him, as if he was one of those homeless people in the library who smell so bad they get a whole table to themselves.

"Play ball!" the ump yelled.

My dad is always razzing the umpires or shouting down advice to Coach Levine. I was afraid he'd be louder than usual, trying to show everybody that everything was normal. Instead, he was so quiet I kept looking around to see if he was still there. And every time I looked, it was the same: his eyes were on the field, but they weren't seeing the game.

We jumped out to a 4–0 lead in the third inning on three doubles, two walks, and an error. Scott Parino wasn't sharp on the mound—lots of balls were hard hit—but he was hanging in there. Then, in the bottom of the fourth, he gave up a single and a walk to Sammamish's first two batters. The next guy popped out to first base, but the batter after that drove in both runners with a double down the third base line.

Parino stranded him at second, but Sammamish loaded the bases in the top of the sixth. From behind me I heard parents cheering Parino, yet it was the one voice I didn't hear that made my head pound.

When the last inning finally rolled around, Levine sent me down with Bill Diggs to warm up. I thought I'd feel better once I was doing something. I threw easily to Diggs, stretching my arm and my back out. To anybody watching, everything looked normal, but I felt as if I were leaning over the Grand Canyon.

Out of the corner of my eye I watched Robby Richardson ground out to end our half of the inning. Levine pointed his finger at me, then headed to home plate to tell the umpire I was coming in. "Go get 'em," Diggs said as I walked past him.

People say the mental part of being a closer is hard, but I love the challenge. I close out games by closing off everything that isn't essential. I don't hear anything I don't need to hear; I don't see anything I don't need to see. I focus on home plate, the catcher's glove, and the ball in my hand. When that's my whole world, I'm in control.

But that day I heard the buzzing in the stands, felt the difference in the way people looked at me. I knew my dad was in the stands watching me, counting on me to show them all.

I gave myself a shake; I had to focus. I looked to Ted Hearn for the sign, then went into my wind-up and delivered. My motion was almost right, but almost doesn't cut it. "Ball one!" the umpire roared as my pitch sailed high. The ball came back to me. Seconds later I was delivering another pitch. "Ball two!" Then "Ball three!" And "Ball four!" The batter trotted to first. Levine stood and leaned against the fence. Up in the bleachers my dad stood. "Come on, Shane!" he shouted, breaking his game-long silence.

A new batter stepped in. My head was spinning. I squeezed the ball tight . . . too tight. "Ball one! Ball two! Ball three! Take your base!"

Levine trotted out. "You okay?"

"Yeah," I said, though the roaring inside my brain was so loud I could hardly hear him.

"All right then. Do it."

From the bleachers I heard my dad. "Throw strikes, Shane! Throw strikes!"

Hearn flashed the sign: fastball. I nodded, checked the runners, delivered. Normally the ball explodes out of my hand. But this fastball was a joke; it went right over the heart of the plate, with no speed and no movement.

The guy's bat came through the strike zone like lightning. The sound told the whole story. He got it all—a towering drive to left field. Our left fielder, Alvin Powell, just looked up and watched it fly far over the fence and onto the soccer field behind. The hitter pumped his fist in the air as he rounded first base. The Sammamish guys swarmed him as he touched home plate.

My teammates stood at their positions and watched Sammamish celebrate, too stunned to move. Finally Greg trotted in, and the others trailed behind. Only I stayed put. Levine finally came out and got me. "It happens to every closer sometime. You'll get 'em next time, Shane."

I packed my stuff quickly and cleared out. In the car, neither my dad nor I said anything as we cruised along the freeway. "Was it me, Shane?" he finally asked when we were five minutes from our home. "Tell me the truth."

"It wasn't you. I just had a bad game."

He looked straight ahead. "Because if it was me, you say the word, and I'll stay away from your games."

"It wasn't you, Dad," I repeated, my voice rising.

He turned into Sound Ridge, waving to Simon as we drove through the gate. "We may be down, Shane, but we're not out. We're going to beat them. It may take a while, but we're going to come out on top."

Our next game was at home on Saturday afternoon against Liberty, a terrible team. "Why don't you skip this one," I told Dad that morning. "We're going to kill them. There's a ninety-nine percent chance I won't even pitch."

"I'm not skipping any of your games," he said. "Besides, don't be so sure of yourself. That's how good teams lose."

All morning I watched him closely, looking to see if he was drinking. I never saw him go to the liquor cabinet, never smelled anything on his breath. But he wasn't right in the car, and he wasn't right in the stands. It was that silence again, that silence that wasn't him.

A blowout. That's what I wanted. A game where we would score twelve runs in the first three innings. Then if I pitched or didn't pitch, it wouldn't matter. I needed some time to catch my breath, to pull myself together.

But Liberty saved their best game of the year for us. In the field their guys were making one great play after another, and with each solid play you could feel their confidence soar. They scored twice in the third, and that 2–0 lead held all the way to the bottom of the sixth.

That's when their starter ran out of gas. His pitches lost velocity, and they were all belt high. Two singles and a passed ball brought our right fielder, Beanie Cutler, to the plate with a chance to tie the game. "Just give us a little hit!" guys shouted from the bench.

Cutler stepped in, then drove the first pitch he saw off the center-field wall on a bounce. Both base runners scored easily. When the Liberty center fielder couldn't find the handle on the ball, Cutler took off for third. The relay from the shortstop was wild, sailing into the fence. "Go!" Coach Levine shouted, and Cutler was off for home. He slid home ahead of the throw, and just like that we were up one run.

"Shane!" Levine called to me. "Get warmed up."

I didn't have much time. Our next two batters hit the ball hard, but right at their shortstop. I'd thrown only about ten pitches along the sideline when I found myself heading out to the mound to protect a one-run lead.

As I took my warm-up tosses, I told myself that the last game had been a fluke, that I was the same pitcher I always was, and that I was better than the Liberty batters—a lot better. But when the first hitter stepped in, there was a roaring inside my brain, like a 747 taking off.

The inning was a nightmare. I walked the first batter on four pitches—none of them close to the plate. I hit the next batter in the foot with a fastball. Levine came out and said something—I don't know what. Liberty's DH ripped the second pitch he saw into the rightfield corner for a triple. After that I don't remember much. I know that there were at least two more doubles, and four more runs scored, and the last out was a fly ball to center that missed being a grand slam by about ten feet.

The ride home was eerie. In the past when I'd screwed up, my dad rode me hard, going over every little thing I'd done wrong. I never liked being yelled at, but now I wanted him to chew me out. I wanted him to be him. I should have said something. If not to him, then to Mom. I knew something was wrong, but I just stayed quiet.

That night Marian had her first nightmare. Her screams woke me up. I hurried to her room, but Mom was already there, holding her tight, rocking her back and forth. "Hush, hush," Mom whispered, "I'm right here."

CHAPTER 7 Monday morning I thought I was the first one up, but when I went downstairs I saw Dad in the sunroom overlooking our backyard, the *Seattle Times* spread in front of him. When he noticed me, he quickly folded the local section of the paper and stuffed it into the pocket of his robe. "You're up early, Shane."

"A little."

"Sit down. I'll make you some hot chocolate."

"You don't have to."

"I want to," he said, and he went through the double glass doors into the kitchen.

In my whole life he'd never made me hot chocolate, and I wasn't sure he knew how to do it, but he managed okay. "It's good," I said, after taking a sip of the steaming cup he placed in front of me.

He stood watching me drink as if he'd never seen me before.

"Everything okay?" I asked.

"Of course everything is okay. What wouldn't be okay?"

"I don't know. Nothing."

A minute ticked away. Another. In the yard a robin was hunting worms.

"You like Shorelake?" he asked.

"Yeah, I guess."

"Did you ever think about going to another school? Maybe Whitman?"

For a moment I didn't understand. Whitman was the closest public high school, but Dad hated the public schools. He insisted they were full of drugs and guns and kids who didn't know how to read but got straight A's anyway.

Then I understood.

Money.

"I guess it would be okay. I just don't know anybody who goes to Whitman."

He tilted his head. "You could make friends anywhere, Shane." He paused. "But if you want to stay at Shorelake, you'll stay at Shorelake."

"No, Dad," I said. "I don't have to stay at Shorelake. I'll go to Whitman. Really."

He reached over and squeezed my shoulder. "We'll put it on the back burner for now. Nothing has to be decided right away." He paused. "Don't mention anything about changing schools to your mother or sister, okay?"

At school that morning, I headed straight to the library. The *Times* was on a rack right by the front door. You're not supposed to take newspapers away from the periodicals section, but I waited until Mrs. Johnson, the librarian, wasn't looking, tucked it under my coat, and headed to the back corner.

I pulled the local section out. On the front page was a photograph of the big billboard in front of my dad's Lexus dealership. His face was grinning out. To the side, in big bold letters, was the headline: "Car Dealer Linked to Drug Lords." And then in smaller type: "Accountant Cooperating with Police."

I read through the article slowly, but all I could take in were phrases. "Mexican drug kingpins . . . phony transactions . . . racketeering charges . . . prison."

CHAPTER 8 "I have a meeting today," Dad said when he came downstairs the next morning. "I might be able to make it to the game, but I'll be late. You'll have to get a ride from somebody else." His face was a pasty white; his voice quavered.

I was in the breakfast nook with Marian and my mother. All of us were halfheartedly eating microwaved waffles. "Don't worry about it, Dad," I said. "Coach can take me."

He turned and went through the kitchen, into the small library off the living room. Mom excused herself and followed. I couldn't see them, but I heard them talking in low tones. I poked at my waffle. Marian's face was long; her brown eyes were sad. I wanted to tell her that everything was going to be okay, but I couldn't say the words.

A few minutes later Dad came back, without Mom. He crouched next to Marian and took her hands in his. "I want you to know," he said softly, "that I love you." He looked at me. "That I love both of you. You know that, don't you?"

"Yes," Marian said.

I nodded.

He stood to his full height. "Good luck with your game." Then he went through the door leading to the garage. A couple of minutes later I heard his car race down the block.

By then Mom had returned. Marian looked at her. "What's happening?"

"Your dad has a meeting, honey. That's all."

"Is something bad going to happen to him?"

"Remember what your dad said. As long as we stick by one another, nothing really bad can happen to any of us. Right?"

• • •

Our game was against Inglemoor High, a big suburban school on the north shore of Lake Washington. I thought about telling Coach Levine I was feeling sick and skipping the game. What difference would it make to anybody? He'd given me two chances, and I'd blown them both. He wouldn't give me a third. Besides, it didn't seem right to be playing a baseball game with my dad in trouble.

But I didn't want to go home to Mom with her cigarettes and Marian with her sad face, so when school ended I made my way to Coach Levine's office. "Can you give me a ride to the game?" I asked.

"Anytime." He pointed to a duffel bag filled with baseballs and catcher's gear. "Give me a hand with that?"

I was afraid he'd want to make small talk as we drove, but instead he tuned the radio to KJR, and for the entire ride we listened to callers grouse about the Mariners or the Sonics. As we pulled into the parking lot by the field, he reached forward and flicked the radio off. "Look, Shane," he said, turning toward me, "I read the newspaper. I know this is a tough time for you and your family—"

"I know what you're going to say," I said, interrupting. "That you're not going to pitch me for a while. I understand. I've stunk it up; it's what I deserve."

"You should let people finish, Shane. Because I was going to say the exact opposite. I think that you need to keep pitching. That you need baseball; that baseball might keep you from going crazy." He paused. "Besides, without solid relief pitching, Clarke and Parino will wear out, pure and simple. If we're going to get anywhere in the playoffs, we're going to need you. But you've got to be clear in your head. When you're out on the mound, you have to think baseball and leave the other stuff behind. So what do you say? Can you do that?"

"I'll try."

In the early innings, I kept checking the parking lot, half expecting to see my dad's Lexus. But it wasn't there and it wasn't there and it wasn't there. Finally I knew he wasn't coming, and I was able to watch the baseball game.

It was a tight game. Inglemoor's pitcher had been All-League the year before. A lefty, he had long brown hair and a fastball that seemed to come from first base. He had our batters backing away from the plate, taking feeble swings. The only hit we got was a little dribbler up the third base line in the fourth that Greg beat out.

Terry Clarke started for us. He wasn't as good, but he was lucky, and that works too. Inglemoor had some solid hits—a couple of doubles and one triple—but they couldn't put anything together. After six innings the game was scoreless.

Then, with one out in the top of the seventh, their pitcher plunked Beanie Cutler in the back with a sailing fastball. Cutler went down hard, and stayed down for a couple of minutes. That seemed to rattle the pitcher, because he walked Stan Cantfield, our next hitter, on four pitches—all of which were way outside. Two on with one out was the closest thing to a rally we'd had all game. If we could squeeze across one run, we might steal a victory.

That's when I heard Levine's voice. "Hunter, get ready."

There are some days when you just have it. The ball fit perfectly between my fingertips, as if it were made only for me. My pitches were popping Bill Diggs's glove. I felt loose and fast.

But it didn't look as if I'd get in, at least not then. Whatever their coach said worked, because our next hitter, Alvin Powell, went down on three fastball strikes. That meant it was up to Andy Chase, and Chase had already struck out swinging twice. If he made an out, Levine would probably send Clarke back out to the mound and save me in case the game went into extra innings.

The pitcher got two quick strikes on Chase, then barely missed getting a called strike three. The next pitch was some sort of changeup. Chase was way out in front, but he did manage to hold back his swing enough to slice a pop-up down the first base line.

It was trouble for Inglemoor the minute it left the bat. The right fielder got a bad break on the ball, and he wasn't the fastest guy anyway. Their first baseman turned the wrong way as he headed back. When he tried to right himself, his feet got tangled up, and he flopped to the ground. The ball landed two feet fair and then immediately spun into foul territory. With two outs, Cutler and Cantfield had taken off at the crack of the bat and scored easily. We had the lead.

Robby Richardson struck out on three pitches—no changeups for him. As our guys took the field for the last half inning, I looked to Levine, and he pointed his finger at me. I threw one final warm-up pitch to Diggs, then ran out to the mound.

Our fans rose to their feet and cheered for me. "You can do it, Shane! . . . One, two, three! . . . Show 'em your stuff."

I tried to throw my warm-up pitches just like I always did. Maybe ninety percent, maybe less. But it was hard not to let everything fly. The umpire signaled that I had one more. I fired it in. Ted Hearn threw the ball down to second; it went around the horn. "Batter up!" the umpire called, and I stepped onto the rubber.

The parents behind our bench kept cheering, but at that instant, my world got small. It was only me, the plate, and the catcher's glove—and I knew I was all right. I worked the ball inside and outside, up and down in the zone. With each strike, with each out, the roar from our fans grew louder, but it was distant, like thunder in the mountains. Not until the last Inglemoor hitter went down swinging did I let myself see or hear anything other than home plate and the umpire's voice. When his right arm went up in the air and he shouted "Strike three!" my teammates surrounded me, pounding me on the back and shaking my hand. By the time I reached the bench, my cheeks hurt from smiling so much.

CHAPTER 9 On the ride home, as Levine told me how awesome I'd been, I looked out the window at the shiny sports cars flying by us in the fast lane. I felt I belonged in one of them. I dreamed baseball dreams, imagining how sweet it would be to pitch in the major leagues, to get the final out to win a big league game.

When we pulled off the freeway, the stop-and-go traffic snapped me out of it. In ten minutes I'd be home again. Home. When I'd see my dad, he'd ask me how I'd done. I'd describe the strikeouts, and he'd smile. "I won't miss your next game. I promise."

How could I tell him the truth? How could I tell him that I *wanted* him to miss my next game, and the game after that, and the game after that? That it was *because* he'd missed the game that I'd pitched well?

Levine stopped at the Sound Ridge gate. I leaned toward the driver's seat to wave to Simon. Instead of smiling at me and saying something, he barely made eye contact, waving the van through quickly.

Levine drove slowly. "It's left up here, isn't it?" he said.

"Yeah, and then two quick rights after that."

"I sort of remember. But tell me if I go wrong."

Normally our neighborhood is quiet, but that afternoon people were on their front lawns in groups of two or three, whispering.

The road bent around a corner, and my home came into view. Two aid cars, a fire truck, and a police car were in front. Levine looked at me quickly. "That's your house, isn't it?"

I nodded.

He pulled up to the curb. "You stay in the car. Let me find out what's going on."

It was my home and my family, but I sat and watched as he went up to a uniformed policeman standing in front of my house. I saw Levine talking to the policeman and the policeman answer. I saw Levine's shoulders slump, his body sag. He turned and looked at me and then turned back to the police-man. For a long time he simply stood there. Finally he walked back toward the van.

As he approached, a wave of panic came over me. I didn't want him to reach me, ever. I was safe in the van. The win-dows were rolled up; the doors were closed. If I could sit in the van forever, then nothing would ever touch me.

Levine opened the door and slid into the driver's seat. For a while neither of us said or did anything. We just sat. Finally he turned in his seat and looked me in the eye. "Your father is dead. He shot himself."

I stared at him. "That's not true."

"Shane," he said, but I didn't wait to hear any more.

I jumped out of the van and raced toward the house. A policeman tried to stop me. I pushed right past him. That's when I saw my mom. She had her arm around Marian. When our eyes met, her face seemed to crumple. Still hug-ging Marian, she reached out toward me. I went to her and she hugged me.

When she let me go, Rausch came over to us. I wanted to hit him the instant I saw him. I thought Mom would tell him to go straight to hell, but she didn't.

"I called the Ramada Inn over by Northgate," he said. "I got you a suite. A couple of small rooms, a little kitchen area. If you'd like, I could take you there now."

"Thank you," she said. "I would like to leave, at least for tonight."

"Would you like me to have an officer pack some clothes for you?"

Mom shook her head. "No. We'll do it."

Rausch nodded and stepped aside.

"Now listen to me, both of you," Mom said. "I want you to go up to your rooms and pack what you'll need for a couple of days. As soon as you have it, come right back out. Don't take too long, okay?"

There were two policemen sitting on our sofa in the front room, a police photographer in the kitchen, and a medic coming down the stairs. As soon as they saw us, they stopped talking and seemed to try to melt into the walls.

Upstairs I saw a piece of yellow tape across the doorway leading to my father's study. His body was probably still in there. That's why we had to leave so quickly. Mom didn't want us to see them take his body out, and I didn't want to see it either.

I went into my room and quickly grabbed two pairs of pants, a couple of shirts, underwear, socks. I stuffed everything into an old duffel bag I had in the closet. Then I hurried downstairs and onto the front lawn and waited for Mom and Marian.

Rausch drove us to the Ramada Inn. The three of us sat in the back seat of his big police cruiser. Mom held Marian's hand. I looked out the window at all the cars on all the roads.

That night in the hotel, Mom called Marian and me to the kitchen table. "You need to see this," she said as she carefully placed a single sheet of paper on the table. The handwriting was shaky, but I recognized it as Dad's:

I'm sorry. I didn't mean for any of this to happen.

CHAPTER 10 My aunt Cella came in from San Francisco the next morning. There are a ton of details after someone dies, and she took charge of them. She called the funeral home, the church, the florist, the newspapers, my father's brothers back in Philadelphia, and about a dozen other people.

All that time Mom sat at the little kitchen table, chain-smoking. Marian sat with her; in fact, Marian couldn't stand to be away from her. But I hated being in that crummy room in that crummy hotel, so I'd go for long walks, hours and hours.

North Acres Park is near there. Those days were bright and sunny, but I was drawn to the forested part of the park. It's not safe back there. Two years ago some crazy kid with a gun shot his girlfriend in those woods, and that part of the park is used for drug deals and sex deals. My dad had told me to stay away. But now I didn't care about the danger. I'd walk the dark trails, thinking how I'd been grinning away on the base-ball diamond while he'd been sitting upstairs in his study, a gun in his hand.

The funeral was on Saturday. We were never churchgoers, so the minister who spoke didn't even know my dad. The stuff he said—that Dad was kind and loving and cared about his family and friends—you could have said about your dog.

Our neighbors were there, and so were my teammates. Greg, Coach Levine, Cody—they had sad looks on their faces, but I knew what they were thinking: that my dad was a crim-inal and he'd taken the coward's way out. A coward! As if any one of them would ever have the courage to put a gun to his head and pull the trigger.

On Tuesday Aunt Cella left. Before she did, she took me aside. "It must seem like the world is over for you right now, Shane," she said, "but it isn't. Time doesn't stop. You've got to go on with your own life, or it'll pass you by. There are people who end up like pieces of lost luggage. Don't be one of them."

"I won't," I said, but it was lie. I wasn't going to go on with anything. I wanted to be a piece of lost luggage.

A few days later we moved back into our house. We'd always had a cleaning lady twice a week who vacuumed the house and mopped the kitchen and bathroom floors, but Aunt Cella had had the entire place cleaned, top to bottom. The kitchen and bathroom floors, the porcelain, the windows—all of them shone like one of the new cars in my dad's showroom. The only place I didn't enter was my dad's study. No one did. That door was closed when we stepped into the house at ten in the morning, and it was closed when I went to bed at ten that night.

I was tired but couldn't sleep. I kept imagining how the gunshot must have sounded, how my mother must have rushed upstairs, what she must have said to Marian to get her downstairs, and how she must have been terrified to open the door.

But she'd done it; she'd opened the door and gone in.

I got out of bed. A long hallway led from my bedroom to the study. Enough moonlight came through the skylight so that I could make my way without turning on a lamp and running the risk of awakening Mom or Marian. When I reached the door to Dad's study, I put my hand on the knob and stood there for a long time. Finally, I turned the knob and stepped in.

Once inside, I quietly closed the door behind me, then flicked the light on. At first everything seemed the same. Dad's desk was right where it belonged, pulled up in front of the big double windows. His green desk lamp stood in one corner, his sleek Bose radio on the small table. The leather chair was there, and so were his computer and his printer and his fax machine and his paper shredder.

I sat in his leather chair. My eyes went around the room again, but more slowly. Everything was in its right place, but it was all wrong. Dad never let our cleaning lady into his study, never let Mom straighten anything. His desk was always cluttered, and usually stacks of papers were piled up on the floor. Now it was too clean.

Something else was wrong, too: the carpet. It was new. It had the same deep red color and Turkish design with curlicues and intricate patterns. But this one had more blue in it, while the old one had been creamier. It struck me as odd. Why would Aunt Cella buy something brand-new? Then I knew. Blood. There must have been lots of blood.

I don't know how long I sat at Dad's desk, five minutes or twenty-five. I don't know how long I would have stayed if the door hadn't opened and my mother hadn't stepped in.

"Shane," she whispered, "what are you doing in here?"

"I let him down, Mom."

"No, no, no," she said, coming to me. "Don't say that. Don't think that. What happened isn't your fault. None of it.

Your father just couldn't see his way anymore. He loved you, and he loved Marian, and he knew you loved him. He always knew it, even at the end. He just couldn't see his way."

CHAPTER 11 After breakfast on Saturday, Mom took Marian to the house of her friend Harmony. Marian was nearly crying at the breakfast table, but Mom made her go anyway. About ten minutes after Marian left, a silver BMW pulled up in front of the house, and a well-dressed woman came up the walkway. Mom opened the door for her. "Please come in."

While I waited downstairs, Mom took the woman through the house. The woman took notes and mouthed compliments. "Lovely details. I can see the house has had a lot of TLC."

The woman was in the house for over an hour before she and Mom made their way back to the front door. "I'll work these numbers up," the woman said, "and call you. I doubt you'll have any trouble getting a good price. The market is hot right now."

"You're selling the house?" I said to my mother once the woman had left.

She sat down on the sofa and looked out the window. My eyes followed hers. Right then the sprinkling system kicked on, the little spurts of water giving way to steady fountains. "I have no choice," she said.

"What do you mean?"

"I think you know, Shane."

I did know. Criminals don't get to keep their money. And neither do the families of criminals. Not even suicide changes that.

"Will we have anything at all?"

She managed a smile. "We'll have a little." The telephone rang. She let it ring twice, then stood up. "I'd better get that."

She took the call in the kitchen. I sat on the sofa where she'd been and looked out. The sun was shining out of a blue sky. Our front lawn was deep green, our flower beds filled with tulips and daffodils. The cherry trees were in full bloom. It was impossible to think that soon some stranger would be sitting where I sat, looking out our windows, eating in our kitchen, sleeping in our rooms.

If it had been up to me, I'd have skipped the rest of the school year and waited until fall to start some new school, but Mom wouldn't hear of it. "You've got to get your credits. I expect you to graduate on time and go to college."

Marian wasn't any happier about returning to school than I was. After Mom dropped us off at Shorelake, we stood at the bottom of the stairs for a long time before we finally climbed up, and when we reached the spot where we usually split, Marian hugged me, which she never does. "I'll meet you here right after school ends," I said. She nodded, then trudged away.

I had ten minutes before school was to start, just long enough. I cut straight to the gym and knocked on Coach Levine's door.

"Come in," he called.

He'd been working at his computer, but he stopped as soon as he saw me. "Shane," he said, standing up. "It's good to have you back. Sit down."

"Coach, I just wanted you to know that I'm quitting the team."

His mouth turned down. "Are you sure that's such a good idea?"

"I'm sure."

"Well, I'm not," he said. "I think that—"

"Here's my uniform," I said, putting a grocery bag on the floor just inside the door. The five-minute bell rang. "I've got to go."

"Wait a second, Shane," he called, but I didn't turn back.

My first-period class was social studies with Mrs. Judd. I wanted to hide in the back and let the minutes tick away, but I'd hardly sat down when an office assistant brought a note into the room. Mrs. Judd read it, then turned to me. "Shane, you're to report to Mr. Porter."

Porter was the vice principal, a little bald guy with big ears. He met me at the door to his office, had me sit on his cheap sofa. He sat across from me at his desk, his hands folded together, his thumbs tapping each other. "I want you to know how saddened all of us at Shorelake are," he said. "We think of this school as a family, so whatever happens to one of us happens to all of us." He cleared his throat. "It takes time to get over a shock. We know that. So you're excused from all the class work that you missed. As for the rest of the year, do what you can, but don't worry. Do you understand what I'm saying, Shane?"

"I understand."

"There's one more thing. Tell your mother that if tuition is a problem for you and your sister, she's not to worry. We have funds for situations like this."

"I will," I said.

"All right then. That covers it."

He stuck his hand across the desk, and I shook it. "You can go back to class, Shane. And remember, we're here to help. Don't be afraid to ask."

As I made my way down the long empty hallway leading to Mrs. Judd's room, I realized there must have been a meeting about me, with the principal and the vice principal and my teachers. They must have talked about my father's suicide, about the charges against him, about our money. I wanted to walk right out the main door and never come back.

In the halls and at lunch I avoided Greg and Cody and the other guys on the team. When school ended, I saw them heading in small groups toward the baseball diamonds. That was harder. I still didn't want to talk with them, have them "help" me, but I did want to step up onto the pitcher's mound and fire fastball after fastball right past them. I wanted to strike out the world.

I hung around the library for a few minutes, waiting for the campus to empty. Finally I dragged myself down the main set of stairs. Marian was waiting at the bottom. "How was your day?" I asked.

"Okay."

We headed up to 145th.

"Isn't Mom going to pick us up?" Marian asked.

"I don't think so. If she were, she'd be here."

The bus took us to the gate of Sound Ridge, but from there we had to walk. That was the first time I'd ever done that. It was a hot, still day. I'd never noticed how long the roads were. Marian didn't complain as we trudged along, but when at last she saw our house, she let out a sigh of relief. Then she spotted the For Sale sign planted on the lawn. I could feel her tense up. When we opened the front door, we saw the real estate agent sitting on the sofa. "And hello to both of you," she said cheerily.

CHAPTER 12 They say time cures everything, but wherever I turned, my father's suicide was there: his chair in the front room, his magazines in the mail, his Lexus in the garage, his crackers in the kitchen.

Things went a little better at school. I kept to myself, and within a week my classmates had basically forgotten about me and my father. How much had they really cared in the first place?

I didn't want to follow the baseball team, but I couldn't keep from checking the scores, which were posted in the main hallway. You want to think you're important to the team, no matter who you are. I figured Scott Parino and Terry Clarke would wear out without me to finish games for them. But those two stepped up to the challenge, and the whole team caught fire, winning everything in sight. The last two games of the regular season were such routs—15–2, 17–1—

that the umpires called them after five innings.

Clarke and Parino kept rolling when the playoffs began, shutting down Bothell, Redmond, and Edmonds in the district tournament, Stanwood and Ferris in the state. When Clarke shut out Gonzaga to put Shorelake into the championship game, my feelings were all over the place. Sometimes I felt as if those guys were still my teammates and that I wanted them to win. Other times I'd picture Greg and Cody holding the trophy over their heads, and I'd want anyone but them to win.

The championship game against Lincoln was on a Saturday afternoon. That same Saturday the real estate agent had arranged another open house. During the previous open houses, Mom had taken Marian and me to a matinee. She wanted me to go again that day, but I couldn't stay away from the game.

They played at Graves field on the University of Washington campus. I picked up a bus on Greenwood Avenue, and then transferred once down by the zoo. After that it was a short bus ride to the baseball field. I showed my student body card and got in for a couple of bucks. Shorelake had the third-base dugout, but I didn't want to sit near anybody who knew me, so I headed down the first base line.

According to the *Seattle Times,* Lincoln had a great pitcher, a blond kid named David Johansen. Watching him warm up, I could tell he was the real deal. There was a looseness in his arm, in his body, that oozed confidence.

Still, nerves can hit anybody, and he started out nervous. We batted first, and Johansen walked Brian Coombs on four pitches, none of them close to the plate. Coach Levine had Jeff Newman bunt, figuring the game would be tight and playing for one run. The third baseman fielded, fired down to second to try to force Coombs. He would have had him, too, but his throw sailed out into center field, and Coombs trotted to third. Shorelake fans were up and screaming, and they kept screaming as Brad Greenberg, who was the DH, blooped a single into short left. Coombs scored, but Newman had to hold at third.

The Lincoln coach called time and trotted to the mound. I watched, wondering what he was saying. Then something unexpected happened—Johansen laughed, and the coach laughed along with him. The umpire came out and broke up the conversation, but whatever the coach had said worked. Johansen struck out Beanie Cutler, Alvin Powell, and Greg Taylor. What had looked like a big inning had fizzled out.

Parino came out and took his warm-ups. He was deliberate with all his movements, as if he were afraid of wasting one ounce of energy. He struck out Lincoln's leadoff batter, then gave up a double. The runner took third base on a groundout. A base hit would have tied the score, and the momentum would have shifted right back to Lincoln, but Parino got a pop-up for the third out.

After that, the game settled into a classic pitchers' duel. Johansen looked like Cy Young. He had a moving fastball and a nasty curve, and he was wild enough to keep batters scared. Hitters jumped back—afraid they were going to be hit—only to have the umpire yell "Strike!" As the innings rolled by, that run in the first inning seemed like a miracle.

By the sixth inning, Parino was exhausted. He took forever between pitches, and all he threw was change-of-speed stuff: little curve balls and changeups. His fastball had stopped popping Hearn's mitt. The Lincoln hitters weren't able to string together any hits, but in every inning they were getting better and better cuts.

Johansen didn't pitch the seventh for Lincoln. Instead they brought in a reliever. The guy's arm was fresh, and he struck out Greg looking, got Cody to bounce to first, and then fanned Richardson. Before Parino could catch his breath, he was trudging back out to the mound.

My fingers wrapped themselves tightly around the wires of the chainlink fence as Parino lobbed his warm-ups in to Hearn. The ball went around the horn, and then it was crunch time. The leadoff batter for Lincoln was their center fielder, a fast kid who batted from an exaggerated crouch. Parino started him off with two dead-arm fastballs that were a foot outside, then threw a strike, then threw two more balls. The center fielder, representing the tying run, clapped his hands together and trotted down to first.

Lincoln's big first baseman stepped into the batter's box. Parino tried to sneak a first-pitch fastball by him, but he sent a single whistling into left field. Had the ball been up in the air, it would have gone four hundred feet.

Coach Levine called time and went out to talk with Parino. I tried to imagine what he would say, because there really wasn't anything to say. Clarke had pitched a complete game on Thursday. There was nobody warming up, nobody to warm up. Finally Levine patted Parino on the back, then returned to the bench.

Parino peered in, got the sign from Hearn, checked the Lincoln base runners, delivered. High—ball one.

The Lincoln fans roared with delight. Again Parino went into his stretch, delivered. High again—ball two. The Lincoln fans were stomping on the bleachers, screaming.

Parino checked the runners, came to the plate. The batter swung, stinging a line shot into deep left center. Coombs was off with the crack of the bat. For a moment I thought he'd track it down. But he stumbled a little, then flung himself out in a wild dive. The ball landed about two feet from his outstretched glove, took a big bounce, and skipped all the way to the fence.

The tying run scored before Coombs reached the ball; the winning run came across before the relay throw to the plate was even made. Immediately, the entire Lincoln team charged out of the dugout. Within seconds, parents and girl-friends and buddies joined them on the field. They mobbed the guy who'd scored the winning run, then high-fived one another. They were state champions.

I left as quickly as I could. I found a seat alone in the back of the bus. Once the guys thought it through, they'd blame me. They'd say I was like my dad, a coward and a quitter, that if I'd stuck with them, they'd have won it all.

The next week was finals' week. I'd taken advantage of Mr. Porter's offer, skipping most assignments, not doing the reading for social studies or English, missing labs in biology and Spanish. At first the teachers had been sympathetic, but after a while I could see the irritation in their eyes.

I didn't sweat my final exams either, writing a sentence or

two when I knew I was expected to produce a page. After that I'd pull out a book and pretend to read when all I was doing was listening to the scratching of pencils on paper.

As soon as I finished my last exam, I headed for the stairs leading off campus. John Schwartz, the dean of men, stopped me. "Where do you think you're going? There's an end-of-the-year assembly. Required."

Schwartz had been a famous athlete in his time—baseball and boxing—and he was big enough and gruff enough to scare almost everybody. But I was past being scared.

"I'm going home. And I'm never coming back."

For an instant he looked like he might challenge me, but then he recognized me. "No, Shane, I don't suppose you will." He moved aside, then motioned with his hand. "Go."

CHAPTER 13 Instead of getting better, Marian got worse. Whenever someone came to look at the house, she'd lock herself in her room. Sometimes she wouldn't come out even when they were gone. And then, late at night, she'd wake up screaming.

It was wearing Mom down. She had dark circles under her eyes, and her hair looked gray and drab. "Marian," she said, her voice tired, "I wish we didn't have to move, either. But we have lawyers to pay, and we owe money to the government. The only way we can get money to pay those bills is to sell the house. I've told you this over and over. You have to accept it."

One day in early July, when Mom was out in the garden, Marian turned to me. "Will we be homeless?" she asked.

I had to smile. "Is that what you're worried about? Because if it is, you can relax. We're not going to be homeless, that I promise."

"How do you know?"

"I just know."

"Some kids are. I read about them in *Weekly Reader* at school. They live in cars and pretend they have a home so that other kids won't know. But the other kids do know, and so do their teachers."

"We're not going to live in a car," I snapped. "Stop being idiotic."

But later I wondered. Mom wasn't working. She owed money to lots of different people. Where would we get money?

All through July strangers were constantly roaming through our house, poking into our closets, asking questions. I could pick out the people who knew about Dad by the way they looked at Mom and Marian and me. They felt sorry for us, but they didn't want to get too close to us either, and they weren't sure they wanted anything to do with a house that had had a suicide. Other homes in Sound Ridge sold, but not ours. One Saturday both Lexuses were gone from the garage, and in their place was a ten-year-old Honda Accord. "We never really owned them," Mom explained. "They belonged to the dealership."

In early August the Robertsons, a family from San Jose, came to look at the house. The man was a hotshot lawyer who'd recently been hired by Microsoft. He hardly spoke, and he kept looking out the window at his gleaming white Mercedes, as if he were afraid someone might steal it. But his wife was one of those people who never shut up. They had a daughter, Anna, who was Marian's age, and a son, Reese, who was my age. "Wouldn't it be nice if the kids became friends?" the woman said, as if we were all going to live together in the house.

She did the same things everybody else did—opened closet doors, poked around in our basement and attic looking at stuff that wasn't hers. "Are the winters as cold and rainy as people say? That's the one thing I worry about. I love the sun. We all do."

"They're not that bad," Mom answered. "And our summers are beautiful."

Three times that week the white Mercedes pulled up in front of our home, and each time Mom grew more anxious. "Both of you," she snapped, "on your best behavior."

The last time, the realtor came with all the papers that needed to be signed, and Mom and the Robertsons sat at the kitchen table going over them. I thought Marian would be in tears, but instead she found her Hula-Hoops in the garage and took Anna onto the deck, where they played, laughing away.

I was the one who was falling apart. I tried to hide out in my room, but after a few minutes Mom came up. "Shane," she said, her voice full of fake cheeriness, "I'm sure you and Reese could find something to do. This will take a while, and I don't think he wants to sit alone in the front room." Reese was standing behind her, a stupid smile on his face.

Mom returned downstairs, and he stepped into my room. "What an awesome room," he said. "I've got a Barry Bonds poster that'll look great on that wall. I suppose you're a Mariners fan. Maybe I'll become one, but right now the Giants are my team. Can you believe the guy hit seventy-three home runs? My dad says Willie Mays was even better."

I couldn't stand the way he took over my room with his eyes or the way he talked as if we were old friends. I wanted him out. "You play baseball?" I asked. "Or do you just watch it on television?"

"I play. Center field. How about you?" There was a challenge in his voice.

"I'm a pitcher." I paused. "How about if we play catch in the yard?"

"I don't have my glove with me."

"No problem. I've got an extra one."

He followed me downstairs and into the yard. My dad's old glove was lying in a box by the back door. I brushed aside a spider's web. "This okay?" I said, handing it to him.

He slipped his hand in. "Sure."

My first few tosses were soft, but little by little I started throwing harder. My dad's glove is a million years old. There's so little padding he used to slide a sponge inside to protect his hand when I threw hard. The sponge was in the box, but I didn't give it to Reese. I threw a fastball as hard as I could. The ball smacked into his glove.

"Wow!" he said, taking off the glove and shaking his hand, a pained smile on his face. "Go easy, will you? That hurt."

"I thought you said you were a ballplayer."

"I'm a center fielder, not a catcher. And this is definitely not a catcher's mitt."

"There's nothing wrong with that glove."

"I didn't say there was. I just said it wasn't a catcher's mitt."

He tossed the ball back. I threw it to him again, fast—but not my fastest. The ball went back and forth a half dozen times or so.

"I'd like to hit against you sometime," he said.

"No, you wouldn't," I said.

"Why not?"

"Because I'd strike you out."

He held the ball. "You're pretty sure of yourself, aren't you?"

The screen door opened. "Reese!" his mother called. "Time to go."

I followed him into the house. I could tell by the way the realtor was grinning that the papers had been signed. I walked right through the kitchen toward the stairs, but before I could escape I heard Mom chirping away. "You're going to love living here. It is so safe. Nothing but good families."

The next weekend we had a big yard sale. Everything in the basement and attic and about three-fourths of the things from the rest of the house went. Mom's books, my old bicycles, almost all of Marian's stuffed animals, old clothes—you name it, we sold it. Marian liked playing saleslady, making change for customers and all that, but I hated everything about it. It was like having your whole life lying on your front lawn for people to pick over.

Some of our neighbors didn't come. Sound Ridge was too fancy for yard sales, and Mom was breaking an unwritten neighborhood rule by having one. But lots of people couldn't resist a bargain. Most of them were millionaires, but if something was ten bucks, they'd want it for five; and if it was a buck they'd offer fifty cents. I would have told them to drop dead, which is why Mom didn't let me do any of the selling. She was polite through it all. "Well, that's done," she said as she counted the money on Sunday night. "Now we can move on."

CHAPTER 14 On Monday morning Mom called me into the kitchen. "Shane, I'm going to be out quite a bit now. I've got to find a place for us to live. While I'm gone, I want you to be kind to Marian."

"I'm never mean to her."

"I didn't say you were. I said I want you to be kind. There's a difference." She paused. "Look, you know how frightened she is. With me out of the house, it's up to you to make her feel safe. Do you understand what I'm saying?"

I nodded. "I understand."

"Good." She looked at me. "How about you, Shane? Anything going on inside you that I should know about?"

"I'm fine, Mom. Don't worry about me."

That morning, and every morning, Mom scoured the *Seattle Times* classified ads, highlighting any ad that looked reasonable. After breakfast she'd go out, leaving Marian with me.

Marian would slip upstairs to her room as soon as Mom left. She had her pet rats there. Before my father killed himself, she rarely took the rats out of their cage. But she played with them the first day we moved back into the house after the funeral, and ever since she'd have them out all the time. I'd hear her singing to them, talking to them, having them talk to one another. Sometimes I'd ask her if she wanted to go over to Harmony's house, or Anna's. "Not today," she'd say.

While she was upstairs, I'd go through the newspaper. I'd kill an hour or so checking on the Mariners and going over the box scores of the other games. Then I'd spend the rest of the day listening to the radio, sleeping a little, and eating some.

The last page of the Wednesday sports section is dedicated to youth sports. All the summer baseball tournaments were going full tilt. Levine coached a select team made up entirely of Shorelake players. While I was stuck in the duplex, Greg and Cody and the other guys were traveling up and down the coast playing baseball.

The Robertsons were moving in on August 31. On August 15, Mom still hadn't found a place for us to live. She was drinking more wine than usual at dinner, and at night she'd sit on the back porch smoking one cigarette after another. I thought about what Marian had said about families living in their cars, and I was no longer so certain she was crazy. Then, while Mom was apartment hunting one day, the phone rang. "Tell your mom the place on 138th came through."

"Who are you?" I asked.

The voice laughed. "I'm sorry. I'm Lisa Rodriguez. Your community service rep." I hadn't even known we had a community service rep. I took down her name and number. "Tell her it's the little duplex off Greenwood, just inside the city limits, not too far from where you live now. She'll know which one."

When Mom came home that afternoon, I gave her the message. Her face brightened. She went straight to the phone. "Ms. Rodriguez, please."

Marian and I stood watching as Mom spoke, her voice growing more and more excited. "And the rent? . . . Oh, yes, that is reasonable. . . . I'm sure we will. . . . We'll be by first thing tomorrow. . . . This is such a relief. I can't thank you enough."

When Mom hung up the telephone, she bowed her head and cried.

"What's the matter, Mom?" Marian asked.

"Nothing's the matter," Mom replied, lifting her head and wiping away the tears. Then she hugged Marian tightly. "As a matter of fact, everything is wonderful."

She went to the telephone and ordered a pizza from Romio's. "And we'll rent a movie, too. Some big Hollywood musical, *South Pacific* or something like that. We'll microwave some popcorn and just relax. Okay?"

When the pizza arrived, she started to pour herself a glass of wine but stopped. With Marian and me watching, she poured down the drain all the wine that was left in one bottle, and then she opened two other bottles and poured the wine out. Once that was done, she took her cigarettes out of her purse, broke them in half, and threw them in the garbage. Then she turned and smiled at both of us. "No more of that," she said. "I promise."

CHAPTER 15 "Now don't be expecting much," Mom said as we drove to see the house the next morning. "It's not what you're used to. But it's clean, and we're all together, and we're healthy, and that's all that matters."

I wasn't expecting much, but I still swallowed hard when she pulled up in front of a small, mustard-yellow house. There were bicycles and big-wheel toys strewn about in the front yard, which was more like a dandelion patch than a lawn. I saw the letters *S.H.A.* stenciled onto the garbage cans that were out in the open at the end of the driveway.

"Why are there two front doors?" Marian asked as we headed up the walkway and onto the porch.

"It's a duplex, honey," Mom said, taking out the keys. "We don't have the whole house, only half of it."

It took some doing, but the door finally opened. Inside, a stairway led straight up. "I'll show you the bedrooms later," Mom said. "Let's do the main floor first."

It didn't take long. There was a tiny living room, a kitchen that was like a hallway, and a little breakfast nook that wasn't much bigger than the breakfast table we'd sold.

Upstairs were two bedrooms. Put together, they weren't as big as my room in Sound Ridge. "Marian and I will share this one," Mom said opening the door to the larger one, "and you'll have the other one."

A puke-yellow bathroom was wedged between the two rooms. Mom turned the handle on the faucet, then flushed the toilet. "I can't say I agree with the choice of colors," she said, "but everything works."

We trooped back downstairs. "Well, what do you think?" she asked.

"It's nice," Marian said.

"What does *S.H.A.* stand for?" I asked.

Mom's face lost color. "Pardon me?"

"*S.H.A.,*" I repeated. "What does it stand for?"

"Seattle Housing Authority."

"So we're in city housing?"

She looked me in the eye. "Yes, Shane, we are."

I went back to the car, unloaded the few boxes we'd brought from our home, and carried them into the front room. As I started to unpack them, Mom picked up her keys. "I have to sign some papers. I'll be back in an hour."

I finished unpacking the boxes. At the bottom of the last one was the board game Candy Land, which I thought we'd sold at the yard sale. When Marian saw it, her eyes brightened. "Let's play," she said.

"Aren't you a little old for Candy Land?"

"There's nothing else to do," she said.

I don't know if the people in the unit next to us were talking loudly or whether the walls were paper-thin, but if we'd wanted to, we could have heard every word. Instead, Marian and I tuned them out. We just turned over the little cards with their yellow and green boxes, as well as the occasional picture card that jumped us around the board. Candy Land is a stupid game for anybody over six years old, but that day I enjoyed it. I was as intent on each card as Marian was.

We'd played for ten or fifteen minutes, each of us close to winning, only to be dropped down by some bit of bad luck. finally Marian was almost at the top. A card of any color and the game would be hers.

Eagerly she reached for the stack and flipped over a card. But instead of a color card, she'd pulled Mr. Plum, the worst card in the deck. She dropped all the way down to the bottom. Her face fell. A few minutes later, I won. "Do you want to play again?" I asked.

She shook her head. "I'll just read." She got her book and headed upstairs to the little room she'd be sharing with Mom. I heard the door click as she closed it.

I felt bad, but what could I have done? If she were younger, I would have cheated for her, but I couldn't do that anymore. She'd have seen me, and she'd have been angry. Besides, there was a truth to the game. Some people pull Queen Frostine and move all the way to the top. Others get Mr. Plum and just about drop off the board. She'd drawn Mr. Plum, so she might as well get used to it.

PART TWO

CHAPTER 1 The new place was a dump, and I hated it. But by then I hated the house in Sound Ridge, too, hated that I was hiding in my own house, not wanting to see any of the neighbors, all the time feeling that they were watching us, talking about us, waiting for us to leave. *Goodbye to all of you,* I thought when we'd finally finished loading the last box and were driving through the gates for the last time.

It took one full afternoon to unload our Ryder truck. Even though we'd gotten rid of three-fourths of the stuff we had, the new place still couldn't hold everything we'd kept. We ended up taking ten boxes to the basement and leaving them in the area reserved for us.

"Somebody could steal this," I said to Mom.

She laughed sardonically. "I wish somebody would."

Daytime wasn't so bad. I kept busy painting the entire unit, top to bottom, closets to windows. But at night it was different. Sleep wouldn't come, my mind would start racing, and pretty soon I'd be seething. City housing. Why had Mom brought us here? I saw everything—the cramped rooms, the cracked bathroom tiles, the water-stained ceilings, the weed-filled lawn—through Dad's eyes. He would never have lived here. Never.

Right before school started, Mom got a job as a waitress at Pasta Bella working the dinner shift, from six to midnight. "I won't get home until after one," she said, "so I'm counting on you to look after Marian. Make sure she does her homework, takes a shower, gets to bed on time. You understand?"

"Yeah, sure. You want me to baby-sit."

Her eyes flashed. "I want you to do more than baby-sit. I want you to be her friend, talk to her. But since that doesn't seem to be happening, then yes, I'll settle for simple baby-sitting."

"That's not fair," I said, defending myself. "All Marian does is play with her rats or read. I can't make her talk if she doesn't want to."

Mom frowned. "Fair enough, Shane. But if she ever does want to talk, I want you to be here to listen."

My new school, Whitman High, began an hour before Marian's. Mom and Marian were still sleeping when I ate breakfast in the kitchen. The only company I had was the old black electric clock whose second hand would go slowly between the two and the three, and then race to catch up.

After I finished my cereal, I packed my backpack, pulled the door shut behind me, and walked to the bus stop, which was at Greenwood and 140th, just two blocks from the duplex.

As I waited for the bus, I thought back to the year before when my dad had driven Marian and me to Shorelake. Every morning we'd come right down Greenwood Avenue, past the very spot where I was standing. Sometimes my dad would nod toward the clumps of Whitman kids waiting for the school bus. They'd be smoking cigarettes, nuzzling their girlfriends or boyfriends, or just standing there, shoulders hunched. "Look at them," Dad would say, his voice filled with contempt. "Just look at them."

That morning I pawed the ground, glancing up every so often, hoping to see the ugly yellow school bus that would get me off the street. Where was it? Would it ever come?

It wasn't the bus that came but something else, and for a moment I couldn't breathe. A white Mercedes, gleaming in the early-morning sunshine, was gliding toward me. Mesmerized, I stared until I was sure: Reese Robertson.

He was sitting in the front seat next to his dad; both of them were laughing. I turned away, hoping they'd drive right by. But the traffic light turned red, and the Mercedes eased to a stop in front of where I stood.

I turned around and faced the little closed shops on Greenwood, determined not to look back. But I had to look. I turned around just as Reese glanced out his window. Our eyes met, and in that second there was a flash of recognition, and then we both looked away. The light turned green; the Mercedes drove off.

My bus pulled up a minute later. I flopped onto the first available seat, my heart pounding. Greenwood was the main arterial from Sound Ridge to Shorelake Academy. I'd seen Reese today; tomorrow it might be Greg, and the day after that Cody. I could stand in the back of the crowd of kids, I could pull a cap down over my face, but they'd see me.

It was the first day of my junior year of high school, but all I thought about was the bus stop. And I thought about it at home after school let out. I hated myself for letting it get to me. A thousand times I told myself that I didn't care who saw me.

The next morning, and every morning, I tried to look down at the ground or off into space. But I couldn't. The chance that a Shorelake guy might be in the next car worked on me like a magnet. I had to look.

I tried to time it so that I'd get to the stop just a minute or two early, and the bus would come, and that would be that. But when the bus was late, which was at least half the time, someone would see me. It didn't matter who it was—Greg, Cody, Reese Robertson—it was always the same. Our eyes would meet, and then we'd both look away, as if we'd never known each other.

CHAPTER 2 Whitman High is a crowded school— more than fifteen hundred kids jammed onto a campus about half the size of Shorelake's. There's no place to go off by yourself; everywhere you turn there are people. The kids in my classes had friends from earlier years. I knew no one, and no one seemed interested in knowing me.

But that was okay. You meet kids, and pretty soon they ask what your name is and where you live, and all that. My dad's name had been in the paper and on the television news for money laundering, for drug dealing, for killing himself. The more you talk, the greater the chance that somebody will figure things out. It was best not to talk to anyone. I went to school, wandered through the day, and came home.

We never discussed it, but I think Marian was doing the same thing. She'd come home from Broadview-Thompson, her new middle school, and go up to the room she shared with Mom, where she'd do her homework. At around five Mom would call us for a quick dinner. Once Mom left for work, Marian would finish her homework at the kitchen table, then watch television for an hour or so. After that, she'd take her shower and go to her room to read. By nine o'-clock she had the light out. It almost seemed as if sleeping was her favorite thing.

The first couple of weeks I was glad to be left alone. But after a while I wished Marian would stay downstairs and talk. There were things I wanted to know about the day Dad had died. Had he said anything to her or to Mom before he went to his study? What happened right after the shot? Did Mom go upstairs? Did Marian?

And I guess I was lonely, too. There was nobody to talk to at school. Mom was gone all the time. Even if Marian didn't want to talk about Dad, it would have been okay by me to play Monopoly or Clue. In a way, it was a joke. Before Dad had died, Marian always wanted to hang out with me and I always brushed her aside. Now, when I wouldn't have minded doing stuff with her, she was the one with her door closed.

In October I hooked up with this skinny, pasty-faced kid

named Lonnie Gibson. Maybe I should say he hooked up with me. He was at the bus stop every morning and afternoon, and he was in my music elective at the end of the day.

Lonnie was a wild man in class—singing off-key on purpose and always laughing at the music teacher, Mr. Bull. He didn't even care about Mr. Stimmel, the school principal. "What are they going to do? Throw me out?" he said.

Lonnie lived in an apartment near the AM-PM Mini Mart on 145th. I'd noticed the place because it was city housing, too. "Stop by some night," he was always saying. "We could hang out together."

"I've got to look after my little sister," I said.

He shrugged. "Well, if you change your mind, come by."

It was a Monday night, around nine-thirty. I had homework, but I didn't feel like doing it. I'd been a good student at Shorelake Academy—Dad would have killed me if I hadn't come home with high grades—but I was near the bottom at Whitman. I was downstairs watching the Bears play the Vikings on *Monday Night Football*. The game was late in the fourth quarter, with the Vikings leading 26–3. They had the ball and were running out the clock. A run over left tackle; a run over right tackle; an off-side penalty. I found myself thinking about Lonnie. Hanging out with him had to be better than sitting alone in a crummy, claustrophobic duplex while watching a lousy football game.

I flicked the television off, then went upstairs and stood outside Marian's door. Her light was off. I turned the knob and peeked in. She was asleep, her breathing slow and regular. She was still waking up with nightmares, but that was always later, at two or three. I closed the door, grabbed a jacket from my room, then slipped quietly down the stairs and out into the night.

Lonnie was standing in front of his housing complex next to a tall guy I didn't know. "Hey, Shane," he shouted the instant he saw me, his eyes lighting up. "Good to see you." He reached out and shook my hand high, then did the little knuckle thing, as if we were in some sort of street gang. "This is Justin," he said, nodding toward the tall guy, and then Justin shook my hand in the same way.

Justin was older than Lonnie and me, probably eighteen or nineteen. His hair was dyed black, he had a wispy goatee, and he wore a long black trench coat. He reached deep into his pocket and pulled out a pack of Camels, shaking the pack so the tips of the cigarettes came up. Lonnie took one, so I did too.

I'd smoked a couple of times when I was a freshman but hadn't had any cigarettes since. I was afraid I'd cough like crazy and they'd laugh at me, so on the first puff I barely inhaled. The hot smoke burned, but I didn't cough. On my second puff I inhaled a little deeper.

The three of us stood under the streetlight, leaning against an old blue Chrysler, smoking and talking about girls and cars and TV shows. Justin looked at his watch. "It's after ten. Let's see if that little Vietnamese woman is working the minimart."

I looked at Lonnie.

"You'll see," he said.

The market was about a half block away. When we reached it, Lonnie went inside while Justin and I waited around the corner. A minute later Lonnie came back, a grin on his face. "It's her, and she's alone."

"You sure?" Justin asked.

"I'm sure."

"Piece of cake," Justin said. He nodded toward me. "Is this guy okay?"

"Shane'll do fine," Lonnie said and then turned to me. "Just do what I tell you, when I tell you. Okay?"

"What am I supposed to do?" I said.

"Just do what I tell you. There's nothing to it."

For the next five minutes, we hung out around the corner from the store. I wanted to ask what was what, but I bit back the words. Justin kept watching the gas pumps. Finally, when three cars pulled up simultaneously, he took off his trench coat. "Wear this," he said, handing it to me. "And do exactly what Lonnie tells you to do."

As we walked toward the store, Lonnie filled me in on the plan. "We'll go in first. Then Justin will come in and grab some candy. He'll drop a whole bunch of change on the counter. While the lady is sorting it out, you slip Mickey Stouts—the twenty-four-ounce size—inside this coat, as many as you can get. The pockets are deep."

"What if she sees me?" I asked.

He pushed the door open, and I stepped inside. "She won't," he whispered. "She'll have all that change on the counter, three cars out front to watch, and I'll be standing in front of you, screening you. There's no chance she'll see you.

We do it all the time with just two guys. With three there's even less risk."

I could feel my body tighten as we stood in front of the refrigerators. It was like being on the pitcher's mound—every one of my senses was on alert. Out of the corner of my eye, I could see Justin push the door open, grab a large bag of M&M's, and take it to the cash register. I heard the clatter of coins as he dropped them onto the counter. The Vietnamese woman lowered her head to sort them out. "Now!" Lonnie whispered.

I slid the glass refrigerator door open, grabbed a couple of Mickey Stouts, and slipped both into the deep inside pockets of Justin's trench coat. I reached in a second time, grabbed two more bottles, and slipped them inside the pockets. My hands went back a third time. When I looked around, the woman was still counting Justin's change, and there was still more room in the trench coat, but that was it for me. I turned, and Lonnie followed me as I walked quickly—but not too quickly—toward the door. At the door Lonnie touched me on the shoulder and pointed to the cover of some magazine. "Nice looking, isn't she?"

Once I was around the corner, I broke into a run. The six beer bottles clanked against one another inside the coat. "Slow down!" Lonnie called out after me. "We're safe. Don't break them."

A minute later Justin caught up with us. "How many did you get?" he asked.

"Six."

"Only six? The coat holds ten."

Lonnie stuck up for me. "Six is good and you know it. My first time I only got two."

We slipped into the alley behind Lonnie's apartment and sat next to the garbage cans. I put all six Mickeys in front of us. Lonnie and Justin each grabbed one and unscrewed the top, so I did the same.

My dad had let me have a few sips of beer a couple of times, but I'd never liked the taste. It was too bitter, and now I had forty-eight ounces of it to drink. I was glad Justin had bought the M&M's. I'd take a swig, then reach into the bag and grab some before taking my next swig.

"You ever drink before?" Justin asked me when he'd finished the first Mickey and reached for his second.

"Sure."

He laughed. "Liar."

"I'm not lying."

"Yeah, you are. But don't sweat it. It's like with girls. Everybody has a first time, and then they can't wait for a second and third."

Lonnie finished his beer and started on his second. Only my second stood untouched. "If you're not going to drink that Mickey, I'll take it," Justin said.

The M&M's and beer were getting scrambled in my stomach, and I felt as if I'd swallowed some cigarette smoke too. But I wasn't going to drink any less than they did. "I want it," I said.

I didn't exactly get drunk, but I did lose track of time. It was eleven-forty-five before I looked at my watch. Occasionally Mom got home just after midnight. "I've got to go," I said.

"See you tomorrow," Lonnie mumbled.

● ● ●

I made it back to the apartment at 12:05. I checked on Marian
. . . sound asleep. I thought I'd have to pretend to be asleep
when Mom came in, but as soon as I lay down, I was out. If
my alarm hadn't gone off, I'd have slept until noon.

After that, I started sneaking out nearly every night.
Whenever the Vietnamese woman worked the market, which
was most of the time, we stole beer. We shared the risk by taking turns, but the whole thing was like stealing candy from a
baby.

One day when we were drinking, I told them about my dad
killing himself. I don't know why, it just came out. "Wow,"
Lonnie said, "that's really tough. Do you know why he did it?"

"He was involved with some drug dealers from Mexico.
He did the money-laundering part. You know." They nodded
as if they did. "He was headed to prison."

Justin's eyes widened. "Your dad was a big-time drug
dealer?"

I felt strangely proud of him. "We used to have packages of
cash coming to our front door, the size of shoeboxes, two or
three times a month. We lived in a big house in Sound Ridge,
and we had two Lexuses and all sorts of computers and a huge
entertainment center. Anything I wanted my dad got for me."

"You're full of it," Justin said.

"It's true," I insisted. "You could look it up in the newspaper. It all happened just six months ago. Last year I went to
Shorelake."

"Really?"

"Really."

For a while no one said anything. Lonnie finished one Mickey, then opened another. "My dad might as well be dead; I never see him."

Justin grinned. "Maybe that's because he's not really your dad. Maybe your mom was fooling around on the side, and he knows it. Your mom's kind of hot looking still, with those tight sweaters she always wears. She must have been something when she was younger."

"Shut up."

CHAPTER 3 It was the night before Halloween. Mom was working, Marian was asleep, and I was sprawled out in the alley drinking my third bottle of Mickey Stout with Lonnie and Justin. Justin had started telling a joke about this good-looking girl and a mirror. "Mirror, mirror, on the wall," he was saying, but before he could finish, two cop cars pulled into the alley, one from each direction, their spotlights on us.

In a flash Justin was gone, bounding over the cyclone fence and racing through somebody's backyard. But Lonnie and I didn't move quickly enough, and before I knew what was happening, the big hands of a policeman had pulled me to my feet and spun me around so that my face was against the fence. The cop patted me down, and then I felt handcuffs go on.

"Wait," I said, "you don't understand."

"Get in the back seat, kid," the cop said. "I understand perfectly. And you will too, real soon."

I thought the cop would call my mom at work and then take me home. Instead, he got on the freeway and drove toward downtown Seattle. Lonnie looked out the window as if we were just going for a pleasant drive; I felt sick to my stomach.

"Where are you taking us?" I asked.

"Youth Detention Center," the cop answered.

"Can't you just take me home?" I said. "I won't ever do it again. I promise."

He didn't answer.

The Youth Detention Center turned out to be a newer building in the Central District. Once we went through the big double doors, Lonnie was taken into one room and I was led to another. A woman—I don't know if she was a cop or not—asked me a bunch of questions. Name, address, phone number. That sort of thing. Next, a younger guy with blue eyes and an earring called me into his office. "Tell me about it," he said.

"That was the first time I've ever done anything like that. I swear it was."

He smiled. "There's a surveillance camera in that mini-mart, kid. The owner's been on to you for a while now. So try again."

"All right. I've done it before. But I won't ever do it again. I promise."

He nodded. "Well, that's a start. Now how about telling me about the young man who jumped the fence."

"I don't know anything about him," I muttered.

"You know his name, don't you?" His voice was sharper.

"It began with a *D* or a *B,* I think. Ask Lonnie. He knew him a lot better."

His face went rigid. "There are two ways this can come out, Shane. I can ignore all the evidence on those videotapes and pretend this is your first offense. If I do that, the judge will probably put you on probation and have you do community service. The second way is much worse. Because I could go through all those videotapes, count the times you stole beer, tell the judge that you won't cooperate, and recommend that you do a month or two in here, locked up. There are some pretty tough kids here, and you don't look that tough. So I'll ask you again. What was the other boy's name?"

My throat was so dry I could hardly speak. "Justin."

"Justin what?"

"I don't know. And that's the truth."

"I suppose you don't know where he lives either."

"I don't. I told you—he was Lonnie's friend."

"You're sure?"

"I'm sure."

He folded his hands on his desk and stared at me. "All right. But if it turns out that you're lying to me, you will regret it."

"I'm not lying. I swear to you. I'm not. I only just met him a few weeks ago."

He went to the door, opened it, and a second later my mother came in. Her eyes were moist, but she wasn't crying. Marian was hanging on to her coat, half asleep.

"You can take him now," he said. "I'll be in touch about the court date."

"Thank you," my mother said. "Thank you very much."

In the car she didn't say a word, maybe because Marian was in the back seat, sleeping. She just drove. Once we got home, she half carried, half guided Marian to her room. "You can't do this to me, Shane," she said when she came downstairs. "You just can't."

"I'm sorry."

"Sorry isn't good enough. I have to be able to trust you. You left Marian alone. Not just once, but over and over. What if there was a fire, or a break-in? We don't know anything about our neighbors. What if one of them is a sex offender?"

"Oh, Mom, don't get carried away."

She slammed her fist on the table. "I'm not getting carried away. We're not in Sound Ridge anymore. Understand? Do you want to go down to the police station tomorrow and read about all the sex offenders who live in this neighborhood? Do you? Because I did, and it's not pretty reading." The room went silent. After a long time, Mom looked up at me. "And what about you?"

"What do you mean?"

"I mean, what are your plans for yourself?"

I shrugged. "I don't know."

"Are you going to be a criminal?"

"No," I said angrily. "I'm not going to be a criminal."

"Well, that's good news. So what are your grades like so far at school?"

"They're okay."

"Really. So you can go out and get drunk every night and still get okay grades in school."

"I didn't get drunk every night, Mom."

"That's not what the police say."

"Well, the police are wrong."

"So what are your grades? A's?"

"No, they're not A's."

"Are they B's?"

"No."

"C's? D's? F's?"

"I don't know what they are."

"I can guess."

I stood. "All right. You've made your point. I'll stay here with Marian. I promise. Okay? And I'll hit the books more. What more do you want from me?"

Her eyes flashed. "Don't use that tone with me, young man. And to answer your question: I don't want anything *from* you. It's what I want *for* you. And that's everything. Do you understand? I want everything for you, just like I want everything for Marian. And I will not stand by and let you throw your life away. Not without a fight. Now go to your room."

I had to return to the Youth Detention Center a week later. Standing in the front of the room in a sports coat I'd out-grown, I waited while a gray-haired judge paged through a stack of papers. He had glasses on the end of his nose, and every so often he'd look at me over their top. Finally he closed my file, took off his glasses, and leaned forward. "I guess you've had a tough go of it recently," he said.

"I guess so," I answered, my voice quiet in that silent room.

"Life can sometimes deal out some bad hands."

I nodded.

His eyes narrowed. "But other people have tough times too. Your mother, for example. I don't suppose you'd say that these last months have been easy for her, would you?"

"No, I wouldn't."

"I wouldn't either," he said. "I wouldn't either." I expected him to go into a long lecture, but all he did was lean back in his big chair and stare at me. Finally he spoke. "Shane, I'm putting you on probation for a year. That means a probation officer will be watching you closely. He'll make house calls, check with your teachers and principal, that sort of thing. You'll also have to make restitution to the minimart, of course." He looked to my mom. "Does your son have his own savings account?"

"Yes, Your Honor," Mom answered. "He has a couple of hundred dollars of his own."

The judge looked back to me. "You now have a hundred dollars less."

I nodded, then turned to leave.

"I'm not done with you quite yet, young man." The judge's voice wasn't loud, but somehow it filled the room. I turned back. "I'll tell you when I'm finished."

I stood motionless as he read through a paper, the glasses back on the end of his nose. "I see you're a baseball player."

"I used to be," I said.

"Good enough. Besides the probation and the restitution to the minimart, you'll perform twenty hours of community service. There's a Boys' and Girls' Club down in Ballard, which isn't too far from Whitman High. Mr. Cornelius Grandison runs the program there, and he needs somebody to get the baseball diamond in shape for the upcoming season. That somebody will be you. Every day you will report to him after school until your twenty hours are complete. I, on the other hand, will never see you again. Is that correct?"

For a moment I didn't understand. Then I got it. "Yes, sir," I said.

"Good." He took off his glasses. "Now you can leave."

CHAPTER 4 After school the next Monday, I caught a city bus to the Boys' and Girls' Club to start my community service. A girl about my age was at the front counter. She was nice looking, with brown eyes and long brown hair. Before everything had happened, I'd have been interested, but I just didn't care enough anymore. "I'm supposed to meet Cornelius Grandison," I muttered.

She looked down at a clipboard. "Are you Shane?"

"Yeah," I said, embarrassed that she knew why I was there.

"Mr. Grandison is working on the baseball diamond." She motioned toward a door leading out.

"What's he look like?" I asked.

She smiled. "Don't worry. You won't miss him."

I pushed the door open and stepped outside, wondering what she meant. I looked around the baseball diamond, then did a double take. Standing on the pitcher's mound was a huge black man. He had to be at least six feet five and close to three hundred pounds.

He spotted me. "You the kid from Shorelake?" he called out.

"I don't go there anymore," I said, annoyed that he knew things about me when I didn't know anything about him.

"What's your name again?"

"Shane."

"Well, get over here, Shane."

I walked toward him. Not fast, but if a guy is six five, you don't crawl. When I reached him, he held out his hand. I thought he'd squeeze my hand hard, showing me how tough he was, but it was a normal handshake.

"How many hours you going to work each day, Shane?"

"Two," I said.

He nodded. "You owe twenty hours of time, so I've got you Monday to Friday for two weeks. Right?"

"Looks that way."

He stared at me. "It *is* that way." He paused. "I read your file. You're a ballplayer."

"Used to be."

"What do you mean *used to be*? Aren't you playing anymore?"

"I don't have a team."

"What about your new school? You go to Whitman, don't you?"

I nodded. "Yeah, but there's no way I'm playing for them."

"Why not? You too good for them or something?"

"Look, I have to work for you, and I know it. But I don't have to answer a bunch of questions."

He snorted. "A tough guy. I should have known—stealing beer from a little Asian lady. That's real tough. I'm just surprised that a tough guy like you would be a quitter."

The word *quitter* made my spine stiffen. My dad had always said that that was the worst thing anyone could call you. But I knew Grandison's game. He was baiting me. Then, once I got talking, he'd prove to me how stupid I was and tell me everything I should do with my life. Instead of answering, I looked off to the side. For a while neither of us said anything.

Finally he picked up a shovel and thrust it into my hand. "See that pile of dirt by third base? This infield has about a thousand holes in it. You use that dirt to fill them. Then tamp it down, and fill it again. When you've done that, come inside and get me. Okay?"

It was November, not exactly the warmest month of the year. As I worked, a light rain started to fall, and the wind picked up. I'd fill a wheelbarrow with dirt, then work my way around the infield filling in holes. The biggest hole was right at home plate, but there were smaller ones everywhere.

That first day all I did was fill holes. On day two Grandison had me water the field, refill the new holes that appeared, then rake the infield. After that I rolled a big, drumlike thing over the whole infield to make it level.

When I finished the infield, Grandison put me to work in the outfield. That didn't have to be perfect, but there were lots of holes, and it was hard work pushing the wheelbarrow back and forth. I got blisters on my hands, and my back ached every night, but still I kept at it until I got it done. If anybody sprained an ankle on that field, it wasn't going to be my fault. When the infield and outfield were in good shape, I worked on the foul territory and the screened-off pitching area. I spent the last two days painting the backstop and the benches green. Every time I finished something, I expected him to start in with the questions again, but he never did.

On my last day, Grandison came out and checked my work. "This field looks good," he said, nodding his head up and down. "Better than it's looked in a long time."

"Thanks," I said. It did look good, and I was proud of it.

"No, I'm the one who owes the thanks. You're a good worker, Shane. On that first day I didn't think you would be, but you are."

We walked back into the main building. Grandison opened a door and had me sit down in his office, which was about the size of a closet. He filled out some forms and made me sign in a couple of places. Then he looked at me.

"You love baseball, don't you?"

"It's okay."

He smiled. "You can't fool me. Juvenile Court has sent me lots of kids. I always put them to work on that field, and they mostly dog it." He chuckled. "Sometimes when they finish, the field is in worse shape than when they started. I don't know how they manage that." He pointed his long finger at me. "But you . . . you're different. You see the game even when there's nobody on the field."

"What?" I said.

"You heard me. You see the game even when the field is empty of players. I know you do, because I see it too."

He was right. As I'd worked, I had seen infielders scooping up grounders, outfielders tracking down fly balls. I squirmed in my chair, not knowing what to say.

He laced his fingers together behind his head and leaned back in his chair. "So tell me why you aren't going to play baseball for Whitman."

"I don't know. I'm just not."

"You're just not," he repeated. "What are you going to do instead?"

I shrugged. "Nothing."

He snorted. "There's a solid use of time."

"Can I go now?" I said.

He looked up at the clock. "No, you can't. I've got you for five more minutes." He paused. "I've read your file, Shane. Read all the newspaper articles about your dad. You've come down a peg or two in the world. But I'm here to tell you that all the stuff you lost—that fancy house and that fancy school—none of it was ever really yours. Your daddy got all of that with dirty money. He got it by bringing drugs into our city, ruining other people's lives, lots of them kids who live in my neighborhood. You're better off without all that. You get what I'm saying?"

The whole time that he was talking about my dad, I wanted to yell at him to stop. When he'd finally finished, I wanted to scream that he was a nothing, a nobody, and that he had no right to say those things, no right at all.

"Are you done?" I said, my voice like ice water.

He glared at me, then waved his hand toward the door. "I'm done. Go on, get out of here."

My heart was pounding like crazy as I headed for home. Why had I worked so hard for him? I should have left his field full of holes.

I took the bus up to Holman Road, and then transferred to the Greenwood bus that would take me home. For the first time in two weeks, all the connections worked; I didn't have to wait for more than five minutes for either bus. As I crossed Greenwood to head home, I heard my name being called. I turned and saw Lonnie Gibson waving at me.

I hadn't seen him since the night the cops had caught us. He asked me a bunch of questions, and I answered them. "How about you?" I said. "What are they making you do?"

Lonnie shrugged. "They kicked me out of Whitman. I go to Hay Alternative School now. It's a total joke. We don't even have books. We just sit around and talk in every class. About what we're feeling, what our needs are, that sort of garbage. And I got forty hours of community service at the Foss House, every single one of them with Mrs. Newby watching my every move. I empty the trash, mop the floors, clean up all sorts of gross stuff. Yesterday I found an old lady's teeth behind a toilet. I'm telling you, Shane, some of those people are *old*. I hope somebody shoots me before I get like that."

A bus came into view. "I got to go," he said. "Every time I miss an hour, I have to serve five to make up for it." He started walking toward the bus stop, then turned back to me. "Why don't you come around tonight? We can hang out like we used to, only not get ourselves arrested. What do you say?"

"Maybe."

"Do it. Those were good times."

CHAPTER 5 School . . . home . . . school . . . home. That was my life. The only time I saw my mother was at dinner, and then she pumped me with questions: "What's happening with your classes these days? . . . Anything important coming up? . . . How are you feeling?" She was trying to connect with me, but I didn't know what was going on inside me, so how could I tell her? Anyway, she had enough worries without my adding to them. She was working constantly, always taking overtime. And every couple of nights, I'd hear Marian cry out, then listen to her sob while Mom soothed her.

One Thursday evening, right before Christmas break, Mom had to take a night off from work because Mr. Kraybill, the social worker assigned to supervise me, was making his first house visit. I hated the idea of being checked on, but he could visit whenever he wanted—judge's order. When Kraybill showed up at our front door, he looked the opposite of what I'd expected. I thought he'd be flabby and old, but he was a skinny man with a narrow face, brown curly hair, and a wispy beard. He looked like he ran about ten miles every day.

After he settled himself on our sofa, he pulled out a file and flipped through it. I sat in the chair across from him and watched. Mom was bouncing up and down, bringing him coffee and little cakes, plumping his pillow. I think she was afraid he could cart me off to jail if he wanted to. "I'm fine," he said over and over. "Really, you don't have to bother."

He flipped through a thick stack of papers. "You got a good report from Mr. Grandison, Shane. You finished the community service right on time, didn't miss a day, worked hard. Grandison's a good man, isn't he?"

"He was okay," I said.

He tilted his head. "You didn't like him?"

"Not particularly."

"Really?" Kraybill's eyes sought out mine. "Most people do."

"He was okay."

"So you said."

Kraybill stared at me, then his eyes went back down to his papers. When he spoke again, his voice was clipped. "Your grades aren't as good as when you were at Shorelake. Any ideas why?"

"I guess Whitman's harder," I said.

A pained smile came to his face. "That's an interesting statement. Given the reputations of the two schools, I doubt there are five people in this city who'd agree with you."

Ten seconds went by. Then ten more. Finally my mom hopped up. "Can I get you more coffee?"

"Yes, thank you," Kraybill said, handing his coffee cup to her. He ran his fingers through his beard. "What are you interested in, Shane?"

"What do you mean?"

"A young man has to have interests. Yours clearly isn't school these days. So what is it? You got a girlfriend? You play a musical instrument? Do any sports?"

I shook my head. "I'm not interested in anything."

"Nothing?"

"Not really."

He picked up a picture from the coffee table. It was of me in my Shorelake baseball uniform. "You used to play baseball. You were pretty good, too, weren't you?"

"I was okay," I said.

"Are you going to play for Whitman this year?"

"Did you talk to Grandison about me?"

"No. Why?"

"Because he was after me to play baseball, too."

"And what did you tell him?"

"That I wasn't interested."

Kraybill closed his file folder and turned to my mother. "I'm going to arrange for Shane to see a psychologist. The county provides vouchers so that—"

My body went rigid. "I won't go," I said.

"Pardon me?"

"I won't go."

He smiled. "You don't seem to understand something here, Shane. You are under court supervision. Which means you are under *my* supervision. You follow my directions, or I'll bring you back before the judge with the recommendation that you spend a month under lock and key. And when that month is over, you'll *still* have to do what I say."

I remembered the kids I'd seen that night at the Youth Detention Center, their orange jump suits and angry eyes. I swallowed. "But I don't need to see a psychologist," I said.

"Is that so?" He paused. "Very well. I'll tell you why I disagree, and then you tell me where I'm wrong. If you convince me, then I'll drop my recommendation. But if you don't convince me, then you're going to do what I want you to do. You follow me?"

I nodded.

"Here's how I see it. You're sixteen years old. Before your

father killed himself, you were a student athlete with friends. Now you're doing nothing at school, you're doing nothing after school, you're doing nothing on weekends. The only friend you've made is Donny or Lonnie or whatever his name is, and he's a sad case, if ever there was one. You've stayed out of trouble for a few weeks, but it won't last. It can't last. A good psychologist might be able to jump-start you again, get you back among the living. Otherwise you're going to fall in with a bunch of losers."

I thought for a long time. "What if I jump-start myself?"

"How?"

"Baseball. If I play on the Whitman High team, then I'd have an interest, wouldn't I? I'd have a reason to keep my grades up; I'd have something to do after school and on weekends. That's what you want, right?"

"You said you weren't trying out."

"I wasn't going to. But I will if it means I don't have to see a psychologist."

He stared at me for a long time, so long I wanted to look away. But I somehow felt if I did, he'd say no. So I made myself look right back at him. "Fair enough," he said at last. "Baseball it is. But let me be crystal clear about this. I'll be in touch with your coach to make sure you attend every practice and every game, and that you give one hundred percent effort. So don't try to scam me."

"I won't."

With that, he stood up and made his way to the front door. When he opened it, he looked back at me. "You don't know who the baseball coach at Whitman is, do you?"

"No," I said, "I don't."

A funny smile came to his face. "He's a good man. I think you'll like him."

Once Kraybill was gone, Mom turned on me. "Shane, what is wrong with you? You were rude. Plain rude. The man was here to help you. To help us. Can't you see that?"

"I don't need his help," I said.

She laughed. "Is that right? You're doing so well on your own."

I was going to say something back, but instead I went to my room, lay down on my bed, and stared at the ceiling. I didn't know why I'd acted the way I did with Kraybill. Just like I didn't know why I couldn't concentrate at school, why I muttered only one-word answers whenever my mother asked me anything, why I was tired all the time. Everybody acted as if I *wanted* to be this way.

My baseball glove was sitting on top of my dresser, a baseball in the pocket. I got up, slipped the glove onto my left hand. Then I tossed the ball into the pocket. My dad had said that doing that over and over would make me a better pitcher. I don't know if that's true, but hearing the ball smack into the pocket used to send a charge of electricity through my body. There was no electricity that night. After about ten tosses, I put the glove back on the dresser.

We didn't get a tree until Christmas Eve. It was a scrawny thing, one side of it nearly bare. We turned that side to the wall, stuck on some ornaments, lights, and tinsel, and stepped back and looked at it. I don't know about Mom or Marian, but what I saw wasn't the ornaments on the tree but all the lights, ornaments, and decorations that were either sold at the yard sale or boxed up in the basement.

"It's small," Marian said, "but it's pretty."

"It is," Mom said. "It's very pretty. Don't you think so, Shane?"

"Yeah. It's great."

We looked at each other, not sure what to do next. For as far back as I can remember, Dad had taken us out on Christmas Eve for a long ride in a brand-new Lexus, which he'd brought home from the dealership especially for that night. He'd drive us through Olympic Manor and then over to Candy Cane Lane. He'd have Christmas music going on the CD player, and he'd turn the heat up so we could keep the windows down for a better look at the brightly decorated houses. "Everybody happy?" he'd ask, and we'd all say we were. At around ten o'clock we'd go to Pike Place Market for gelato. If it wasn't too cold, we'd walk down to the waterfront and look at the lights on the boats out on Puget Sound. Every year he'd make the same joke: "You two had better enjoy your ice cream, because tomorrow all that's going to be under the tree are lumps of coal." And every year Marian and I would laugh as if we'd never heard the joke before.

Nobody suggested going out that Christmas Eve. By ten o'clock, Mom and Marian were in their room, asleep. I kicked around downstairs a little longer but finally gave up and went to bed.

Christmas Day wasn't much better, though Mom tried. She made us a big breakfast—sausage and eggs and muffins—

and she wrapped everything she could think of, so that there were plenty of gifts under the tree. But Dad wasn't there making jokes and talking loud and fast, and there was nothing she could do about that.

CHAPTER 6 January was cold and rainy. The beginning of baseball season seemed as far off as the moon. Kraybill called my mom every week to check on me, and I think he called Whitman, too, though I'm not sure about that. If he did, he got good reports. I kept my head down and my mouth shut in the classroom, but I kept my ears open. I wouldn't say my grades soared, but by February, when the days started to grow a little longer and a little warmer, I was passing all my classes.

Finally the first day of tryouts rolled around. I packed my glove and cleats in my backpack and carried them from class to class. Every time I opened the backpack and saw them, a knot would form in my stomach. The prospect of joining a team made me go cold.

When the final bell rang, I thought about skipping practice entirely. Then I remembered Kraybill and his gray eyes, and I knew I didn't want to test him. I forced myself to take the long walk to the baseball field.

I'd never been back to that part of the campus. I figured it would be as run-down as the rest of the school. Surprisingly, the outfield grass was level, and somebody had filled the few holes with fresh dirt. They'd done a good job, too, as good a job as I'd done at the Boys' and Girls' Club. The infield was freshly raked, no rocks or holes anywhere. I stepped onto the pitcher's mound. It was better than the one at Shorelake. Firm, with a long gentle slope—not sticking up like a pimple the way some mounds do.

Somebody cared.

I sat down on the grass behind first base, took off my tennis shoes, and while lacing up my cleats, let my eyes wander. There were no more than twenty or twenty-five guys trying out. They were hanging out in groups of three or four, though a couple of guys were alone like me. Most of them seemed reasonably athletic, but two or three of them looked more like big-time pizza eaters than big-time ballplayers. One of the heavy guys was wearing sandals, and he didn't look as if he was going to change. There was nobody around who looked like a coach.

Once my shoes were laced up, I stretched. My hamstrings were incredibly tight, and my back was stiff. I've always been limber, so for a while I couldn't figure out what was wrong. Then I realized that I'd done nothing for nine months.

I was still stretching when a beat-up blue van pulled up next to the field. I thought I'd seen that van before, but I couldn't remember where. The door opened and a huge black man got out.

Cornelius Grandison.

What was he doing there? Had Kraybill sent him? Was he checking on me? Then I remembered Kraybill's question: *You don't know who the baseball coach at Whitman is, do you?*

As soon as Grandison stepped out of his junky van, guys

crowded around him. You could tell immediately that they liked him a lot and that he liked them. Others—newcomers like me, no doubt—hung back.

After a few minutes, Grandison broke free, blew his whistle, and waved for all of us to come closer. I moved forward, but not too far forward. His eye caught mine anyway and rested on me for a few seconds. He sort of nodded, and I nodded back.

When we were quiet, he introduced himself, then gave us the beginning-of-the-season pep talk. It was the same talk Coach Levine had given at Shorelake, only there was stuff about getting along with people of different races.

When Coach Grandison finished, he told us to play long toss to warm up. Guys partnered with friends; I stood around until the only person left was the heavyset guy wearing sandals.

If you'd asked me before practice began, I'd have told you I didn't care how I did. But once I saw that Grandison was the coach, I wanted him to know I could play.

The sandals guy was no ballplayer. He threw moon balls, high floaters that barely reached me. I threw him line drives that had so much zip they scared him. Grandison noticed. Toward the end of the warm-ups he came and stood next to me, not saying anything for a while. Then he blew his whistle and called the team together. "I want you to see something," he said. He turned to me. "Shane. Your name is Shane, isn't it?"

I nodded.

"Throw the ball to your buddy there. Just like you were doing."

I threw the ball, making the sandal guy's glove snap.

"Everybody see that?" He looked at me. "Keep throwing,

Shane." I threw again; again the glove snapped. "See how he uses his legs, how he bends his back? He's not all arm like some of you. He uses the other muscles, and that takes the strain off his arm. That's good mechanics."

Next he had everyone run a lap, but he held me back for a moment. "Your Shorelake coach teach you to throw like that?" he asked.

"My dad taught me to throw."

"Well, your dad did a good job."

CHAPTER 7 Calling those four days tryouts was a joke. At Shorelake there'd been fifty guys fighting for eighteen spots. Coach Levine had assistant coaches and volunteers with clipboards all over the place. They timed and measured everything: our height, our weight, how long it took us to go from home to first, first to second, second to third. They noted how the outfielders tracked fly balls, how the infielders handled grounders. They put a speed gun on the pitchers, charted how every player did in every drill, and at the end of the day gave those pieces of paper to Coach Levine.

At Whitman it was just Coach Grandison with just one clipboard with just one piece of paper on it, and I never once saw him write anything down. Maybe that was because he didn't need to. On the second day four guys—including my sandals buddy—didn't return. On the third day five more guys quit, bringing us down to sixteen, and three of them couldn't hit the ball out of the infield to save their lives.

By Friday, the last day of tryouts, fifteen of us were left. At the end of our final drill, Grandison announced we were all on the team. The guys around me smiled and punched each other, acting as if making the team meant something. "We play hard; we play together," Grandison said, "and we'll win our share of games."

I didn't blame him for saying that. What else could he say? Grandison had turned that dump of a field into something the Mariners could have played on. But it would take more than a rake and a love of baseball to turn the team into winners. I started to trudge off the field, but Grandison called me back. "I want to talk to you, Shane. Wait a second, will you?"

He wanted to talk to about five other guys, too, so I ended up standing there for a good ten minutes. Finally it was only him and me.

"Something wrong?" he asked.

"What do you mean?"

"You don't seem particularly happy about making the team."

"Come on," I said. "Everybody who tried out made the team."

He nodded. "I suppose tryouts are a little different at Shorelake."

I snorted in disbelief. "You could say that."

He looked at me quizzically. "Just how are they different, exactly?"

"You really want to know?"

"Yeah, I really do."

"Well, here it's you and that old pitching machine, and

that's it. At Shorelake they have three pitching machines, a pop-fly machine, two speed guns, two enclosed batting cages, an assistant coach, and a bunch of parent volunteers." I stopped. "You want me to go on, or is that enough?"

He smiled. "No, no, don't stop. Go on. This is interesting."

"Besides all that, there are the guys. Last year fifty tried out, and most of them could play. Shorelake has a varsity, a junior varsity, and a freshman team. You don't even have enough guys to field a JV team."

Grandison squinted into the sun. "So it was a lot better there, is that what you're saying?"

"It was another world."

He nodded. "Tell me something, Shane. How far is it from the pitcher's mound to home plate over there at Shorelake?"

"What?"

"You heard me."

"Sixty feet six inches."

"And from base to base. Was it ninety feet at Shorelake?"

"Of course it was," I said, wondering if he'd lost his mind.

"And how many guys on the field at one time?"

Suddenly I understood what he was doing. "Look, you can stop. I get your point."

His eyes went fiery. "Do you? I wonder."

With that, he turned and walked away.

I had to skip my shower to catch the bus home. It was nearly empty, but I still went way to the back, hunched up in a corner, and looked out the window. I found myself wondering about Shorelake. How had tryouts gone? Had they found somebody to take my spot? Then I stopped myself. Better to think of nothing than to think of that.

CHAPTER 8 As it turned out, the Whitman team wasn't as bad as I thought it would be. We had no bench at all, but the starting nine was solid. That was Coach Grandison's doing. He took the best three position players and put them right up the middle: Benny Gold behind the plate, Brian Fletcher at shortstop, and Jeff Walton in center field. If you're solid up the middle, you can generally get by.

The other position players were adequate, though Kenny Miller out in left field was about as slow an outfielder as you'll ever see. But Miller could hit a little, and Pedro Hernandez, our first baseman, could hit a ton.

The pitching wasn't bad either. The two starters had decent stuff. Hank Fowler, one of the few seniors on the team, was a big redheaded kid who threw nothing but fastballs. Cory Minton was smaller, with dark eyes, dark hair, and a body like a fireplug. He threw curves and changeups and an occasional fastball. That was the whole staff. There were no returning relief pitchers, not one. From what I picked up in practice, the year before those two guys had pitched every single inning.

Our opening game was on a Saturday. The Monday before, Coach Grandison took me off to the side and then called Gold over. "Get warm," Grandison said to me.

Gold crouched down, and I threw about fifteen warm-up tosses, picking up the speed on each just a little. When my arm felt loose, I looked at Grandison.

"All right," he said, "let it rip."

So I did, burning the ball in, throwing as if it were mid-season. After about ten fastballs, Gold popped up out of his stance and pulled his glove off. "That hurts," he said, smiling and blowing on his palm. "If you're going to throw like that, I've got to get a sponge."

Grandison turned to Gold. "Is he as fast as Fowler?"

"Faster."

Grandison nodded. "All right, Benny. That's enough. You go take some swings."

"Sure, Coach," Gold said, and he trotted off.

"You got anything other than that fastball?" Grandison asked when we were alone.

"Sometimes I throw a changeup."

"No curve?"

"My dad never let me throw one. He said it would ruin my arm."

Grandison nodded. "Good for him. How many pitches you good for?"

I shrugged. "Thirty, thirty-five."

"And then?"

"I lose speed and guys hit me."

Grandison looked across the field to where Minton and Fowler were tossing the ball around. "They're decent pitchers, both of them. But they don't have that closer's instinct. It gets tight late, and they want out of the game." He stopped. "What I'm saying here is between you and me. Understand?"

I nodded. "Yeah, I understand."

"You're going to be the key to our season, Shane. We went four and fourteen last year, but we lost eight of those fourteen in the last couple of innings. Win them all, and we go twelve and six. If you can throw that fastball over the plate in the late innings of a tight game and mix in the changeup to keep hitters off balance, we'll win them."

• • •

At the end of Tuesday's workout, Coach Grandison passed out a flyer about a team picnic. It was for that Friday, in place of practice. "You can bring your family," he said. "We'll have burgers and hot dogs and Wiffle balls and kites. I've arranged for the school van for those of you who need a ride, so I want to see everyone there. Understood?"

As we walked off the field, Minton sidled over to me and a couple of the other new guys. "You won't believe Grandison's daughter," he said. "But don't let him catch you checking her out, or you won't play for a month."

A dozen times that week I heard about how good the food was to eat and how good Grandison's daughter was to look at. But when Friday afternoon came, I didn't feel like going. So instead of piling into the school van, I went home. For the first time since baseball season had started, I was home before Mom had left for work. For a while I sat in the front room while she put together dinner for Marian and me. "Can I help with something?" I asked, feeling guilty that she was working and I was doing nothing.

We ate early—roasted chicken, rice, and French bread. While Mom got herself ready for work, Marian and I washed the dishes. "You want to do something?" I asked once Mom was gone. "Play Monopoly or Sorry or something like that?"

She shook her head. "I'm just going to watch TV."

The phone rang. "Aren't you going to answer it?" Marian asked, turning back.

"I want to hear who it is first," I said.

The answering machine clicked on. "Shane, you there?

This is Coach Grandison. If you're there, pick up the phone."
There was a long pause, followed by the dial tone.

"Why didn't you pick it up?" Marian asked.

"I didn't want to talk to him."

"Why not?"

"I just didn't want to."

CHAPTER 9 Opening game was Saturday at three at
Rainier Beach High. Even back when we lived in Sound Ridge
and my mom didn't have to work, she rarely went to my
games. She wasn't coming to this one, either. "You know how
I get, Shane. I feel sick to my stomach waiting for you to
pitch. And then when you do pitch, I can't watch. Besides, I'd
have to rush to make it to work."

At practice Grandison had told us that if we needed a
ride, we were to meet him in front of the school at one-thir-
ty. I figured I'd be the only person without a ride, but Miguel
Alvarez, our backup catcher, was there before me. We hadn't
waited for more than a few minutes before Grandison pulled
up. When we'd loaded all the stuff—helmets, bats, catcher's
gear—into the back, Grandison slammed the doors shut and
then turned on me. "Where were you yesterday, Shane?"

"I had to look after my little sister," I said.

"Didn't you hear me say you could bring your family?"

"She didn't want to go."

"Why not?"

"I don't know. She just didn't."

He considered that for a moment. "Next time you don't want to do something, just say it. Don't blame it on your sister."

I felt myself flush. "I'm not lying. My sis—"

He stopped me cold. "The more you talk, the less I want to hear. Get in the back of the van and keep quiet."

That's what I did. And even though he didn't say anything else, I could feel his anger. Before the game, the guys talked about the Wiffle ball game and the tank top Grandison's daughter wore. From what I could tell, I was the only player who hadn't shown up, not that anybody other than Grandison seemed to have noticed.

When warm-ups were over, I took a seat at the end of the bench next to Alvarez. There weren't many parents or kids in the bleachers, but I could feel the buzz of opening day. Our leadoff hitter, Jim Wilson, nubbed a little roller down the third base line. Their guy got to the ball okay, but his throw was wild. By the time their right fielder ran it down, Wilson, who can fly, was standing at third. Kurt Lind, batting second, struck out. It didn't matter, though, because Pedro Hernandez unloaded a long home run to left field, giving us two quick runs. We scored twice more in the second inning on doubles by Jeff Walton and Benny Gold, and I thought we might blow them out. But after the second inning, the Rainier Beach pitcher settled down and our bats went quiet.

Cory Minton was steady on the mound. He didn't overpower anyone, but he kept the ball low. In the early innings, the Rainier Beach hitters were overanxious, and they pounded those low pitches into the dirt for easy groundouts. But little by little they started to time Minton. They put together a couple of hits and a walk to push across one run in the fourth, and they scored another on a triple and a groundout in the fifth.

By the sixth, Minton was done. You could see it in his face and in the length of time he took between pitches. Rainier Beach's leadoff hitter smacked a single to left. "Hunter!" It was Grandison's voice. "Get warmed up. Fast." I nudged Alvarez. He grabbed his catcher's mitt, and the two of us hustled up the first base line.

As I warmed up, I kept one eye on the game. Minton threw one ball, then another. The hitter dug in and ripped the next pitch on a line, but right at Brian Fletcher for the first out. But the next batter laced a double down the right field line, putting runners at second and third. I speeded my warm-ups. Grandison looked down at me. I shook my head *no*. There was still some tightness in my shoulder. I'd need a few more throws to get loose.

Minton went into the stretch, delivered. The crack of the bat was so loud both Alvarez and I stopped to watch the flight of the ball.

It was a towering drive to left center. Walton broke on the ball, raced to the base of the fence. I was sure it was gone, but at the last second Walton leaped. His glove was about six inches over the top of the fence, but he pulled the ball back in. The runner at third tagged and scored, cutting our lead to 4–3, but without Walton's incredible play we would have been down 5–4.

Grandison walked slowly out to the mound. I fired one

pitch, then another, to Alvarez. I saw Grandison look over to me. This time I nodded, and he waved me into the game.

I was sweating like crazy when I took the ball from Grandison. "Get him out," he said, and I nodded, my throat too dry to talk. It was the first time I'd been on the mound in a real game since the day my father died. I could almost feel him as I took my final warm-up tosses. "Play ball!" the umpire called. Gold settled in behind the plate.

The situation was pretty simple. Two out, tying runner at second. The batter was their first baseman, a guy with legs like tree trunks.

I was pumped—too pumped. My first pitch was wild high. Gold jumped to his feet, but the ball sailed over his mitt to the backstop. The runner at second trotted down to third— ninety feet from tying the score.

My next two pitches were a little better, but not much. Both were high and outside, but at least Gold could get to them.

With the count 3–0, Grandison called time and trotted out to me. "You want to walk him?" he asked. "Take our chances with the next guy?"

I looked to the on-deck circle. The next batter was a left-handed contact hitter, the kind of guy who puts the ball in play. You never know what's going to happen with hitters like that. "I can get this guy out."

Grandison nodded. "Okay. Just trust your ability. Be fluid."

As he trotted off the field, I crouched down and retied my shoelaces. If I could go slower, my pitches would be faster. I stood up, and smooth as silk, went into my wind-up. I hadn't tried at all, but the ball was a bullet that smacked into Gold's mitt. "Strike one!" the umpire shouted.

From the bench, Grandison clapped his hands together. "Two more just like that, Shane. Just like that."

I got the sign from Gold, went into my motion, delivered. Everything was easy, and the result was another bullet at the knees. "Strike two!" the umpire shouted.

The crowd, loud to begin with, got louder. "Don't overthrow!" I whispered to myself as I went into my motion for the payoff pitch. Again everything seemed effortless, yet the ball exploded out of my hand. This time the batter swung, but the ball was in Gold's mitt before he got the barrel of his bat over the plate. "Strike three!" the umpire yelled.

As I trotted off the mound, the guys behind me whooped and hollered, and when I sat on the bench, they came over and patted me on the shoulder and the top of my head. "Way to go, Shane!" I hardly looked at them. I had another inning to get through.

But that strikeout breathed life into my teammates' bats. We pounded the ball all over the park in the top of the seventh, bringing home five runs on four hits, two walks, and an error.

With a six-run lead, I wasn't going to nibble at the corners. Everything in the bottom of the seventh was right over the plate. Nothing but strikes—hit it if you can, but they couldn't. There was a pop-up to first, a comebacker, and a strikeout.

When the umpire yelled "Strike three!" on the last batter, my teammates rushed the pitcher's mound. I high-fived them all. Grandison came out to me, too. "You the man!" he said, a grin on his face.

I made my way to the bench and as I packed my bag, Kurt Lind came over. "My dad's going to buy us all burgers at Red

Robin. You want to come?" It was the kind of thing my dad used to do at Shorelake after we'd won a game.

I looked across the parking lot to a big van where a bunch of the guys were standing and talking. Even Benny Gold, who hardly talked to anybody, was with them.

"Sorry," I said. "I've got to get home."

"Ah, go with them, Shane," Grandison said from behind me.

I didn't like him listening in on my conversations.

"I've got to go home."

Grandison frowned. "Your sister again?"

"As a matter of fact, it is."

Lind put up his hand. "Next time."

CHAPTER 10 But I didn't hang out with the guys after the next game or the game after that, either. When I closed out the fourth victory of our season by striking out the side, Kurt Lind didn't bother asking me.

"You like being an outsider or something?" Grandison said when he dropped me off in front of the duplex.

I shrugged. "I don't mind."

"I suppose it's easier," he growled. "If you become friends with people, you have to talk to them, get to know them. You can't spend so much time thinking about yourself, can you?"

"Thanks for the ride." I slammed the van door shut and headed inside the house.

It was around then that Marian made a new friend, Kaitlin McGinley. Kaitlin had red hair and freckles and was quick to laugh. She also had an older sister and brother and two younger sisters. They lived a block away in an old ramshackle house that looked as if it would collapse in a windstorm. Marian went there every chance she got and stayed as long as she could. She was full of stories about the McGinleys' dogs, their creepy attic, and the Ping-Pong tournaments in the waterlogged basement. She was smiling again, and her nightmares had almost stopped.

On more and more school nights, I was alone in the duplex while Marian did her homework at Kaitlin's. You wouldn't think it would matter. When she'd been home, we didn't talk much. She'd go upstairs and read, and I'd stay downstairs and watch television. But there's something about being the only one in a house that's different.

After that fourth victory, I couldn't find anything I wanted to watch on TV. Bored, I stretched out on the sofa and flipped through the *Seattle Times*. In the sports section, there was an article about Shorelake's team. I tried not to read it, but I couldn't resist.

They were crushing their opponents, winning games by scores like 10–2 and 14–1. The writer talked about how good their two starters were, and how many complete games they'd thrown. There was no mention of any relief pitchers.

One name did jump out at me—Reese Robertson. I'd thought he was a total braggart when he'd talked about wanting to hit against me, but according to the article, the guy was some kind of hitting machine. He'd been all-state in California as a sophomore. He was hitting over .500 for Shorelake, with two home runs, a bunch of RBI. He stole bases and caught everything that was anywhere near him. I read the article over and over again, and every time I read it, I hated him more.

We won our fifth game by thumping Cleveland 7–3 on Saturday afternoon. I pitched another perfect seventh to close it out. Guys were pumped at practice on Monday, but it wasn't the Cleveland game Grandison talked about. It was the next game, Thursday's nonleague game against Woodway. "You've all heard about what happened over at Woodway High, haven't you?" he said.

I'd seen the article in the newspaper—there'd been a big drinking party at Richmond Beach, with nearly the whole team involved. A fight had broken out, the police were called, and a half dozen players were arrested. "The school has decided to shut the entire team down, to forfeit all games for the rest of the year." Grandison paused. "I don't want anything like that happening to this team. You hear me? No drinking, no drugs. No cigarettes. No chewing tobacco. No nothing."

It was nice to get the forfeit, but when you're on a winning streak, you want to keep playing. The coming weekend was the only weekend all season when we didn't have a game. "So we won't play until next week?" Benny Gold asked.

"That's how it looks right now," Grandison said. "But I've got an idea that I'm working on. Pretty exciting, too. That is, if you guys want to play. Only it wouldn't be Thursday. It would be Friday. How about it? You willing to give up your Friday night?"

"Yeah, sure," guys called out.

"Who'd it be against?" Cory Minton asked.

"I'm not saying," Grandison answered mysteriously. "Not until it's definite. But it's a good team, a team I've wanted to play for a long time. We beat them, and we'll get some attention."

CHAPTER 11 When I got home that night, there was a note on the kitchen table. "Had to start work early. There are some burritos in the fridge for you and Marian. Love, Mom."

I microwaved the burritos, and Marian and I ate them. As I was washing the dishes, a crazy idea came to me. But the more I considered it, the less crazy it seemed. When the dishes were dry and put away, I went to the front room where Marian was reading. "There's something I need to check on the Internet. You want to come to the library with me?"

She shook her head. "I'm going to Kaitlin's. We're doing a science project."

She looked excited; I could tell she wanted to talk. "What's it on?"

"It's an invention. We're going to use my rat wheel to generate electricity. The rat runs in the wheel, and the lights go on."

"How much light?"

"Not much. But it's the theory that counts. You could get lots of lights."

"If you had lots of rats."

"You're making fun of me."

"No, no. It's a good invention."

At the library, I was first in line for a computer with Internet access. I didn't think any of the people would ever log off, but at last an old man stood up and stretched. It took him about ten minutes to put on his coat and pick up his papers and pencils. Finally the computer was mine.

Immediately I logged on to Shorelake's website and went straight to their baseball schedule. There it was. "Saturday, April 3, Woodway High." Next to it was a single word: "Cancelled."

I was right.

Shorelake didn't play Seattle teams. Their schedule was filled with games against other private schools and the suburban high schools. But the Woodway forfeit had left a hole in their schedule, a hole that only Whitman could fill. Coach Levine wouldn't want a long layoff. A game against us was a natural.

I stared at the screen. Part of me didn't want to play them. I hated thinking about them sitting in the dugout talking about me and my dad. But another part of me remembered Greg, Cody, and Reese driving by me in the mornings, pretending they didn't see me. Well, they wouldn't see my fastball either.

I pictured the seventh inning. Somehow we'd be up a run, and I'd get the call to close the game. I'd mow them down. Their last hitter would be Reese Robertson. *I'd like to hit against you sometime.* That's what he'd said. I'd make him eat those words. The Shorelake parents and players would be up and screaming, but I'd strike him out on three pitches.

The whole thing was a fantasy, but it wasn't a crazy fantasy, like imagining that I was going to fly to the moon. They were better than us, no doubt about it, but baseball is a quirky game. On any given night, anything can happen.

When I got home, I couldn't settle down. Finally I dug out Coach Grandison's phone number. It rang about ten times before he answered. "Did you get the Friday game?" I asked him.

"Who is this?"

I scrambled. "It's me. Shane. My mom asked me to call so she can get somebody to look after my sister if I'm not going to be home."

There was a long pause.

"Is there a game?" I repeated.

"Yeah, there's a game," he said. "And it's against your old school, Shorelake. But you already figured that out, didn't you?"

"No," I said too quickly. "I mean it occurred to me it might be against them, but it's no big deal to me who we play."

"Right," he said, "just another game."

CHAPTER 12 The game was at five o'clock at Woodland Park, field one. We were already warming up when the Shorelake bus pulled into the parking lot, and the players spilled out of it and onto the field. When I'd been on the Shorelake team, I hadn't thought anything of our uniforms. Now, across the field from them, I noticed. Black and white pinstripes, just like the Yankees, with major-league-style warm-up jackets. They looked like professionals, and they walked with the swagger of guys who knew they were better than us, and knew that we knew it.

I tossed the ball to Miguel Alvarez, and he tossed it back. Out of the corner of my eye I saw someone running. I looked over, and Greg was trotting toward me, a smile on his face. When he reached me, he stuck out his hand. "Good to see you, Shane."

I shook it. "Good to see you, too."

We both stood there looking at each other, at the field.

"This is great, isn't it?" he said. "Getting to play against each other."

"Yeah. It is."

"I've been following your games in the paper. Seems like you're doing pretty well, and your team too."

"We've done okay," I said.

"Okay? You're unbeaten, and you haven't given up a run all year, have you?"

I shook my head. "Not yet."

He smiled. "That's more than okay. That's outstanding."

"You guys aren't doing so bad either."

He nodded. "We've got a good team. Reese—that guy who moved into your house—he can hit."

"That's what I hear."

"No. I mean he can *really* hit. He'll be a major leaguer someday, no doubt about it." He paused. "Well, I should get back to my team. I only wanted to say hello and wish you luck. We should get together sometime."

I shook his hand a second time. "Yeah. We should."

With that he trotted off.

A couple of minutes later Reese Robertson stepped into the batting cage to take his swings. Outside the batter's box, he didn't look like much, not all that big or muscular. But inside the batter's box, he seemed to grow. The bat was on his shoulder, and then it was whipping through the strike zone with incredible speed. His head was down on every pitch, his arms extended. He took five swings, and every swing resulted in a line shot somewhere. The balls jumped off his bat, one-hopping the fences or sailing right over them.

As Robertson was taking his cuts, my eyes shifted to our starter, Hank Fowler. He was watching Robertson, his eyes wide and his mouth hanging open. I should have gone over to Fowler then; I should have told him that anybody could hit in batting practice. But I didn't, and Fowler's eyes grew wider and wider with every crack of Robertson's bat.

"Play ball!" the home plate umpire shouted. I found a spot at the far end of the bench, stretched my legs out, ripped open a pack of sunflower seeds, and shoved a handful in my mouth.

Fowler started the game strong, striking out the first two Shorelake batters, bringing Robertson to the plate. It was Fowler's chance to send a message to the Shorelake team, to set the tone for the game. He needed to show them that he could handle their best. The fans in the bleachers knew it too. There was shouting from both sides. "Strike him out! . . . Get a hit!"

Fowler rocked and delivered. A good fastball for a called strike. Robertson tapped home plate once, twice. Fowler peered in, got the sign, went into his motion again, delivered. "Strike two!" Another fastball, and for the second time Robertson didn't swing.

On the bench, we were up, shouting for the strikeout to end the inning. Fowler went into his wind-up, came to home plate. It was yet another fastball, but this time, quick as lightning, Robertson swung. The ball jumped off his bat, a line shot into left center. If Robertson had gotten under it even a little, it would have gone out of the park. As it was, it was a solid single, but with two out, Robertson decided to try to stretch it into a double.

Jeff Walton ran down the ball quickly, wheeled and fired to second. The throw was on the money, only it was head high. Robertson slid in hard, bowling over Kurt Lind, our second baseman, as he tried to put down the tag. The ball dribbled out of Lind's glove toward the pitcher's mound. Robertson popped up on the bag, clapping his hands, a smile creasing his face. But Lind stayed down, clutching his knee, which had twisted under the force of the slide.

Coach Grandison raced out, and so did Mr. Burns, the guy in charge of first aid for our team. They checked Lind's knee, gently feeling for any damage. Finally Lind stood up and jogged a few steps. All the parents clapped for him. I could see Grandison ask Lind if he was okay. Lind flexed his knee a couple of times, grimaced, but nodded. "I can play."

When a guy goes down clutching his knee, all you can think is that he might be done for the year. You're not thinking about the next batter, the next pitch. So when it was time for Fowler to pitch again, he wasn't ready.

His first pitch was a fastball down the middle with not much on it. The Shorelake hitter didn't cream it, but he did smack it on the ground toward the hole between second and first base. I'd seen Lind make the play on balls hit harder than that one. Now, unsure of his knee, he barely moved. The ball scooted into right field for a single. Robertson, off at the crack of the bat, scored easily. I watched him walk back to the bench, high-fiving the on-deck batter on his way. He sat down in the middle of the bench, a big smile on his face.

That was the first run of the inning, but it wasn't the last. Robertson had sucked the confidence right out of Fowler. Instead of rearing back and throwing, he started guiding the ball. He gave up another single, a walk, and then a pair of doubles—one to left center and the other a rope down the right field line. By the time the top of the first was over, we were down 5–0. The guys coming in from the field had their heads down.

Before Grandison took his spot in the third-base coach's box, he strode up and down our bench, clapping his hands. "Look alive, gentlemen! There's a lot of baseball left to be played."

It worked, at least a little. Guys sat up and chattered as Jim Wilson, our leadoff hitter, stepped into the batter's box. "Come on, Jimbo! Get a hit." One run. That's all we needed. One lousy run would make us feel that we belonged on the field with Shorelake.

Scott Parino was pitching for Shorelake. He looked bigger than I remembered, as if he'd been lifting weights, and his fastball seemed faster. His first pitch to Wilson was a strike on the outside corner. He followed that with a fastball inside—sending Wilson spinning out of the way. On the bench we all jumped up, hollering at Parino, even though we knew the pitch wasn't really that close.

Wilson stepped back in. Parino's next pitch was another fastball, right down the middle. It was the kind of pitch Wilson normally handles. But this time he managed only a weak swing and popped out to second. Lind, still limping, tapped the first pitch he saw right back to the mound. Two pitches later Pedro Hernandez popped out to the catcher, and the first was over.

Fowler struggled through the second, giving up a walk and a single, but no runs. I felt myself hoping again. All we had to do was hold them down for a few innings, then chip away—a run here, a run there, and we'd be right back in it.

I looked down the bench at the guys. They were leaning forward, elbows on knees, chins resting on their hands. For the first time I wished I'd gone to the barbecue, hung out with them at lunch or before school. Then I could have walked up and down the bench, encouraging them, pumping them up. Instead, all I could do was sit on my hands and watch as Parino shut us down in the second inning.

Fowler started the third inning strong, blowing away Shorelake's first two hitters with a combination of fastballs and changeups. He was pumped to strike out the side—too pumped. His first pitch to the third hitter sailed over the guy's head all the way to the backstop. His next pitch wasn't much closer. Two more balls put that batter on first. *No big deal,* I thought. But then came an infield hit and an error by our third baseman, Paul Barrett. Just like that the bases were loaded—with Robertson stepping to the plate.

Fowler was intimidated. You could see it. His first pitch was a foot outside; the one after that was two feet outside. With the count 2–0, there was nothing he could do but serve up a fastball and hope for the best. Fowler rubbed up the baseball, went into his wind-up, and threw his best fastball down the middle. Robertson was waiting for it. He sent a rocket into the left-center-field alley. The ball skipped past Walton, rolling all the way to the fence. With two outs, the runners had taken off at the crack of the bat. The first two scored standing. The throw home to try to nail the third guy was wild, and he scored too. And standing on third base, no more than twenty feet away from me, was Robertson, clapping his hands and grinning ear to ear, his team ahead 8–0.

The game was over. In the top of the third, it was completely over. After Robertson's big hit, players on both teams started swinging at the first pitch, just trying to finish the game. Grandison still called out encouragement to batters, but there was no urgency in his voice. On the Shorelake bench, guys were punching one another, laughing and joking, hardly watching the action on the field, moving around simply to keep warm. Even guys on our team were making jokes, only quietly.

The score was 11–0 after four innings. In the fifth, Grandison took out Fowler and put in Cory Minton, who did a little better, getting through the fifth without giving up a run. But in the top of the sixth, Robertson—who else?—hit a mammoth home run to left center to push Shorelake's lead to 13–0.

When Minton returned to the bench after recording the third out, Grandison came over to me. "Shane, do you want to pitch? Because if you do, the seventh is yours. If not, I'll let Minton finish. Your call."

For a moment I couldn't say anything. Did I want to pitch? I didn't really know. Then I felt a surge of cold fury. "I'll pitch." I grabbed my glove, tapped Alvarez on the shoulder, and headed for the sidelines.

CHAPTER 13 It was cold and getting colder when I finally took the mound to pitch the seventh against Shorelake. A low fog was hanging over the outfield, making it tough for the hitters to pick up the ball, and I was going to make it tougher.

The leadoff batter was a sub, a guy I didn't know. I teased him with a changeup outside, then came in with a fastball on the hands. He took a weak swing and dribbled the ball right to me. I tossed the ball to first for the out.

One down, two to go.

Brian Coombs was up next. We'd never been friends, but he nodded at me and half smiled, generally acting as if he expected me to smile back. I gave him nothing—nothing but fastballs that he couldn't touch. Three pitches, three strikes. Two down.

The ball went around the diamond and came back to me. I rubbed it up, then turned to face the final batter of the night. I looked, then looked again.

Reese Robertson.

I'd been so focused I hadn't noticed him on deck. But now that he was there, facing me, I knew this was what had to be, that it was somehow fated.

Something odd happened next. The guys on the Shorelake bench stood up. They started screaming and hollering. "You can do it, Reese! . . . Just a single, that's all you need."

I didn't get it. They were up by what . . . thirteen runs? You'd think that would be enough. Then the chant started: "Cycle! Cycle! Cycle!"

That's when I understood.

Hitting for the cycle is the rarest accomplishment in baseball, rarer even than a no-hitter. A hitter has to get a single, a double, a triple, and a home run all in one game. It takes power and speed and luck. Some great ballplayers go their whole careers and never do it, not at any level. All Robertson needed was a single, and he'd have done it. Just a measly little single.

He wasn't going to get it. Not off me.

I stepped onto the rubber and glared down at him, but he didn't register anything. He was so calm, so confident. There was nothing personal in the way he looked at me. Benny Gold put down one finger, calling for the fastball on the outside corner. I nodded and let it fly. Most guys can't take a full swing at my fastball; their bats aren't quick enough. But Robertson was on it; he just swung right under it. "Strike one!" the umpire yelled. Robertson stepped out, pulled on his batting gloves a little, trying to act cool, but the speed on my fastball had surprised him.

I wound up, delivered. Another fastball, but this time I'd thrown it about six inches outside, figuring he'd be overeager. I was right. He swung awkwardly, barely fouling it back. "Strike two!" the umpire called.

He stepped out, took a deep breath, adjusted his gloves again, then stepped back in. For a second his eyes met mine and locked. Blue friendly eyes, confident eyes.

Gold gave me the sign for another fastball. I nodded. Then Gold crouched down and held his glove a good foot outside. He thought we could get Robertson to go fishing and strike out. But Robertson was a smart batter. He peeked down at Gold and saw how far outside he was set up. Immediately he crowded close to the plate, thinking he'd be able to lean out and poke the outside pitch into right field for the hit he needed to complete the cycle.

Robertson's strategy might have worked if I'd thrown to Gold's glove. Instead, I reared back and fired the ball harder than any ball I've ever thrown in my life. Only I didn't throw it outside. I threw it inside. Up and in.

High heat.

It was the last thing in the world Robertson was expecting. He was leaning out over the plate, looking for something outside and low. By the time he understood what was really coming, he was lost. His cleats might as well have been bolted to the ground.

He was lost, but the ball found him. It found him as if it were some heat-seeking missile. At the last fraction of a second he threw his hands up and tried to duck away, but it did him no good. I heard the ball hit him, hit him so solidly it sounded as if it had hit his bat. It caught him half on the skull, half on the helmet, shattering it. He wobbled, and then he went down. A few seconds later blood was flowing from his nose, and his legs started flopping around.

Everyone stood frozen for what seemed like minutes but was probably only seconds. A woman in the bleachers screamed. Gold and the umpire were on their knees, leaning over Robertson. Coach Levine ran out, followed by Grandison and other people from the stands. So many people were crowded around Robertson that I couldn't see him.

I did see his mother, though. She stood off to the side, covering her mouth with her hands, tears running down her face. She looked nothing like the woman who had gone through our house, checking each closet and light switch, talking and talking and talking.

A minute later I heard a siren in the distance. It grew louder and louder. finally an aid car pulled onto the field, right up to home plate. Two medics jumped out. Everyone stepped back.

They bent over Robertson, taking his pulse I guess, or maybe checking his heart. I couldn't really see. They put a brace around his neck. After that they moved him onto a stretcher, then slid the stretcher into the back of the aid car. Reese's mom and dad climbed in with him, and they went tearing off the field, siren screaming.

At home plate Grandison, Levine, and the umpire conferred. It didn't take long. Grandison turned and waved us all in. "Game's over, men," he said.

All of the other guys either had a parent at the game or were going home with a friend. I was the only one getting a ride home in the school van. I packed the gear, threw it in the back, and got in.

Grandison didn't come right away. As I waited, I told myself what some of my teammates had also said as they were leaving: that it wasn't my fault, that it was an accident. Robertson had been leaning out over the plate. I was moving him back, like any good pitcher would. That's all. Just moving him off the plate. If he'd fallen down or jumped back, he'd have been fine. Not that he wasn't fine anyway. He'd had his helmet on. So how serious could it be?

Grandison got into the van. "They've taken him to Children's Hospital. I'm going to go there right now. You want to come along?"

"I have to get home," I said. "My mom is at work. I have to—"

"Look after your sister," Grandison interrupted. "All right. I'll take you home. I don't have time to argue."

CHAPTER 14 When I opened the door to the duplex, all the lights were off. On the kitchen table was a note. "Marian's sleeping over at the McGinleys. There's a plate of food for you in the refrigerator. Hope you had a good game. Try to get to bed early. Love, Mom."

It was deli food: a ham and Swiss cheese sandwich on rye bread, a dill pickle, and potato salad. There was a raspberry Snapple there, too.

At any other time I'd have wolfed it down, but that night I picked at it before throwing it away. I even poured most of the Snapple down the drain.

I took a shower, then looked around the place. It was such a dump. I wanted to go somewhere and do something, but I didn't know where or what. I ended up sitting in front of the television watching *Xena* and *Hercules* until it was nearly midnight. Lots of times I stay awake until I hear my mom come in at around one, but that night I was out as soon as my head hit the pillow.

In the middle of the night I had a dream. I was back on the field, and everything was happening again, only in slow motion. I saw Reese leaning out over the plate. I saw the ball flying toward his head. Closer . . . closer . . . closer. "Hit the dirt!" I shouted in my dream. "Hit the dirt!" Then I heard it again, the sound of the baseball crushing bone. Not helmet. Bone. Only now I wasn't dreaming but sitting straight up, sweat pouring off me.

Had I killed him? It happens sometimes in baseball. It even happened to a major league player once. Ray Chapman was his name. He died not on the field but the next day, or maybe it was the day after that, at the hospital. Carl Mays hit him. Chapman got up after he was hit, took a couple of steps, then fell.

Reese hadn't even gotten up. I thought of the blood that had come from his nose. Where was that blood from? Was it from his brain? Then I thought of the blood on the carpet in my father's study.

I got out of bed, made my way downstairs, and opened the phone book. It took a while, but I found the number of Children's Hospital and punched it in. "I'm calling about Reese Robertson," I said, trying to keep my voice calm. "He was admitted earlier tonight. I want to know if he's okay."

"One moment," the voice said. Music came on—the Beatles singing "Here Comes the Sun." It played and played. I was about to hang up and start over when the line came alive. "Night nurse, intensive care unit. How can I help you?"

"Reese Robertson," I said. "He was hit with a—"

"I know who he is," she interrupted, sounding annoyed.

"I'm a friend of his. How is he? Is he okay?"

"He's not okay, but with a little bit of good luck, he's going to be okay."

"So he's not going to die or be brain damaged or anything?"

She sighed. "No, he's not going to die, and he's not going to be brain damaged or anything. If you give me your name, I'll tell him you called."

"That's okay," I said, and I quickly hung up.

CHAPTER 15 At breakfast the next morning, Mom seemed more tired than usual. She didn't ask anything about the game. Marian came back around noon, her friend Kaitlin trailing behind her. "Did you have a good time?" Mom asked them.

"Uh-huh," Marian answered, and the two of them went upstairs and closed the door.

At one I ate a sandwich. Normally I'd have watched sports on television or maybe listened to CDs, but I was too itchy to stay in the house. I pulled my shoes on. "I'm going down to Market Street in Ballard," I said to Mom. "To that new music store."

"Okay, but be home by five."

I bought an all-day bus pass—on weekends they're cheaper than two one-way rides—and got off in Ballard. I walked up and down Market, went into the Secret Garden Bookstore and the Dollar Store, checked out the CDs. Finally I got an Italian soda at Dutch Treat and sat outside. I took a long time drinking that soda.

As I finished, I looked up and saw the forty-four bus coming—the bus to Children's Hospital. Suddenly I knew what I'd been wanting to do all day. I stood up, dodged cars as I crossed Market Street, and waved down the bus driver.

He stopped, but he was angry. "Don't do that again," he said as I climbed the steps. "No bus ride is worth getting hit for."

"I won't," I said as I showed him my pass.

As the bus bumped along, I felt better. I'd go see Reese, tell him I was sorry. We'd shake hands just like major leaguers would, and it would be over. Just past the University of Washington I gave the cord a tug and hopped off.

Children's Hospital is perched on a hill above Sandpoint Way. When we'd passed it in the car before, it had always seemed like just another big building. But that day, with the birch trees blowing in the wind and dark gray clouds racing across the sky, it was spooky. As I trudged up the hill, the hospital seemed to grow larger. Car after car passed by. I could see parents looking out. They'd see me but look right through me.

I walked past one parking lot, then another, then another. For every one of those cars, there was a sick kid. It was hard to believe there were that many sick kids in the whole world. An ambulance sped up the hill past me, its siren strangely silent.

I felt the urge to turn around, head down the hill, and catch the first bus back to my duplex. Instead, I forced myself to keep going. Once I got this over with, I'd be fine. Besides, Reese wouldn't be with the really sick kids, the bald kids with cancer who were fighting for their lives. He'd be with guys who had normal stuff—like broken legs and arms. That's what most of the kids would have. They were here for a day, maybe two, and then they went home all fixed up and better. The hospital wasn't a graveyard.

I finally reached the main entrance. I stepped on the black

rubber mat, and the doors opened automatically. Inside, there was a cleaning lady mopping the floor. She looked up, read the confusion in my face. "Reception is over there," she said, pointing. "They'll get you where you want to go."

"Thanks," I said.

On the counter was a bouquet of flowers, the biggest bouquet I'd ever seen. Sitting at a desk in front of a computer was a woman with reddish hair and big arms. "Can I help you?"

"Reese Robertson's room. I'm a friend."

She typed his name into the computer and then gave me the number—B3213—on a slip of paper. "Now here's how you get there."

As she gave directions, a woman about my mom's age with dark hair and dark eyes came up beside me. I looked at her and smiled, and she smiled back, but her eyes were brimming with tears.

The woman behind the counter stopped talking. I hadn't listened carefully to her directions, but I couldn't ask her to repeat them, not with the sad woman waiting. So I thanked her, walked to the elevators, and got in. A few seconds later the doors opened and I stepped out.

The hospital was big. It seemed as if wherever I turned, there was a new hallway with other hallways opening off it. Nurses, doctors, orderlies, bustled about. Wheelchairs and gurneys and linen carts lined the halls. I wanted to ask for help, but everyone looked busy or worried or both.

I turned a corner and came to an area with sleeping bags and mattresses on the floor. Some parents were sleeping there. Others, with bags under their eyes and coffee cups in their hands, whispered with one another or looked out the window. I walked down the corridor quickly, not making eye contact with anyone.

Finally I found myself in front of a long breezeway that connected one wing of the hospital with another. There was a sign above the breezeway: To Rooms 3000–3400. That had been the problem; the hospital had two different wings, and I'd been in the wrong one.

Relieved, I headed down the walkway. All along the walls were plaques with names etched on them. Not cheap plastic plaques, but classy ones, like the ones you get for being MVP on a team.

I was almost at the other side before I stopped to read a few. For a time I didn't get it. There was a name, then two dates. Sometimes the dates would be a few days or weeks apart, but other times there'd be years between them.

Then I understood. The day the kid was born; the day he or she died. I looked back along the breezeway. It seemed as if there were thousands upon thousands of plaques there. My face went hot, and I felt dizzy. Suddenly I didn't know what I was doing in the hospital. I picked up my pace, walking faster and faster, but now I wasn't looking for Reese Robertson's room; I was looking for exit signs.

I found them, all right. Too many of them. I went up this hallway, down that one, following the green lights and the black arrows. I turned left, then right, then left, breaking into a clammy, nervous sweat. I had to get out, but the place was like a huge maze.

I turned a corner, looked up, and saw the sign B3213

above an open door. For a split second I stood frozen outside the door. Then I slowly turned my head and looked in. Reese was lying in bed, his head heavily bandaged. Sitting next to him on either side of the bed were his mom and his dad. His mom was holding his hand.

Reese looked away from his mom and right at me. Our eyes met and locked, just like before I'd thrown the pitch.

"Pardon me."

An orderly was standing behind me, pushing an IV cart. His voice snapped me out of whatever reverie I'd fallen into. My eyes broke free from Reese's. And then I was walking again, walking so fast I was almost running. I didn't want to talk to Reese. Let his parents and teammates talk to him. What happened wasn't my fault. I didn't mean to hit him; he was leaning out over the plate. He should have gotten out of the way.

I couldn't find an elevator, but I did see an open door. Inside, a girl about Marian's age was sitting in a chair. She was thin and pale, and she had an oxygen mask over her face. A nurse was with her. "Breathe, Natasha," the nurse was saying. "Let's clear those lungs." Natasha breathed in deeply, smiling at me as she did so.

The nurse followed her eyes to me. "Can I help you?" she said, her voice irritated.

"I'm sorry. I can't find the elevator."

"Go out the door you just came in, turn right, and walk about twenty steps. You can't miss it." Then she turned back to the girl. "Breathe deeply."

I took the elevator to the ground floor, finally got out of

the hospital, and hustled down the hill to the bus stop. A spring storm was coming. The birch trees were like wild horses, bending down and then rearing up.

When the bus came at last, I slumped into the first empty seat and stared out the window. Why had I been feeling sorry for him? I was the one whose father was dead. I was the one living in city housing.

In Ballard I only had to wait a couple of minutes for my transfer. Still, I was late. I hustled the final blocks to the duplex. When I stepped inside, Mom had her purse out and was about to leave. "Where have you been? I was worried."

"Nowhere," I mumbled. "Just kicking around. And then the bus didn't come. You know how it is on weekends. Did I miss dinner?"

She nodded. "There's ravioli in the oven. You can eat whenever you want. Marian is over at Kaitlin's, and I'm off to work."

"I'll eat later then," I said, and I started toward the stairs when my mom's voice stopped me.

"What's this I hear about the game?"

"What do you mean?" I said, looking back.

"Coach Grandison called. He told me you hit a boy in the head with a pitch. He wanted to know how you were taking it."

I didn't answer.

"Well, how are you taking it?"

I shrugged. "I'm okay. I wish I hadn't hit him, but it's not like I did it on purpose."

"Coach told me to tell you that the boy will be okay."

I nodded. "I knew I couldn't have really hurt him. He was wearing a helmet. And I'm not exactly Randy Johnson."

She looked at me. "Still, Shane, you did hit him. And he's in the hospital. I think you should go see him. I could drive you there tomorrow."

I felt a moment of panic. "I called him at the hospital last night, Mom. I don't have to go see him."

She was surprised. "You did? Then why didn't you say so? What did he say?"

"I didn't talk to him. I only talked to the nurse."

"Did you leave a message?"

"Yeah. I told them to tell him I was sorry."

"What's the boy's name? I'll call a florist and have some flowers sent."

My heart raced; I did not want her to know it was Reese. "Mom, I'm not sending flowers to a guy. He's fine. He's got a lump on his head, that's all. I left a message saying I was sorry. That's enough. He's probably out of the hospital by now, anyway."

She looked at her watch. "All right. If that's the way you want it. But I still think you should do more." She picked up her purse. "Marian should be back by eight-thirty. If she's not, call the McGinleys and tell her to come home. And see that she's in bed, lights out, no later than nine-thirty. Okay?"

CHAPTER 16 English class had hardly begun on Monday when the phone rang in the back of the room. Mrs. Joyner, who had started talking about Emily Dickinson, scowled at the interruption, and she scowled again as she looked at me. "Shane, you're to go to the coach's office." I gathered my books together and headed for the door. "But you are not excused from your homework or from your reading."

The gym is clear across campus from my English class, so it took a while to get there. When I reached it, I could hear voices inside. I waited a moment, then knocked.

Grandison wasn't usually at school in the mornings, but I wasn't surprised when he opened the door. His face was solemn as he motioned me inside. "Shane, this is Mr. Brock, head of the WIAA. He wants to ask you a few questions."

Brock was a big man with short blond hair combed forward like a kid's. He had a gold ring on his little finger—some sort of championship ring—maybe a Super Bowl or World Series ring. His deep voice filled the room. "Nice to meet you, Shane. I knew your father a little. We played against each other when he was at Washington State and I was a Husky. I was sorry to hear what happened."

I never knew what to say when people talked about my dad, so I was relieved when Brock sat down at Grandison's desk and opened a laptop computer. I sat in front of him while Grandison stood off to the side. Brock typed for a moment, then looked at me. "You know why I'm here, don't you, Shane?"

"Because I hit that guy from Shorelake."

"That's right. And that *guy* has a name. Reese Robertson."

Brock leaned back in his chair. Ten seconds ticked by, then another ten. "Do you know what the WIAA is?"

"Not really."

"It stands for Washington Interscholastic Athletic Association. We supervise high school sports, make sure everything is on the up and up. I'd like you to tell me what happened with that pitch."

I swallowed. "It was an accident. I was trying to come inside with a fastball, move him off the plate, but the pitch got away. It sailed up and in, and he was leaning out over the plate. He barely moved."

Brock folded his hands in front of him. "So there was nothing different about that pitch?"

"Only that it got away from me."

Brock typed something, then looked up. "You were losing badly. That must have been tough."

"It's always tough to lose."

"But you know Reese Robertson, don't you? And that made it tougher."

"Not really. I barely know him. His parents bought my old house, but I've only talked to him once or twice in my whole life."

"You don't hold a grudge against him?"

"Why should I hold a grudge?"

"I can think of a few reasons. He's living in your old house; he's going to your old school; he's playing—and starring—on your old team."

"Look," I said, "I didn't hit Reese Robertson because his parents bought my house or because he goes to Shorelake. That'd be stupid."

Brock leaned forward. "I've talked to the Shorelake coaches, the Shorelake parents, the Shorelake players. They think you set Reese up with outside pitches, got him leaning out over the plate, and then went headhunting. They think you hit him on purpose."

"Well, they're wrong," I said, my body getting hot all over.

I paused. I could tell he didn't believe me. "Look. I went to the hospital to see him. Would I do that if I hit him on purpose?"

"You visited Reese?"

"Yeah. I took the bus on Saturday. He's in room B3213," I said. "I didn't talk to him because his mom and dad were with him and nurses were all around him. But I went. And I called the hospital the night it happened to make sure he was okay. If I was such a bad guy, if I hated him so much and wanted to hurt him, I wouldn't do that, would I?"

For a moment Brock stared at me. "I don't know, Shane. Would you?"

"I'm telling you," I said, my voice rising, "it was an accident."

For a long time no one said anything. Finally Brock spoke. "All right, if you say it was an accident, then I guess it was an accident. You can go back to class now."

I stood up, went to the door, then turned back. "What's going to happen? Am I going to be suspended?"

Brock shook his head. "No. You won't be suspended."

CHAPTER 17 I was shaky all day at school. At practice I could feel the eyes of my teammates on me. After we did our stretching and running, Grandison sent me along the sidelines to play catch with Miguel Alvarez. We stood about one hundred feet apart and threw back and forth. Long toss makes your arm stronger without risking injury.

It was exactly what I needed. We got into a nice rhythm,

and time passed by. As I threw to Alvarez, I could hear Grandison barking at the infielders and outfielders, but he might as well have been a million miles away.

I'd been throwing for ten minutes when he strolled over. He'd watched a dozen throws or so when he stopped me. "You feel okay about pitching Wednesday?"

"What do you mean?" I said.

"Just what I said."

"Of course I feel okay. I'm looking forward to it. Why wouldn't I?"

He shrugged. "Some pitchers have trouble throwing hard after they put a guy down."

"If I'd hit him on purpose, then maybe I would," I said. "But the guy was leaning . . ."

Grandison put his hand up. "I've heard it already, Shane. I was there. Remember?"

"Right."

"All right, regular plan then. If Wednesday's is close, you'll be going in."

The Roosevelt Roughriders were a decent team with a decent record: 4–3 or 5–2. Something like that. While watching them as they warmed up before our game, I could sense they weren't likely to make great plays in the field but they'd catch the balls hit to them, and they'd hit any fat pitches that were laid right down the middle.

Cory Minton started. We staked him to an early three-run lead on a bunch of walks and a bases-clearing double by Jeff Walton, but Roosevelt scratched back, scoring a run in the fourth and another in the fifth. Grandison turned to me in the top of the seventh. "Shane, get yourself warmed up. You'll close the game for us."

I grabbed my glove and hustled out, Miguel Alvarez right behind me.

As I loosened along the sidelines, I felt the familiar excitement come back like an old friend. I was done with hospitals, done with explanations. It was time to pitch.

I had great stuff along the sidelines that night. I wasn't throwing any faster than usual, but the ball was moving as if it had a mind of its own. When that happens, everything is simple. All I do is aim for the catcher's glove, and in the last twenty feet or so the ball will tail a few inches inside or outside. I don't really know which way it will go, but that doesn't matter. Batters swing at a ball that looks like it's coming right down the middle, but when their bat crosses the plate, the ball isn't there.

Confident, I stopped throwing and looked out to the field. Benny Gold took a hard swing and hit a mile-high popup that the other team's third baseman caught for the last out in our half of the seventh. I threw one more practice pitch to Alvarez. It tailed down and away, an impossible pitch to hit. Alvarez gave me a little smile and a thumbs-up, and I trotted out to the mound.

"Play ball!" the ump yelled. Gold fired the ball to second; it went around the infield and came back to me. I rubbed it up a little, stepped back onto the mound, and looked toward the plate as the Roosevelt batter stepped in.

That's when the dizziness hit me. It was like being punched in the head. Everything started rocking this way and that. Gold put down one finger for the fastball, the most basic sign, but for an instant I couldn't register what it meant. I stepped off the rubber to get ahold of myself.

Gold popped out of his crouch and took two steps toward me. "You okay?"

"Yeah, I'm okay."

"All right then. Let's go."

I stepped back onto the mound. Quickly, I wound and delivered. But my great stuff was gone. Instead of letting the ball fly free and easy, I choked it. The ball bounced up to home plate. Gold smothered it, fired it back. "Come on, Shane!" he shouted, making a fist with his bare hand. "You can do it." Behind me the infielders were calling out the same thing.

Again I wound, and again I hurried everything. The ball bounced at least ten feet in front of the plate. In the stands I heard laughter. Grandison leaned through the opening from the bench and cupped his hands into a megaphone. "Relax, Shane. Relax."

Gold signaled for another fastball. I nodded, then delivered. I told myself to let the ball go, to fire it in there, but I held back, and the result was a nothing pitch that floated over the heart of the plate.

The Roosevelt hitter swung so hard he nearly corkscrewed himself into the ground, sending a line drive to deep left center that landed about ten feet in front of the fence and then bounced over for a ground-rule double. Roosevelt's players and fans screamed in delight.

Gold got a new baseball from the umpire and carried it out to me. "It's okay," he said, holding his palms down. "It's okay. Just relax and throw the ball."

He returned behind the plate. I tried to pretend there was no batter standing there. I focused entirely on Gold's glove. But as my arm came forward, I guided the ball. Instead of going eighty-five miles an hour, it went seventy-five. The Roosevelt guy, first pitch swinging, caught it solid—a mammoth drive down the left field line. For a moment I thought it might curve foul, but it was out of the park so fast it never had a chance to. The Roosevelt players danced onto the field as their parents whooped and hollered behind them.

My teammates trudged past me back to our bench and started packing their gear. The loss was sudden and unexpected. We'd led the whole game. The whole game!

I stayed on the mound, too stunned to move, until Grandison came and got me. "It happens," he said, patting me on the shoulder. "Some days you just don't have it. You'll get them next time." I nodded, but inside I was in knots. Because I *did* have it. While warming up I'd never been sharper.

When I stepped inside the house that night, Mom had already left for work. Instead of being up in her room, Marian was downstairs. I knew something was bothering her. She would read, get up and wander around, then go back to the sofa. Every once in a while I'd catch her looking at me funny.

Once I had finished my dinner, I went to the front room. "Something wrong?"

She shook her head. "Nothing's wrong."

"Come on. What is it?"

She looked at me angrily. "Don't you know what today is?

One year ago today Dad killed himself. Mom didn't say anything, but I could tell she remembered. And you don't even miss him."

"Come on, Marian," I said, ashamed. "Just because I didn't remember the exact date doesn't mean I don't miss him."

"You don't miss him. All you care about is baseball and being a star pitcher."

"That's not fair, Marian. I don't wake up with nightmares, but that doesn't mean I don't care about Dad. Okay? So lay off."

I could see her flinch at the word *nightmare,* and she immediately opened her book and hid behind it. I went upstairs to my room and lay on the bed. Was she right? Was I forgetting about my own father?

Two of my grandparents had died a few months apart when I was seven. I could sort of picture them if I tried hard, but only sort of. And I never thought of them, except maybe at Christmas. But with my dad it was different. He wasn't getting hazy in my memory. The way he lived and the way he died were clear. Maybe it wasn't that I couldn't remember him. Maybe I didn't want to.

CHAPTER 18 At the next practice I asked Grandison if I could pitch batting practice. When I'd asked before, he'd always said no, afraid to risk an injury. He started to refuse me that day too, but then he stopped himself. "Maybe that's not such a bad idea," he said.

There was an old paint bucket filled with balls right next to the pitching rubber. I picked up a ball and motioned to Kurt Lind. "You ready?"

"Fire away," he said, stepping into the batter's box.

You're not supposed to throw one hundred percent during BP. The idea is for hitters to build their confidence. But you're not supposed to throw so easy that it does them no good.

I laid in a seventy-five-mile-an-hour fastball, which Lind smacked past my ear and into center field. My next four pitches were like the first one, and he creamed three of them, finally leaving the cage flexing his biceps. But that was okay, because I had a plan. I was going to pick up my velocity batter by batter, never getting to full speed, of course, but coming as close as I could without having Grandison chew me out. The five pitches I put up for Brian Fletcher had more zip on them, and as I worked through our hitters, I pushed myself a little harder with each one.

"Last batter," Grandison called to me as Pedro Hernandez stepped in.

This was it. Hernandez was a dead fastball hitter. Anything but my best and he'd be all over it. But if I was on top of my game, I'd have enough to blow the ball by him. I rocked and delivered.

If you were watching from the sidelines, you'd have sworn that I was throwing all out, one hundred percent. I couldn't tell you how I was holding back. But I was. I could feel it, and I could see it in the results. Hernandez sent a line drive down the left field line, then hit a long fly to center that would have been out of half the parks we played in. He fouled the next pitch straight back, his timing perfect. He ripped the final two pitches into left center. After each pitch I vowed to let the next one go, but I held back every time.

On Saturday afternoon we had another away game, this time against the Ingraham Rams. Before the game, I went into the men's room and threw up. I'd never done that before. I'd always been nervous-excited; this was nervous-terrified. When I finished puking, I sat down gulping air for a while, trying to pull myself together.

"Where you been, Hunter?" Grandison barked when I finally returned to the field.

"In the bathroom," I said.

He must have seen something on my face. His anger changed to concern. "You sick?"

"Stomach's a little off."

"Can you pitch?"

"I think so."

"Go down and throw to Alvarez some."

I threw to Miguel Alvarez for ten minutes or so. Right before game time, Grandison came down to watch. "You warmed up?" he asked.

"Yeah."

"All right. Let it rip."

I reared back and fired. Alvarez's glove popped. I threw a second blazer, then a third, and a fourth. Grandison watched them all, then, without a word, he turned and walked away.

When the game started, I took my spot at the end of the bench and watched. I was hoping for a blowout. I didn't care whether it was a win or a loss. All I wanted was a chance to pitch an inning or two without any pressure. I just needed to get a few outs to regain my confidence. Then I'd be all right.

Hank Fowler was pitching for us, and he started strong. He kept the ball low, his fastball had zip, and his control was better than I'd ever seen it. He was ahead in the count against every batter. Ingraham got an infield single in the second, and a bloop double in the fourth, but that was it.

Ingraham's pitcher matched Fowler pitch for pitch, out for out, inning for inning. He wasn't fast, but he had a big-breaking curve ball, which you don't see all that often in high school. The ball started out at the waist or even the chest, and then dropped to the knees. Our hitters were swinging over the top, striking out or hitting soft rollers to the infield. In some games it doesn't seem as if anybody is ever going to score a run, and this was one of them. For six innings all that went up on the scoreboard were zeros.

Jeff Walton led off the top of the seventh for us with the first well-hit ball for either team, a rope into left field. If Ingraham's pitcher hadn't had a no-hitter going, their left fielder would have played the ball on a hop and Walton would have pulled up at first with a solid single. But the left fielder didn't want his pitcher to lose the no-hitter, so he dived for the ball, trying to make a circus catch. The ball short-hopped him, bounded over his shoulder, and rolled and rolled.

Walton can run. And with the left fielder down on his belly, their center fielder had to come over to make the play. The guy had been sleeping; he hadn't made a move to back-up until the ball was past the left fielder. Now he was flying across the outfield as Walton flew around the bases. The center fielder's throw hit the shortstop's glove when Walton was already around third. The smart play might have been to hold him up, but Grandison was waving his arm like crazy. The shortstop double-clutched, then threw high. Walton slid in headfirst with the first run of the game. Our guys were on their feet. "Way to go!" they shouted, high-fiving him as he came to the bench.

From the third-base coach's box I heard Grandison's voice. "Loosen up, Shane."

Ingraham's pitcher struck out the next three batters. Fowler walked out to start the seventh, but there was no bounce in his step, and his warm-up pitches had no zip. If I hadn't been so bad in the last game, Grandison would have had me out there.

Still, there was a decent chance Fowler could finish the game. He was facing the bottom of the Ingraham order, batters he'd handled easily. He worked the count to 3–2 on the first hitter, taking a ton of time between pitches. The payoff pitch was in the dirt, but the guy chased it for a strikeout.

The number-eight hitter wasn't so stupid. He could see that Fowler was struggling, and he worked the count to 3–1 before he took his first swing. The pitch was right down the middle, and he ripped a solid single into left field.

Grandison looked at me along the sideline and then at Fowler. For a moment, I thought he was going to leave Fowler in. But then, just before Fowler started to get the sign for the next batter, Grandison called time and ran onto the field. When he took the ball from Fowler, the players on our bench stood and cheered for him, and so did the parents behind our bench. It was by far Fowler's best game, and it was up to me to save his victory.

I'd been strong along the sidelines. Not as strong as the game before, but strong. And maybe that was better, considering how the other game had finished. I felt confident walking onto the field, confident taking my warm-ups. Everything was going to be okay. But as soon as I saw the batter step in, the lightheadedness came back.

The hitter was their number-nine guy, a little second baseman with no power. I didn't need to be one hundred percent to get him. Ninety percent would have been plenty. And if I could get him to hit a ground ball, we might be able to turn a double play to end the game. One save—that's all I needed.

I went into my stretch, then fired the ball to first to keep the runner close. I stretched again, delivered. The batter swung and sent a ground ball to short, just like I wanted. Only he didn't hit it hard enough. Fletcher had to charge in, and when he fielded the ball, all his momentum was forward. He made the smart play, getting the sure out at first. But the tying run was now at second, and the leadoff batter was standing at the plate.

I'd watched this hitter each time he'd come to the plate. He was a slap hitter, tough to strike out. But if I threw my best fastball, I could blow the ball by him. *Now,* I thought to myself. *Make it happen.*

I blew out some air, stepped onto the rubber. Benny Gold called for the fastball and stuck his glove right over the middle of the plate. If I fired it in there, just cut loose like I had with Alvarez along the sidelines, the batter wouldn't be able to handle it. All I had to do was trust myself. I went into my motion, checked the runner at second, then came straight over the top. He was going to get my best fastball.

Only he didn't.

Instead of exploding out of my hand, the ball came out like a second baseman's throw, straight and clean. The Ingraham hitter's bat flashed through the strike zone, catching the ball solidly and sending a stinging line drive down the left field line. The runner on second scored, and the batter cruised into second standing up.

I'd blown Fowler's victory. The only thing left was to blow the whole game.

I did that on the next pitch, another dead-arm fastball down the middle. Ingraham's hitter rifled it into right center. The runner kicked up a cloud of dust sliding into home, but he could have walked in. For the second straight game, my teammates plodded off the field as the other team celebrated a last-inning victory.

The guys gathered their stuff quickly. Fowler was headed to his parents' car before I took my shoes off. Alvarez and I were the only ones catching a ride with Grandison. We helped him pack the gear and load it into the van. When Grandison slid the door shut, he turned to me. "Your arm okay? You're not injured or anything, are you? Because if you are, tell me. You can hurt yourself if you throw when you're not right."

"My arm is fine," I said.

He turned to Alvarez. "What do you think, Miguel?"

"Shane throws fast along the side. His ball . . . it moves. Faster than Minton. Faster than Fowler. On the side, Shane, he's the best."

Grandison turned back to me. "So what happens when you get in the game?"

"I don't know," I said. But I did know.

And Grandison knew too.

On Sunday afternoon I dragged myself to the library. As usual, all the computers were taken. I wrote my name on a white board and waited while the kid on computer number three played some stupid game in which he stacked blue boxes on top of red ones. Finally his forty minutes ran out, the screen went back to the library's homepage, and it was my turn.

I went to Google and typed in "Shorelake High School." From the way I was looking around and sweating, you'd have thought I was trying to log on to *Playboy*.

Shorelake's homepage came up, and after a couple of clicks I was looking at the baseball team's page. The first thing I saw were the scores, including Saturday's game against Endeavor High, which they'd lost 8–1.

I clicked on a button labeled "Box Score." Slowly, methodically, I went over every name. Ted Hearn had been the starting pitcher; Robby Richardson had gotten two hits; Greg Taylor had smacked a double and scored the run. But the name I wanted to see wasn't there. Some guy named Brad Post was playing center field.

I leaned back in the chair, looked at the ceiling, and closed my eyes. I was being stupid. So what if they'd lost? It wasn't my fault. Besides, one loss was no big deal. Nobody goes unbeaten in baseball. Shorelake would still be a top-ten team. And as for Reese—of course he wouldn't be playing yet.

It had been only a week. He'd be back for the next game probably, and if not that one, then the one after that. Missing two weeks wasn't such a big deal. Twist your ankle and you're out longer. The time off would work out to his benefit. He'd be fresh for the state playoffs, and he'd give Shorelake a lift when he did come back.

CHAPTER 19 But Reese didn't play the next week, or the week after that. And Shorelake didn't win either. The loss to Endeavor was their first of five in a row, dropping them completely out of the state rankings. Ted Hearn's name stopped showing up in the box scores, and so did Greg's. Both of them must have gone down with some injury or other. Their season was falling apart.

And so was mine. Loosening up along the sidelines, I was as fast as ever. Once I got into a game, that same seasick feeling came over me. I just couldn't throw hard, not with a batter standing in. Sometimes I'd get lucky and a hitter would crush the ball right at somebody. But in most games I got bombed, and most games we lost.

One Thursday, after I'd blown yet another lead and cost us another game, Grandison kept me after practice. "I got some information that I thought you'd be interested in hearing. It's about Reese Robertson." His tone was curt.

"What did you hear?" I said, my voice distant.

"You know he hasn't played since that game, don't you?"

"No," I said, "I didn't know that."

Grandison glared at me. "You didn't notice his name wasn't showing up in the box scores or in the Wednesday newspaper?"

I shrugged. "Why would I check Shorelake's box scores?"

His eyes narrowed. "Oh, I don't know, Shane. Maybe because you hit him in the head and sent him to the hospital. But I suppose that hasn't been bothering you, has it?"

"It was an accident," I said. "I've told you that."

"So you have."

There was a long silence.

"So what did you want to tell me?" I said.

"Nothing much. Only that Reese is going to play again, tonight. Shorelake's got a game against Bellevue at Woodland Park. I'm going to the game. I thought you might want to go too."

I shook my head. "I can't go."

"Can't go? Or won't go?"

"Can't go. I've got homework. Besides, I'm not supposed to leave my sister alone."

"So if I called your mom and explained the situation, she'd tell me there was no way you could go?"

I looked down. "I can't go."

"All right," he said, "go on home."

I headed for the gym. I hadn't gone more than ten steps when he called out to me. "Shane, did Miguel Alvarez ever tell you that he's a pitcher?"

I turned back. "No."

"Well, he is. He pitched in relief last year for his high school team in Sacramento. His uncle showed me his stats. He did pretty well. I'm going to give him a chance to pitch for us."

Right away I understood. Grandison was telling me I was done as a closer.

"That's a good idea," I said, my voice blank.

"Starting tomorrow, you'll work in the outfield. You might like it out there. I'm not telling you to quit pitching; I'm just going to give you a break from it for a while."

On the bus ride home I tried to picture myself playing in the outfield, far from the action. For a while I was depressed, but then it didn't seem so bad. I could stand out there on the green grass, run down a fly ball or two, make a throw to second or third now and then.

Back home, I fixed Marian and me dinner—hot dogs, baked beans, and potato chips—then went upstairs to do my English homework and listen to music. But I couldn't get settled; I kept standing up and walking around. At about six-thirty I went downstairs. Marian was watching television. "You done with your homework?"

"Kaitlin's coming over later. We're going to do it together."

"Would you be okay by yourself for a while?"

"Sure, I'll be okay," she said. Her eyes never strayed from the television.

"You won't tell Mom I left you alone."

"I won't be alone. I told you, Kaitlin's coming."

"I'll be back by ten at the latest."

I thought about taking the bus but decided against it. Buses were late half the time, and they didn't run much at night anyway. I went down to the basement, half expecting my bicycle to have been stolen. But there it was, locked to a foundation post. I was surprised that I still knew the combination. I rolled the bike back and forth a couple of times, then checked the tires. They weren't fully inflated, but they weren't flat either.

Woodland Park is about five miles from my house. Most of the way is downhill, so it didn't take me long to reach the park. When I was little, my dad had taken me to a place for dirt bikes, fifty yards away from the third base line. That's where I locked the bike to a tree. I picked out a grassy spot closer to the diamond, sat down, and looked across the field.

Right away I spotted Reese. He was shagging fly balls in center field, making everything look easy, moving well, joking with the other outfielders. He looked exactly the way he'd always looked, and I could feel his teammates feeding off him. A whistle blew, and the Shorelake guys trotted in. A minute later the game started.

Bellevue batted first. Scott Parino was pitching for Shorelake. He had his good stuff early, striking out the first two guys. The third hitter ripped a line drive to right center. It looked like a sure double, but Reese got an incredible jump on the ball and tracked it down, making a sliding, knee-high catch. After that catch, the whole Shorelake team funneled over to him as he trotted in, patting him on the back and grinning. In the stands the parents rose and cheered.

"Nothing wrong with him," I said out loud.

Standing nearby was a man watching his son do bike tricks. "Were you talking to me?" he asked.

"No," I said.

Embarrassed, I walked closer to the field, both to get away from the man and to see Reese hit. I had a feeling something big was going to happen, and I was glad I was there.

In the bottom of the first, Shorelake got a leadoff single, followed by another single, and then a walk. The bases were loaded—the perfect setup for Reese's return. The Shorelake fans rose and cheered as he slowly walked to the batter's box, and they stayed on their feet when the Bellevue pitcher fired his first pitch.

It was a ball, way outside. The second pitch was right down the middle, only Reese took it. "Strike one!" the umpire yelled. The next pitch was yet another belt-high fastball. This time Reese swung, but his left side opened up, and his left foot lurched toward third base. He missed the ball by a foot. "Strike two!" the umpire hollered.

A sick feeling came over me. The Bellevue pitcher, suddenly confident, fired a fastball on the inside corner—his best pitch of the game. Reese jumped back as if the ball were close to hitting him. "Strike three!" the umpire yelled. The Shorelake fans booed the ump momentarily but stood and cheered Reese as he walked back to the bench. The next batter grounded into a double play to end the inning.

Reese didn't bat again until the fourth. Again the cheering was loud, but cheering can't make a guy hit. On the first pitch, he swung weakly and missed. "Hang in there, Reese," I whispered. He took a ball, then a second strike, then waved at a mediocre fastball out over the plate for strike three. When he ran out to center field at the end of the inning, his head was down.

The game stayed scoreless until the top of the fifth. Then Bellevue got to Parino, pushing across five runs on a couple of hits, a couple of walks, and a home run. I thought about leaving, but I couldn't go until Reese had had his final at bat. It came in the sixth inning. He struck out on three pitches, the last one a fastball right down the middle.

Before he was back on the bench, I was on my bike and headed for home. When I opened the door, Marian was sitting on the sofa reading *Harry Potter and the Goblet of Fire* for what had to have been the fifth time.

"You should be in bed," I said.

"As soon as I finish. I've only got two pages to go. Where'd you go, anyway?" Her eyes were on her book, and she was still reading. She could do that—read and talk at the same time.

"A baseball game," I said, suddenly feeling a need to tell someone.

"Who won?"

"Bellevue."

"Is that who you wanted to win?"

"I didn't really care."

"Then why'd you go?"

"You know I hit a guy, don't you?"

She flipped a page. "Sure. Mom told me she thinks you feel really bad about it, though you won't admit it."

"He played tonight. It was his first game since I hit him."

"How'd he do?"

"Not too well."

She closed her book with a loud bang. "Done," she said, and she looked at me for the first time. "But he must be okay if he's playing, right?"

"Right," I said.

She stood up. "I'm glad he's all better. I'm going to bed now. See you in the morning."

"Yeah," I said, "see you in the morning."

CHAPTER 20 Nobody said a word, but I could feel my teammates watching me as I trotted out to right field at the next practice. I shagged fly balls until Grandison called me in for batting practice. I managed to hit the ball hard a couple of times, but I missed more than I hit. When my turn in the batting cage was over, Miguel Alvarez came over to me. "I'm sorry," he said.

"Don't worry about me, Miguel. Just pitch."

"You're better than me."

I laughed. "I'm terrible."

Grandison's voice boomed across the field. "Miguel, come here."

"You'll make it back," Alvarez said before jogging off.

He was taking my position from me, but I still liked him. In another time and place, he could have been a friend.

We had a game Wednesday afternoon against Edmonds. I sat at the end of the bench next to Alvarez, as usual. Only he was the one fighting to keep his nervous energy under control, and I was the guy just watching.

Edmonds broke on top with three runs in the second inning on an error, two walks, and a bases-clearing double down the line. But we fought back, scratching out single runs in the third and fourth innings, before breaking through for three runs in the top of the sixth. When Hank Fowler got the third out in Edmonds' half of the sixth, Grandison called down the bench. "Get loose, Miguel. You're pitching the seventh." We didn't score in the top of the seventh, so our lead was 5–3 as Alvarez made his way to the mound to pitch the bottom of the seventh.

Alvarez hadn't done anything, but by his third warm-up pitch sweat was pouring down his forehead. Usually he had a smile on his face, but he was all business. And he was on. He fired strike after strike. His arm was loose and free—the way mine used to be. He struck out the first Edmonds hitter on three pitches, got the next batter on a grounder to third. The final hitter lifted an easy fly ball out toward Jim Wilson in right field. Wilson settled under it and squeezed it for the third out.

The guys surrounded Alvarez at the mound, pounding him on the back. His grin went from one side of his face to the other. I joined them. "Way to go, Miguel," I said.

"Thanks, Shane. Thanks a lot."

CHAPTER 21 That night I dreamed I was riding my bicycle in the international district, and my dad was driving along in the car next to me. I had my old dirt bike, and I did a wheelie along the sidewalk, a great wheelie, only I smashed into this old Chinese lady's table. The table was made of thin little boards, and they all splintered from the impact.

"I'm sorry," I said, but she didn't seem to hear.

"My table, my table," she said over and over. Then she

started picking up the splintered pieces and trying to piece them together again.

My dad jumped out of his car and came running over. Immediately he pulled out his wallet and gave her one hundred dollars. "Here. Take it. It's more than the table is worth."

The woman didn't stop wailing. "My table, my table, my table."

"Take the money," my dad said angrily. I looked at him, afraid he might hit the old woman. It wasn't his normal face that I saw. Instead, it was that ridiculous, grinning face that had stared down at motorists from the billboard above his dealership on Aurora Avenue. I woke up, my heart racing, my forehead covered in sweat.

I lay there until my heartbeat settled, then went downstairs and made some hot chocolate. As I drank it, I looked out the window. The streetlight must have been out, because everything was incredibly dark. I stared into the darkness and thought about Alvarez and Grandison and pitching. There was nothing to be mad about. Everything ends sometime.

I finished the hot chocolate, but instead of returning to my room, I sat thinking of my dad, wondering what it would be like to be dead. Always before, I'd thought that I didn't want to die, not ever, no matter how old or how sick I was. But that night death seemed peaceful and not scary. It would be like being lost in the darkness, where no one could ever find you.

I spent the next practices running down fly balls in right field. I was okay; I knew how to hit the cutoff man and all that. Grandison gave me a double shift during batting practice, and I managed a few decent hits. But I didn't hit as well as Jim Wilson, and I didn't field as well as he did either. At the end of practice on Friday, Grandison called me over. "I thought you might dog it on me, Shane, but you're working hard, and I'm impressed. Since you've been straight with me, I'll be straight with you. Miguel is going to close out our games for the rest of the year. I'll try to get you an inning or two in right field if I can, but I don't guarantee anything. You may not play again this year."

After that, the season seemed to leak away. Alvarez was okay as a closer but not great. He could bust the ball right by weak hitters, but his fastball was too straight, and the really good hitters drilled him. We lost three of our last six games, two of them in the last inning. I didn't play at all.

I followed Shorelake's season in the newspaper and on the Internet. They finished more poorly than we did, dropping five of their last six. Reese managed a hit now and then, but not too many. It seemed unbelievable that a team once ranked number one in the state could fail to make the play-offs, yet that's what happened.

Coach Grandison gave me a ride home after our last game. "I know this season went sour on you, but I still want you to turn out again next year," he said as I stepped out of the van.

"Why?" I said, surprised he cared. "You've got enough outfielders without me."

"I know I've got outfielders; I still want you to turn out."

I shook my head. "I don't know."

"Think about it, okay?"

I shrugged. "Sure, I'll think about it."

As I watched his van disappear around a corner, I knew that I'd played my last game. For a moment I felt guilty. My dad wouldn't have wanted me to quit. He would have told me to work hard and come back strong to show everybody what I was really made of. I could almost hear him say it.

PART THREE

CHAPTER 1 I was in the kitchen on a Saturday morning eating breakfast. The school year had ended. Mom was at the sink washing dishes. "Have you thought about what you're going to do this summer?" she asked. It was at least the tenth time she'd asked that question in the last week.

"I told you. I'll get a job or something," I said.

"I talked to the manager at Pasta Bella. I can get you work at the restaurant, washing dishes or maybe being a busboy."

"I don't want to work in a restaurant."

"I don't want you to work in a restaurant either. But you're not going to sit around for two and a half months."

"Marian doesn't have anything to do. You're not on her all the time."

"Marian's signed up for a bunch of different camps at the community center. Besides, Marian's different."

That made me mad. "Why? Because I was arrested and she wasn't?"

"I wouldn't have put it that way, but yes."

"I'm done with that. I've told you. You don't have to worry."

She turned and faced me. "Great. I'm glad I don't. But I still want you to have something to do this summer. So if you don't get a job on your own, you're going to work at Pasta Bella." She paused. "You know, Shane, we're not rich. If you earned some money, it would help."

That afternoon I took the bus to Northgate Mall. At store after store I filled out application forms. The managers would take the forms and stick them in a file. "We're not hiring now, but if somebody quits or doesn't work out, we'll give you a call."

For a couple of days I sulked around the house, feeling guilty but still dreading the day when I'd have to start washing dishes. Mom kept looking at me, and I knew I couldn't hold out much longer. I was just about to give up when I got the phone call.

It wasn't from any store manager at Northgate; it was from Coach Grandison. I was surprised to hear his voice and even more surprised to hear his offer. "I've got a summer basketball league starting, and I need referees. You interested? It pays twelve dollars a game, and you'd do three games a day."

"I sure am," I said. "Where?"

"At Bitter Lake Community Center. The program goes all summer. You start tomorrow. A man named Matthew Falk is my partner. He'll train you."

"Tomorrow?" I said.

"Yeah. Tomorrow. Noon. Why? You doing something else?"

"No. It's just that . . ."

"What?"

"Nothing. I'll be there."

When I hung up, I felt excited and then confused. Why had Grandison called me? How did he know I was looking for a job?

Just then Mom came into the room.

"Did you ask Coach Grandison to get me a job?" I said.

For a moment she didn't reply. When she finally spoke, her voice was clipped. "As a matter of fact, I did."

That made me mad. "You should have asked me before you did that."

"Why?"

"Because I would have told you not to."

"Oh, Shane, don't be such a child. There's nothing wrong with asking for help. You don't want to work at Pasta Bella, and I don't want you working there. If Coach Grandison can get you something better, take it."

"You don't understand," I said. "I'm not going out for the baseball team next year. Grandison wouldn't give me this job if he knew that. He'd give it to somebody who is coming back."

"How do you know that?"

"It's obvious."

She considered for a moment. "Okay, say you're right. Then let me ask you this. How do you know you won't turn out for baseball next year?"

"I'm not turning out again. There's no way."

"Do me a favor, Shane. Look where we are today, and think where we were a year ago. Then, if you're still certain you know what you'll be doing next year, call Coach Grandison and tell him you don't want the job and I'll get you the dishwashing job. Right now I'm going to the grocery store. You need anything?"

Once she'd left, I let my eyes wander over the front room: the little sofa, the small television, the bookcases, the coffee table. It was so much my home that it was hard for me to remember the Sound Ridge house. And when I did picture that house, it seemed comically big and showy. Had it been only a year since I'd lived there?

That night I got out the bus schedule. I'd have to transfer once, and of course the times didn't work out at all. The thought of standing at a bus stop every morning and every afternoon was depressing. I already felt sluggish and out of shape.

Then an idea came to me. I could jog the two miles to the community center and then jog home at the end of the day. If I got to the center a little early, I could pump iron in the weight room. I could turn the job into a way to make money *and* get in shape.

After breakfast the next morning, I laced up my shoes and headed off for Bitter Lake. For most of the way, I ran along Second Avenue, a quiet street without the traffic of Greenwood. I was right about my conditioning; by the time I reached Bitter Lake I was dragging.

I headed straight for the weight room but stopped short when I saw the rates: three dollars for a single visit, twenty dollars for ten. "You want to do some lifting?" the man at the main counter called out.

"Not now," I said, feeling my empty pocket. "Maybe tomorrow."

"Go on in. Give it a try. See if you like it. In the summer it's free in the mornings to kids under eighteen."

"Really?" I said. "It doesn't say that here."

"It doesn't? Well, it should."

I pushed the door open and stepped inside. There were maybe ten different stations, and at each station there was a chart explaining how to do the lift properly. I started with the bench press. I had nobody to spot me, so I had to keep the weights on the low side and do lots of repetitions, which is the right way to lift anyway. After the bench presses, I worked through squats and curls, all the regular stuff.

It was hard work, but it was good to feel my muscles strain. I'd pump iron, then rest, then pump some more. When I finally looked up at the clock, it was nearly noon. I did two more reverse curls, then hustled to the gym to start my new job.

I was nervous. I'd played basketball in grade school and junior high. I had a decent outside touch, but I wasn't fast enough to play guard, and I wasn't tall enough to play in the front court, so I lost interest. I knew the rules, or at least most of them, but I wasn't sure about the signals for blocking fouls and charges and that sort of thing.

When I stepped onto the Bitter Lake gym, the first guy I saw was Miguel Alvarez. He smiled and called out, "You refereeing too?"

"Yeah," I said, smiling back.

Seeing him made me realize how much I liked the guy.

You could tell he just wanted things to go well for you and that he'd help you if he could. I couldn't think of anybody I'd rather work with.

In the next few minutes, four more "refs" showed up. Two of them were black guys, Abdul and Jonas, who definitely looked like basketball players. There was also a tough-looking girl named Brandy and her friend Carmen. Both had about fifty earrings in each ear, and their clothes reeked of cigarettes. The six of us stood around until a man came onto the court. "Welcome," he called out. "I'm Matthew Falk. You must be my summer refs."

Falk was a young guy with short gray-blond hair. You could tell he was both strong and fast. He had the easy smile of a coach who is used to being liked by all his players. "This week you'll learn how to ref. Starting next week, you'll be assigned to different gyms in the North End. You'll come here, and we'll drive you to wherever your games are. You'll handle three games a day, Monday to Friday. Pay is twelve bucks a game. Any questions?"

That afternoon we shadowed Falk, watching him as he refereed scrimmages. The next day we took turns doing the refereeing, with him supervising. After the first scrimmage, Falk took me aside. "Remember, this is a rec league. Don't call everything. Blow the whistle only if they can't play through the contact."

On day three Miguel and I did better, except Falk said we should have called a technical foul when this little punk slammed the basketball against the wall and shouted, "This game sucks!"

At night I studied the rule book and practiced the moves refs make: hands on the hips for a block, two arms up for a three pointer. Sometimes I'd get dramatic, pretending I was calling an NBA game: Kobe and Shaq and Kidd and Webber. "What are you doing?" Marian called up. "The whole room's shaking down here."

On Monday Miguel and I were on our own. We were assigned to the Loyal Heights gym, which was closer to town. The players were fifth and sixth graders, and it was only a summer league, but it was work. And I don't mean the running up and down the court. That was easy. The hard part was making the calls as best you could, then tuning out the whining coaches and kids.

Falk watched our last game that day. I thought we'd done terribly, but when the final buzzer sounded, he came onto the court with a smile on his face. "Don't get down on yourselves. You made some mistakes, but that happens. The important thing is you worked as a team, picking up the calls for one another. You're going to do fine."

That evening Mom asked me how the job was going.

"It's good. I like it."

She smiled. "I'm glad."

I quickly settled into a routine. I'd get up around nine, clean up, eat a little, then jog to Bitter Lake. Once I was there, I'd lift weights until noon, when I'd meet up with Miguel. The bus would take us to Loyal Heights, Ballard, Meadowbrook, or wherever we'd been assigned for the week. We'd finish around four and be back at Bitter Lake by four-thirty. I'd run home, shower, and then eat dinner. After dinner I'd watch a baseball game on television or maybe a movie. By eleven I'd be asleep, and the next thing I knew the alarm clock would go off and it would be time to start over again.

CHAPTER 2 My days were set, but sitting around the house alone in the evenings got boring. You can watch only so many baseball games on TV, rent only so many movies.

It was a Wednesday evening, and for Seattle it was hot—close to ninety. Mom was at work. Marian had made a new friend, Laura Curtiss. Along with Kaitlin, they'd gone swimming at Madison Pool. I had some money in my pocket.

There was a mom-and-pop grocery store right on Greenwood, but for some reason I headed to the minimart where Lonnie and I had stolen the beer. When I got there, I stood at the door for a second and peered in. The Vietnamese lady wasn't at the counter, so I pushed the door open, walked to the coolers, and grabbed a Dr. Pepper. As I did, my eyes fell on a long line of Mickey Stouts.

While I stood in line waiting to pay, I wished that Lonnie hadn't gotten kicked out of Whitman. Not that I was going to steal again—that was stupid. But sitting around and talking, hanging out with him, those had been okay.

Outside the store, I looked in the direction of Lonnie's apartment building. Why not go see him? If he was drinking or doing drugs, that didn't mean I had to. I could hang out with him, talk, pass the time.

As I came up to the crosswalk, the light turned red. It was

a long light—the cars flew by me one after the other for what seemed like forever. Finally the light turned green, but I didn't cross. Who was I kidding? If I started hanging out with Lonnie, I'd be drinking again. Or smoking dope, if that's what he was doing. Maybe not the first night or the second, but eventually.

I didn't want to go home, so I headed down 130th toward the Northwest Athletic Complex. Miguel played baseball there in the evenings. "You should come by. It's mainly Mexican guys, and Salvadorans, but there are some Anglos who play."

"I'm done with baseball," I'd told him.

He'd shrugged. "We'll be there if you change your mind. We play every night."

Before I could see the field, I could hear the sound of a baseball game: the crisp snap of a well-thrown ball finding the pocket of a glove, the ping of an aluminum bat making solid contact, the voices of players. I climbed the steps from the street to the field, walked along a tree-lined path, and came out behind the backstop.

I didn't spot Miguel at first, and for a while I wasn't sure I had the right game. Most of the guys were older than me, with mustaches or beards. I heard more Spanish than English. I couldn't have been standing there for more than a minute or two when Miguel's voice rang out. "Shane, over here."

His team was batting. I walked over to his bench.

"You here to play?" he said.

"Just to watch."

"Come on. Play."

"I can't. I didn't bring my glove."

He waved that off. "No problem. You use someone else's. We're short two players." He paused. "You can pitch if you want."

"I'll play, Miguel, but I'm not pitching."

"Okay, Shane. Don't pitch. You play outfield like Coach says. We need a right fielder."

"Right field it is."

"I'll introduce you to the guys." He lowered his voice. "They're good guys mostly, but not all of them. You know what I mean."

He called out six names in about seven seconds. Manny, Jose, Pedro. I nodded to each of them, but I couldn't have matched a single name with a face. Not that it mattered, because none of them took any notice of me. They nodded, then went right back to their conversations.

I sat next to Miguel and watched the game. The talent was about the same as in a high school game, only a couple of the older guys were better than anybody in high school, and a couple were worse. The pitcher—an older guy—adjusted his game to fit the player. He'd throw some serious fastballs to one batter and then throttle way back when the next hitter came up. Miguel's team—it was hard to think of them as *my* team—scored a couple of runs. I was on deck when the third out was made.

I didn't know how I'd get a glove, but Miguel took care of that for me. The guy he asked stared at me suspiciously for a few seconds, then handed it to me. It was a nice glove, a burgundy Rawlings that had been well cared for. I was going to be sure to hand it back to him and not toss it.

I trotted out to right field, surprised at how nervous I felt. I almost wished I was pitching. I'd have been comfortable on the mound, especially in this type of game, but I felt lost in right field.

The other team got a couple of hits and a walk, and with two out they had one run in and runners at second and third. The batter was a lefty, the biggest guy out there. The center fielder called out to me. "Hey, you." With his arm, he was motioning me to move back. I took five steps and looked over. "More!" he shouted. Who was I to argue? I took five more.

On the second pitch, the guy turned on a fastball and crushed it, sending a towering fly ball down the right field line that ended up in the parking lot. That started a huge argument as to whether it was fair or foul. Even though I was taking Spanish in school, I couldn't follow what these guys were saying. A player on our team ended up running down the line pretending to be the ball, curving as he ran. That seemed to do it—the decision was foul. The next pitch was some kind of changeup, which was smart. The batter was angry about losing his home run and ready to crush another ball. He was way out in front, tried to hold up, and ended up sending a bloop toward me in right.

It was just a pickup game, so I probably should have played it on a hop, even if playing it safe would have cost two runs. But I wanted to show these guys that I could play. I got a good jump and sprinted in. At the last second I dived, and the ball stuck in the web of my glove. I hit the ground hard, but the ball stayed put like a scoop of vanilla ice cream on top of a sugar cone.

As I trotted in, my teammates came over and patted me

on the back. "Nice catch! . . . Way to go! . . . *Muy bien.*"

We played for another hour. I struck out and popped up in my two at bats, but I caught every fly ball hit my way. Our team ended up winning by a half dozen runs or so. When the game broke up, Miguel gave me a playful punch in the shoulder. "See? I told you. It's good. You come tomorrow night?"

"Yeah. I'll come tomorrow night."

He reached out and shook my hand. "Good. Good. It's fun."

I had started toward home when he called after me. "Hey, Shane, you know that guy you hit in the head?"

All the good feelings drained out of me. "What about him?"

"He was here yesterday."

"What?"

"The guy you hit," Miguel repeated. "He was here. Yesterday. He played."

"Reese Robertson was here?"

"I don't know his name, but I remember his face."

"It couldn't have been him, Miguel. He wouldn't—" I was about to say that he wouldn't play with a bunch of Latinos in a pickup game, but I caught myself.

"He wouldn't what?" Miguel said, and I could tell he'd mentally finished my sentence for me.

"He wouldn't have the time to play. His coach runs a summer team. He'd be on it."

Miguel shrugged. "Well, then it must have been some guy who looked just like him. I struck him out twice. Fastballs inside."

CHAPTER 3 I played right field again on Thursday night, picking up my first hit, a seeing-eye grounder up the middle, and scoring my first run. I also ran down three fly balls. On Friday night I struck out twice, but I threw out a runner trying to go from first to third on a single. When the other guys saw the strength of my arm, they called me Ichiro, which made me feel pretty good.

Saturday night I got to the field early. Before Miguel said anything, he tossed me a ball. I fired it back, and we fell into a comfortable rhythm. We must have thrown for five minutes before he motioned for me to look out toward center field. "That's him, isn't it? The guy you hit." He waited while I looked. "It is, right? I told you it was him."

My heart was pounding like crazy. Anger surged. Reese just wouldn't go away. "Yeah, that's him."

"You going to say something to him?"

"Why should I? I don't know him."

"You hit him in the head, Shane. You got to say something."

I fired the baseball back to Miguel. "I don't have to do anything."

A pickup game has a life of its own. One minute a bunch of guys are throwing the ball around, and the next the sides are chosen and the game is going. Exactly how it all happens is a mystery, but I made sure I wasn't on Reese's team.

We started in the field, and I quickly hustled out to my position in right field. But I could feel his eyes on me, and I couldn't keep my eyes from drifting toward him.

Miguel was pitching for us. When Reese came up, he took his practice swings and stepped into the batter's box, looking just like the old Reese Robertson. Fast bat, fast hands. Then Miguel threw him an inside fastball, and Reese's left foot buckled and his left side opened up. He squibbed a little dribbler toward the mound, and he was out before he'd taken ten steps out of the box.

We played seven innings that night. Reese batted three more times. Miguel struck him out on three pitches and got him on another pathetic ground ball to the right side. When Reese came up to the plate for the last time, Alberto Guerrero was pitching. Guerrero was probably thirty years old. He liked the game to move, so he grooved pitches down the middle for everybody. Reese fouled off Guerrero's first pitch, then drove the next one over our left fielder's head. I watched as he flew around the bases, his long stride eating up the ground, turning a triple into a home run. Guys on his team swatted him on the back, and I could see his smile from three hundred feet away. But when he sat down on the bench, the smile disappeared as quickly as it had come. If I knew Guerrero had laid the ball in there, then Reese had to know it too.

By nine the sun was setting and a chill wind had come up—quitting time. I'd avoided Reese during the whole game, running to and from right field with my head down. I intended to get myself home in the same way. But as I was heading off the field, I heard his voice behind me. "Shane Hunter."

I turned around. "Yeah?"

"Remember me? I'm Reese—"

"I know who you are," I interrupted.

He stared at me. "I thought you did."

My throat was so dry I could hardly talk, but I made my-self. "What are you doing here, Reese? Shorelake's got a summer team. I went there, remember? You could be travel-ing up and down the coast, playing top teams and staying in fancy hotels. Why are you playing in a crummy pickup game like this when you could be doing that?"

He looked at the ground. "You want to know?"

"Yeah. I want to know."

"All right. I'm here because I haven't been able to hit since that game. And I'm sick and tired of my teammates and coaches treating me with kid gloves. I need to play in games where I can work on getting my stroke back without feeling like I'm in a fishbowl. But if it's not okay with you that I play here, then—"

"No," I said, embarrassed by his directness. "You can play here. You can play wherever you want. It's a free country. I just didn't understand."

"And now you do?"

"Now I do."

"Okay then."

"Okay."

He turned and started toward the parking lot, which was off the first base line. There was only one car there—a brand-new bright red VW Beetle. "Is that yours?" I called out to him.

"Yeah," he said, turning back. "It's a birthday gift. I've only had it a week."

"You shouldn't park it so close to the field. A ball landed there just last week."

"Thanks for the tip."

• • •

You can tell yourself a million times that something is no big deal, but you can't trick your body. It lets you know when things aren't right. All through the next day, my stomach was turning over. I did a terrible job refereeing, and Miguel noticed. "Something bothering you?"

"No. Nothing."

"Then blow the whistle."

At around six-thirty that evening I headed to the baseball diamond for the game. The first thing I did when I climbed the stairs to the field was check out the parking lot. Reese's Beetle was parked as far from the field as possible.

I played catch with Miguel and Jose, trying hard to behave normally. But I caught myself laughing too hard at every little joke anybody made. The whole time, I kept sneaking peeks at Reese. He was in the outfield tossing the ball with the older pitcher, Alberto Guerrero. Finally our eyes caught. Reese gave me the smallest of waves, and I gave him the same back. *All right,* I thought, feeling better. *That's done. Now I can play my own game.*

Only I couldn't. Because every time Reese stepped to the plate, I watched each pitch as if it were the last inning of the World Series. When he struck out, popped up, or hit a soft grounder to the infield—which was most of the time—I'd feel empty inside. I kept thinking that he'd improve, that he had to improve. But one week went by, and then another, and another, and nothing changed.

Not that he struck out every time. He did okay against the older guys, like Guerrero, who had nothing to prove. But against the hard throwers, Reese opened up his left foot and shoulder way too soon, making his swing pitiful. Most guys would have thrown a few bats, or at least let loose now and then with a few choice words. I know I would have. But not Reese. He'd strike out with the bases loaded or hit a little comebacker with runners at second and third, and when he returned to the bench, he'd walk with his head up. Most of the time he even managed a word for the next batter. "Get a hit" or "You can do it."

After striking out in a big situation, most players will carry the strikeout with them onto the field. They'll be thinking about their swing, so they get a late jump on fly balls or throw to the wrong base—stupid things they wouldn't do if they were hitting well. But Reese never let his strikeouts affect the rest of his game. He was all over that outfield, tracking down fly balls hit to left center and right center, diving for line drives that he could have easily let bounce for base hits.

During one game in late July, Miguel struck Reese out four times. The next day I saw Guerrero working with Reese, showing him how to keep his shoulder in. Reese listened and nodded. Guerrero meant well, but Reese knew what to do; he just couldn't get himself to do it.

Reese wasn't getting anywhere, but I was. The weightlifting and running were paying off. The scale showed I'd put on five pounds, but I'd probably lost ten pounds of fat and put on fifteen pounds of muscle. I had more stamina than ever. I was playing okay, especially in the field. I caught everything hit my way, and I threw out any runners who tried to take an extra base on me. At the plate I wasn't much, though I did hit a home run. The ball barely cleared the fence down the right field line, and I hit it off Guerrero, but it was a home run.

• • •

The day after that home run was August 2, my birthday. Mom took the day off, and I skipped the baseball game. We went to Rosita's for dinner and afterward had an ice-cream cake at home. "What did we do for your birthday last year?" Mom asked as we ate.

Marian looked at me.

"I don't think we did anything," I said. "I don't think we did anything for Marian's either, or for yours."

After that, a silence fell over us.

Upstairs in my room, I thought about my dad. When they'd lowered him into the ground, I'd sworn to myself that I'd always remember him, every single day of my life. It had been only sixteen months since his suicide, but already weeks would go by when I wouldn't think of him at all. And now, when I did think of him, I felt mad at him for leaving Mom and me and Marian. If he were alive, I could ask him things, like whether I should play right field or try pitching again, and if there was something I could do for Reese.

CHAPTER 4 In the second half of August we started getting rain showers, and the sun was setting earlier. Still, I figured the baseball games would keep going at least until the World Series ended in late October. But one Monday night toward the end of August, Guerrero brought a soccerball with him. A half dozen guys formed a circle and kicked the ball around; the conversation was all about the national teams of Mexico, Argentina, and Brazil. It was hard to get them to put the soccerball away and start the baseball game. The next evening there were three soccerballs, and the circle of guys kicking the ball grew to a dozen. Those guys were good, too. It seemed as if every one of them could dribble with both feet, turn on a dime, and pass. The ball might as well have been on a string.

After about fifteen minutes, there was a general discussion, mainly in Spanish, about whether to play baseball or soccer. One of the older guys took charge. "*Fútbol?*" he said, and a whole bunch of voices responded. "Baseball?" he called next. Only Reese voted my way.

With that, the whole pack moved to the adjoining soccer field. "Come on, Shane," Miguel said, motioning for me to follow him.

"No way, Miguel. I'm terrible at soccer."

"It's just for fun. Nobody cares."

I laughed. "I care." I turned and started for home.

That's when I saw Reese. He had his baseball glove in his hand. We both stood there, looking at each other for a minute. "As long as we're here, how about if you and me toss the ball around a little?" he said at last.

He stood at shortstop, and I stood between home and first. He had a good, loose arm, and he fired the ball with just the right velocity. "Do you remember the first time we did this?" Reese said after the ball had gone back and forth about twenty times.

"Yeah, I remember."

"You gave me that old glove and then almost burned a hole in my hand. It was sore for a week." I didn't answer. The ball went back and forth a few more times. "I didn't know about your father then, about how he died. My parents never told me, even after we moved in. I didn't find out until I got to Shorelake. So if I acted like a jerk that day, it's because I didn't know."

I held the ball for a moment. "You didn't act like a jerk. If anybody acted like a jerk, it was me."

"I just wanted you to know that I didn't know."

"Forget about it. It's over."

I threw the ball to him, he threw it back, and there was no more talk about my dad.

Reese had brought his bat with him, so after a while we took turns hitting grounders and fly balls to one another. It wasn't a real game or even a real practice, but it was baseball. An hour or so must have passed because the soccer game ended, and Miguel, all sweaty, came over. "You should have played. You kick the ball. You run. You kick the ball. Nothing to it. We could have used you."

I shook my head. "It's not my game, Miguel."

Miguel frowned. "You change your mind, you tell me, and I'll get you in the game tomorrow." He looked to Reese. "Both of you." Then he headed off the field.

Reese looked at his watch. "I should go, too." After he'd taken about ten steps toward his car, he turned to me. "How about you and I throw the ball around again tomorrow?"

"Okay by me," I said.

"Here? Regular time?"

"Yeah."

"All right. See you tomorrow."

For the rest of August it was just me and Reese. We'd play

catch, hit fly balls and grounders to each other. One night when we'd finished, he asked me if I wanted to get something at Starbucks. "Sure," I said. After that we'd always get in his car and drive to the Starbucks down on Greenwood. He'd have hot chocolate and I'd have a mocha. We'd talk baseball mainly, Mariners and Giants and Yankees and Athletics, playoffs and World Series. Afterward he'd drop me off on Greenwood and 140th, and I'd walk the final few blocks home.

He always offered to take me to my house, but I never let him. Mom had planted flowers in front, and I kept the lawn mowed and edged and the walkways swept. I didn't care if Grandison or any of the guys from Whitman saw it. Looking at it, no one would ever guess that it was city housing. I just didn't want Reese to see it.

CHAPTER 5 The Saturday of Labor Day weekend the sun stayed hidden behind gray clouds, and a chill wind blew from the north. My summer job had ended, so I hung out in my room, listening to music and thinking about school.

My mother had the lunch shift that day. She came home at four and called Marian and me downstairs. "Let's the three of us go to the movies tonight. There's a Spielberg film at the Majestic Bay. We could get hamburgers or pizza first. What do you say?"

Marian immediately agreed.

"I can't," I said. "I'm playing baseball."

"Shane, you've played every day this summer. You can miss

once. Besides, it looks like it could start raining any minute."

I thought of Reese alone, waiting. "I told them I was going to show, so I've got to show."

Mom frowned. "All right, do what you think is best."

They left before I did. Mom was still angry. While she was getting her purse, Marian whispered, "You could still come."

"I told you. I can't."

Marian pulled back the curtain and looked at the sky, which was darker than ever. "You're going to be the only one there."

Once they were gone, I went to the kitchen and peeked inside the refrigerator. Most of the time Mom would leave something on a plate for me, but there was nothing. I spread peanut butter on some French bread, poured myself a glass of milk, and looked at the clock. As I ate, a light drizzle began to fall.

I felt stupid walking to the diamond. The drizzle was turning to rain. When I reached the field, a cold wind was blowing across the infield. Marian had been right; there was no sign of Reese and no soccer game going. I zipped up my jacket, shoved my glove between my arm and body, stuffed my hands in my pockets, and stood under a tree. Five minutes, I decided.

Five minutes came and went. I decided to wait five more. Still no Reese. Finally I turned and headed for home. I'd gone about a block when I heard the horn. I looked up as his red Beetle pulled across the center line to the curb right next to me. Reese leaned over and rolled down the window. "Sorry I'm late. There was an accident up by the golf course. It took me ten minutes to get through."

"You still want to do this?" I said, glancing up at the sky.

"I'm game, if you are."

I got in his car, and we drove back to the field. By the time we reached the diamond, the rain had let up a little. "I think it's stopping," I said.

We'd been throwing for about ten minutes when the first bolt of lightning split the sky. The thunder came about five seconds later. Reese held the ball, and we both looked at the clouds. "I think it's moving away from us," I said.

"Maybe," he said, but ten seconds later a series of lightning bolts lit up the sky right over us. The clouds opened. Huge sheets of rain drove us off the field and back to his car. It couldn't have been more than fifty yards, but we both got drenched.

When we settled into his car, we looked at each other—hair plastered to our heads, water dripping down our faces—and laughed. It was the first time we'd ever laughed at anything together. "Starbucks?" he said, starting up the car.

I got my mocha, he got his hot chocolate, and we sat down at a table by the fireplace. I sipped the steaming-hot mocha slowly, enjoying the sweet warmth of it.

"When do you go back to school?" he asked.

"Tuesday. How about you?"

"The same." He took a sip of his chocolate. "Hey, is it true that some of the girls at Whitman flip their tops in the halls?"

"Not that I've ever seen. Where'd you hear that?"

"I don't know. Some guy told me."

"Whitman's not that different from Shorelake," I said. "Kids don't run around shooting each other or having sex in the halls."

After that we both stared into the fire. "Can I ask you something?" Reese said at last.

"Sure. Ask away."

"Why didn't you pitch this summer?"

My face went red. "No reason. I just didn't feel like it."

"But you're going to pitch for Whitman next year, right?"

"No more pitching for me. If I play, and I'm not sure I will, I'll play in the outfield."

"Why did you quit pitching?"

I looked away. For an instant I thought about telling him the truth. But how could I explain to him something I couldn't completely explain to myself? When I looked back, I shrugged. "No reason, really. It's just that being a relief pitcher isn't a whole lot of fun. You sit and you sit, your stomach churning the whole time. And then lots of times you don't even play."

"Still, it must be quite a rush to strike out some guy to end a game."

I thought of how that felt. The ball in my hand; the game on the line; the umpire yelling, "Strike three!"

"Yeah," I admitted. "It is."

He played around with his spoon, then looked at me again. "You still could pitch, couldn't you? If you wanted to. You didn't hurt your arm or anything?"

"No, there's nothing wrong with my arm."

He fiddled with his spoon again. finally his eyes locked on mine. "Would you pitch to me?"

"What?"

"Would you pitch to me? Over the winter. I mean really pitch. Your fastest fastball; your best stuff. We could get together on weekends and over Christmas break. It would be good for both of us."

"What's that supposed to mean?"

"You know what it means."

I looked off to the side, away from him. "Listen, Reese. If you want to get together and throw the ball around in the off-season, I'm all for it. I'll even throw batting practice to you if you want. But that's as far as I'll go."

"So you won't pitch to me."

I looked away. "I told you. No."

He stared at me long and hard, then quickly finished his chocolate and stood up. "I've got to go. You want a ride home?"

"I think I'll stay a little longer," I said. "I'll catch the bus or walk."

He headed to the door.

"You going to be at the field tomorrow?" I asked as he was about to push the door open.

He shook his head. "No. There's no point."

CHAPTER 6 On Tuesday morning I dragged myself to the bus. I figured I'd keep my head down and my eyes forward just like the year before. But back then I knew nobody and nobody knew me. As I stood at the bus stop, kids came over. "Can you believe we're back doing this?" they said, remote smiles on their faces.

There was nothing to do but smile back. "No. It's unreal."

In the hallways before school and during passing periods, guys on the baseball team would slap me on the shoulder and ask how I was doing. Mrs. Guion, my Spanish teacher, grabbed me by the elbow. "When you see Miguel, tell him to come to my classroom. Okay? I need him to help me translate a letter." At lunch I did see him, and after I passed on her message, I sat down and ate lunch with him and Pedro Hernandez and some other guys from the team.

When the school day ended, I headed straight to the bus loading zone. Before I reached it, Coach Grandison spotted me from across the lawn. "Shane, come over here for a minute."

I hustled over. He shook my hand, his eyes shining. "How did the job go?"

"Really well. Thanks for getting it for me."

"You interested in more work? The soccer league needs refs."

"I don't know much about soccer."

"It'll be boys and girls under twelve. You'll get training. The hard part is the parents. They take it pretty seriously."

"If somebody shows me what to do, then sure, I'm interested."

"All right then. You're on. Don't plan anything for Saturday afternoons." He paused. "I talked to Miguel. He says you played right field all summer. He says you're pretty good, that you catch everything in sight and that nobody runs on you."

I shrugged. "I field okay, but I can't hit a lick."

"That'll come. Just keep playing."

Behind me I could hear the bus engines starting. I looked over my shoulder. "Coach," I said, "I've got to—"

"Go. We'll talk more later."

Riding home, I thought about what my aunt Cella had said when my father was buried. I didn't want to hear it then because I didn't want to believe it. But she was right. No matter what happens to you, the world doesn't stop. Either you get on board or you don't.

In late September I was excused from my math class to meet with my counselor, Mr. Ferris. The day before, I'd been asked to fill out a form about my "future plans." What was I interested in? Did I want to become an electrician or a plumber? How about AmeriCorps or VISTA? Was I interested in a technical school, a community college, or a four-year college?

At Shorelake I'd just assumed that I'd end up at some expensive Eastern school that had good sports teams. Duke maybe, or Georgetown. But that was when we had money and I got good grades. Now we didn't have money, and I didn't get good grades. I'd checked the box next to *college* anyway. There didn't seem to be anything else I could check. I knocked softly on Mr. Ferris's door. "Come in," he called out cheerily, and I stepped inside, not looking forward to what he'd have to say to me.

Mr. Ferris is the golf coach, and he looks like a golfer. Polo shirt, khaki pants, fair hair, blue eyes, easy smile. He looked over my form. "So you want to go to college. Well, let's see what your grades look like."

As he flipped through my records, I squirmed in my stiff-backed chair. "I know I got bad grades last year," I said, unable to keep still, "but I'll do better this year. Is there a chance I could still get into the University of Washington?"

UW is right in Seattle. If I was accepted, my only expense would be tuition.

He shook his head. "I don't think so. Not unless your SAT is really, really high. Fourteen hundred or so. If I were you, I'd apply to other schools. Central Washington for sure, and maybe Western Washington. You'd need straight A's in your core classes to get into Western, and A's and B's for Central. I'm talking about math, English, history, science. You'll have to buckle down."

I looked at my hands. "My mom couldn't afford room and board on top of tuition. If I can't get into UW, I don't see how I can go anywhere."

He pushed some papers across his desk toward me. "Don't let money keep you from going to college. Bring these home and show them to your mom. There are scholarships and grants available, and low-cost loans. five years from now you could have a college diploma and not much debt. The key is getting those grades up."

That night I told Mom what Mr. Ferris had said.

"And he said with grants and scholarships, you might not have much debt?"

"Yeah."

"There's no chance for UW?"

"I can't get in, Mom."

For a moment there was silence. Then she smiled. "Well, if you can't, you can't. We'll make other plans."

"I could go to a community college. Then you'd have money for Marian when she's ready for college."

Mom stared off into space. I could feel her thinking. "No," she said at last. "You're going to a four-year college. That's what your father would have wanted, and that's what we're going to do." She paused. "Those other schools sound fine. Especially Western Washington. I've heard nothing but good things about it. We'll take a ride up to Bellingham this weekend and look it over."

We went on Sunday. Western is smaller than UW, but it still felt plenty big. Posted on a kiosk outside the student union building were flyers for sailing lessons in Bellingham Bay, mountain climbing in the Cascades, white-water rafting in Canada, and hang-gliding on the San Juan Islands. There were notices about film clubs, chess clubs, and Internet clubs and announcements of lectures on science, math, and politics. Near the campus were bookstores and coffee shops and movie houses.

"What do you think?" Mom said as we drove home.

"I think it's great," I answered.

She smiled. "So do I. So raise those grades and get yourself admitted."

We got home at four in the afternoon. I walked to the Broadview Library and checked out a couple of SAT practice books. That night I studied for an hour or so. I never did that again, but I did spend fifteen minutes to half an hour on them most nights. And that wasn't the only studying I did. To get C's at Whitman, all you had to do was show up. But A's took study, and I was determined to get A's.

I hardly had time to breathe those days. I was still running every day and lifting weights at least a couple of times a week. I studied at night and refereed soccer games on Saturdays. I had to work those games alone, which made it boring; and some of the parents went ballistic if I missed a call, which made it miserable. But the work put money in my savings account, so I took every game offered.

First-quarter grades were mailed home in early December. I had straight A's. Mom looked at them, then came over and kissed me on the forehead. They posted the honor roll in the hallway outside the cafeteria. That Monday Mrs. Joyner caught me looking at it. "Nice to see your name there, isn't it?" she said.

CHAPTER 7 A couple of weeks later, a little before winter break, Kraybill came back. Seeing him brought back memories I didn't like.

"I didn't think you'd make it, Shane," he said as he drank the cup of coffee my mother offered him. He flipped through a stack of papers. "But everything looks good. School, work, sports—all of it top-notch. No hint of trouble."

"He's a fine young man," my mother said, looking at me and beaming. "And he always was. He made a mistake, he faced it, and he learned from it. Didn't you, Shane?"

I nodded, wishing he'd say whatever it was he had to say and leave.

Kraybill put the file folder down. "Do you see Lonnie Gibson anymore?"

"No."

"Do you go out drinking with anybody? Do drugs now and then? Anything like that?"

"He's done with all that," my mom said, jumping in.

"I've got to ask, Mrs. Hunter. It's my job."

I looked him in the eye. "No."

"Did you know Lonnie was arrested again?"

"No."

"Methamphetamines. He was selling in the University District."

"That's too bad," I said. "But I told you. I never see him anymore."

Kraybill sipped his coffee. "Well, from the looks of it, you won't be seeing me again either. And I'm glad of it." He looked toward Mom. "Thanks for the coffee."

"You're very welcome."

Kraybill stood up and started for the door.

"Can I ask you something?" I said.

He turned back. "Ask away."

"I've got my application in at a couple of colleges. Will they find out about . . ." I stopped.

"About your arrest? Not unless you tell them." He paused. "Anything else on your mind?"

I thought for a second. "No. Nothing."

He smiled. "Make something of yourself, Shane."

Mom walked him to his car. When she returned, she rubbed her hands together. Marian, who'd been listening from the kitchen, had come into the living room. "This is a big day," Mom said, looking at both of us. "I say we all go out for pizza."

"Can we go to Romio's?" Marian asked.

"Of course we can go to Romio's."

I was all for it too, but when we got there, my stomach felt off somehow. I ate a couple of pieces of the garlic bread but didn't even finish my first piece of pizza.

"Are you sick?" Mom said.

"I'm just not hungry."

"Well, don't force yourself to eat."

Marian took another piece off the platter. "More for me!" she said and shoved it into her mouth.

That night I couldn't fall asleep. I tried to make myself think about all the good things that had come my way, but that didn't work. So then I tried to think about nothing, but you can't think about nothing when there's something gnawing away at you.

And Reese Robertson was gnawing away at me.

I went through it all as if it were a movie running in slow motion. My first pitch on the outside corner for a strike. My second pitch even further outside, setting him up, tempting him to lean out over the plate to try to get the base hit he needed to complete the cycle. Finally my third pitch—high and inside. The baseball thudding into his skull . . . his bat flying . . . him crumpling to the ground, his helmet shattered.

CHAPTER 8 Our second Christmas in the house was a lot different from the first. For one thing, the house felt like a home. Now I never thought about how small it was, or that it was really only a duplex, or that there was no backyard. Everything fit just fine.

Mom had been made assistant manager at Pasta Bella.

That meant a bonus for her, and on Christmas Eve she wasn't in the mood for saving. "We'll do that after Christmas," she said. We went to Sky Nursery and bought a noble fir that nearly took up the entire front room. The tree was big enough to hold all the ornaments that Mom had hung on to. We also had some of our old Christmas lights. Dad had always made sure our house was the brightest in Sound Ridge. I couldn't match that, but I ran lights around the outside of the duplex, and the rest I strung up inside. On her day off, Mom baked about ten dozen cookies.

On Christmas morning a stack of gifts were under the tree. Most of them were for Marian. Clothes mainly, but in the heavy box was a Sony CD player. I'd seen Mom looking at a cheaper, off-brand player at Walgreen's, and I know that's what Marian thought she was going to get. "Oh, thank you!" she said as she pulled the Sony out of the box.

I got a sweatshirt, a new pair of pants, some wool socks, and a $100 gift certificate for Olympic Sports. "You're so grown up, I don't know what to buy you anymore," Mom said.

"This is perfect."

"Open your gift," Marian said to Mom. "It's from both of us."

Mom tore off the wrapping paper. Inside was a hand-knitted wool Norwegian sweater, blue and red with a reindeer pattern. Marian had picked it out and contributed some allowance money, and I'd paid the rest. "It's beautiful," Mom said, and she kissed us both. "Absolutely beautiful."

"I told you she'd like it," Marian said as Mom tried it on.

The phone rang. It was Aunt Cella, and we took turns talking to her. Then we cleaned up the wrapping paper and ate breakfast. After that Marian was off. "I want to see what Kaitlin got."

I helped Mom do the breakfast dishes. When we finished, she stretched her arms out and yawned. "Shane, I think I'm going to lie down for a while. I'm beat."

At ten o'clock on Christmas morning, I was alone in the front room with nothing to do. I had ten bucks, so I grabbed my jacket and slipped out the front door.

Once outside, I walked around the neighborhood, not heading anywhere in particular. After about fifteen minutes I found myself at Northwest Athletic Complex. I thought the baseball diamond would be a mud hole, but it wasn't half bad. There was a little pool of water out by second base, and another where the catcher would crouch, but otherwise the field was okay.

I walked across the infield to the pitcher's mound. It was the first time I'd been on a mound in six months. I stared at home plate, remembering how great it had felt to be on the mound with a baseball in my hand and a ball game on the line.

Suddenly I knew that there was something I had to do, something I should have done a long time ago. I walked home quickly. When I opened the front door, Marian, Kaitlin, and Laura Curtiss were on the floor, the Monopoly board spread between them. "Mom still asleep?" I asked.

"Yeah," Marian said. "Why is she so tired anyway?"

"Christmas is hard work," I said.

"You owe me eighteen dollars," Laura said, and Marian went back to her game.

I pulled out the phone book and flipped through it until I found the right page. We have a cordless phone, so I scribbled the number, took the handset to my room, closed the door, and punched in the digits.

"Reese?" I said when the voice at the other end said hello.

"Yeah, this is Reese."

"This is Shane. Shane Hunter."

Silence.

I swallowed. "I'll pitch to you."

More silence.

"Did you hear me?"

"Yeah, I heard you."

"Well, what do you say? Do you want me to or not?"

"You know I do," he said. "But only if you're going to throw your hardest."

"I will. Not right away, of course. But once my arm is loose."

"Fair enough."

"When do you want to start?"

Reese's red Beetle was already in the parking lot when I reached the baseball diamond an hour later. He was by first base, stretching.

We warmed up by playing catch. The tightness in my shoulder surprised me. The weightlifting had made me stronger, but those new muscles were going to take a while to loosen. Reese kept looking at me, waiting for me to say I was ready.

Finally my arm felt reasonably loose. "You want to hit?" I asked.

He nodded. "I've got a bucket of balls in the trunk."

He went to his car and came back a couple of minutes later. "Here's what I thought we'd do," he said. "There are ten baseballs in the bucket. You pitch them; I hit them. We shag them, then do it again. Okay?"

"Sounds good to me."

He picked up his bat, pulled on his batting gloves, headed toward home plate, then turned back. "I left something in the trunk." He dropped his bat and jogged to the parking lot. When he returned, he was wearing a batter's helmet.

I stepped up onto the mound. As I looked at Reese, all I could feel was the hardness of the ball. "Listen, Reese," I said. "I'm going to throw easy today. I haven't pitched in a long time."

"That's okay," he said. "I haven't hit in a long time either."

I rocked and came straight over the top. I was trying to groove a fastball right down the middle, but my pitch was about two feet outside and must have bounced five feet in front of the plate.

Reese started after it anyway, tried to hold up, then finished his swing so awkwardly he nearly fell down. The ball thudded into the wood boards of the backstop. He smiled. "We can only get better."

Again I went into my motion and delivered. The second pitch was a foot outside and a foot high. Reese flailed at it, nubbing the ball off the end of his bat down the first base line.

After that I reached in for another ball and then another. Sometimes I'd throw something resembling a strike. When I did, Reese would take a cut at it. Most of the time his left side flew open, making his swings awkward and ugly. But every once in a while he hung in, and when he did, the ball jumped off his bat into the alleys.

We went through two buckets, then a third bucket, and a fourth. He'd cream about every sixth pitch, his swing as sweet as ever. When the fifth bucket was empty, we picked up the balls and carried the stuff to his car. He opened the trunk, and I stuck the bucket inside. When he closed it, he turned to me. "You want a ride to Greenwood?"

"No," I said. "I feel like walking."

He headed toward the driver's door and opened it. Before he stepped into the car, I called out to him. "There's something I've got to tell you, Reese," I said, not sure what I was going to say.

He stood just outside his car. "What?"

"That pitch I hit you with?"

"What about it?"

"There was nothing accidental about it. I set you up with those outside pitches. When I saw you move closer to the plate, I came in high and tight trying to hit you, and I'm sorry."

You'd have thought I was telling him the weather report. His face didn't register anything.

"Aren't you going to say something?" I asked.

"What do you want me to say?"

"I don't know. Something."

He looked off to the side. "I always thought you were trying to hit me. In fact, I was ninety percent sure. So now I'm one hundred percent sure. It doesn't change much."

I waited, but he didn't say anything else. "So you still want me to pitch to you?"

"Yeah. I do."

"Even though I hit you on purpose?"

"What are you after, Shane? What do you want me to do?"

"I don't know. I guess I thought you'd tell me you hate me, or maybe take a swing at me."

His eyes flashed. "All right. You want me to say this stuff out loud, so I'll say it. Sometimes, after I take a terrible swing, I think of that pitch and what it did to me, and I hate you. I hate you so much I want to smash your face in. But then I stop myself from hating you, and I force myself to think about my swing. Hating you won't get me back to where I was. Standing in against that fastball of yours will. I need you to pitch to me. I need to be able to hit against you. I wish I didn't, but I do."

For a while I let his words hang there. Finally I spoke. "You'll hit again, Reese. By the time baseball season rolls around, you'll be as good as you ever were."

He frowned. "How do you know what I'm going to be able to do? You got a crystal ball or something?"

"I know because we'll work at it until you can. I'll pitch to you until my arm falls off if that's what it takes."

The anger slowly went out of his eyes. "Well, I hope you're right."

"I am right. You'll see."

He opened the door to his car and slid into the front seat.

"Tomorrow?" I said.

"Not tomorrow," he answered. "My grandparents are visiting. The day after?"

"Okay then. The day after."

He pulled the car door shut and drove away.

CHAPTER 9 Two days later I was back at the ball field. It was a raw, gray day. Even though I arrived twenty minutes early, Reese was already there. We played catch for a while, then I moved back fifty feet, and we played long toss. It takes a while to loosen up on cool days, and we weren't in any hurry anyway. "You want to hit?" I said after a while.

"Might as well."

I didn't worry about speed, only about mechanics. I tried to stay closed, to drive with my legs and the trunk of my body. The more you ask your arm to do, the more likely that you'll hurt yourself. Get power from your legs, and your arm will hold up.

I wasn't wild like I'd been the first day. Major leaguers paint the corners, working inside and out, up and down. But that's not me. I just fire pitch after pitch right down the middle and hope for some movement.

Maybe because I was in a better flow, Reese was driving my pitches to all fields, hard ground balls and line drives. I threw fifty pitches that day, and I'd guess he hit twenty of them on the button.

"One more bucket," he said when I told him I was done.

I shook my head. "I don't want to hurt my arm."

I helped him carry the stuff to his car.

"Your swing looked good," I said. "Real good."

He smiled. "Yeah, I'm terrific in batting practice."

"I was throwing pretty hard."

"Look, Shane. It went well. I hung in there and hit the ball solid. But that wasn't close to being your best stuff, and you know it."

"It was a step," I insisted. "For both of us."

Other than two days when the rain absolutely poured down, Reese and I met every afternoon for the rest of winter break. Each time, I threw the ball a little harder, and each time, Reese hit a little better. But I couldn't get myself to cut loose, not all the way.

The Wednesday after New Year's, I was back in the school cafeteria eating lunch with Miguel and Pedro Hernandez when Kurt Lind came over. "Did you hear about the new guy who just transferred in? The baseball player?"

"Is he a second baseman?" Pedro joked. "Because we sure could use a new second baseman."

Kurt ignored Pedro, focusing his eyes on Miguel and me. "He's a Korean guy, a center fielder. He just moved up here from Oregon. Kim something is his name. He's in my PE class. He runs like the wind. I mean faster than fast. He's hard to understand, but I think he said his team went to the Oregon state finals last year."

"That's good," Miguel said. "We can always use a fast guy."

"There's more," Kurt went on. "You know the McDermott twins—Jim and Tim—the wide receivers on the football team?"

"They're going to play second base," Pedro said.

"No," Kurt snapped. "They're both first basemen, and Grandison told me that you're going to be a ball boy."

Pedro laughed.

"I don't know the McDermotts," I said, "but I know who they are."

"Well, they're turning out for baseball too. They're great athletes. Big and strong." He paused. "I'm telling you, we could be really, really good."

"If those guys pan out," I said.

Kurt smiled. "I know, I know. But if you don't dream in the off-season, when do you dream?"

The weeks rolled by, one after the other. School in the day, study at night, baseball with Reese on the Saturdays and Sundays when it wasn't raining, and on some of the days when it was.

After school one Friday in mid-February, I walked out to take a look at the baseball diamond. The mound was in good shape, which surprised me. Then Grandison's blue van pulled up onto the field, rakes and shovels and bags of dirt in the back. He'd already been hard at work.

He got out, waved to me, and walked over. "Getting the itch?"

"Yeah, I guess I am."

He pulled one of the shovels out of the truck.

He looked at me. "How come you're up there on the mound? I thought you were an outfielder now."

I looked him in the eye. "I'm not an outfielder. I'm a pitcher. Or at least I'm going to try to be one, if you'll let me."

For a long moment his eyes stayed locked on mine. Then he nodded. "All right. If that's what you want. A team can never have too many pitchers." He held out a shovel. "I seem to recall you're pretty good at fixing up a field. Can you give me a hand?"

"Sure," I said, taking the shovel from him.

We worked for more than an hour. At first I was cold, but once I'd broken a sweat, I felt good. There's a pleasure in seeing something take form as you work. "That's enough," Grandison said as the twilight darkened. "Get in and I'll give you a ride home."

We packed up the tools and I hopped in the van. He pulled off the school grounds and into traffic. He had the radio tuned to a jazz station, but as we crawled along Greenwood he flicked it off. "Miguel says you've been working out with Reese Robertson," he said, his eyes fixed on the road. "Is that true?"

I felt the blood rush to my face. "Yeah. It's true."

Grandison nodded. "And how's Reese doing?"

I swallowed. "I don't know. Okay, I guess. He's afraid he won't be able to stand in against a really good fastball."

"You've got a really good fastball. Aren't you throwing it to him?"

"I've been holding back a little."

The traffic light at 130th turned red. Grandison slowed to a stop, then looked over at me. "Why? Something wrong with your arm?"

"Nothing's wrong with my arm."

The traffic started moving again. Grandison made a left turn, then pointed to the duplex. "That's where you live, right?"

"That's it," I said. He pulled into the driveway and I stepped out of the van. "Thanks, Coach."

He leaned across the seat toward me. "Pitch to him, Shane."

• • •

I saw Reese the next day. It was a bright, sunny day. Cold, but spring was in the air. We could both feel the baseball season sneaking up on us.

We went through our normal routine. A little catch, some fly balls, some grounders. Then I took the mound. The first couple of buckets were basically like the ones I'd thrown the week before. I was going maybe ninety percent. And he was tagging me.

His swing was pure, the prettiest swing I'd ever seen. He kept his arms in tight, bat just off his shoulder, and then—the explosion. Everything forward, everything smooth. Hips, legs, arms, all working together, almost perfectly. But only *almost*. Because he was still pulling off just a little. Someone who didn't know baseball wouldn't have noticed. But instead of driving inside pitches to straightaway left field, he was lifting them to center and right center. And instead of going 350 feet or more, those drives were carrying 280.

We finished shagging the second bucket and headed back toward the infield. "Baseball season starts pretty soon," he said as we reached the infield.

"Yeah," I said, "it does."

"Don't you think it's time to find out?"

I was as ready as I'd ever be. I was throwing free and easy. Two-seam fastballs, four-seam fastballs. Everything was over the plate or just off it. That shakiness, that roaring in the ears I'd felt last spring—none of that had come back.

"Yeah. I guess it is."

A steady breeze was coming from the west. But as I walked up onto the mound, I suddenly felt hot. For an instant I panicked. Was I losing it? But then a deep calm came over me. This wasn't fear; it was adrenaline. This was what I loved about pitching.

Reese stepped in and nodded to me. I rolled the ball around in my hand, getting the two-seam grip I wanted. When I had it, I nodded back. But the truth is I didn't see him. At least I didn't see him as Reese. He was a batter, my enemy, and all I wanted to do was to strike him out.

I could feel the power in my arm, waiting. For weeks I'd been throwing in the low eighties, effortlessly, the way I used to throw in the high seventies. I'd added five miles per hour on my fastball. Minimum. That would put my top speed near ninety. There were major leaguers who didn't throw that fast.

You hear about players getting in the zone. That's where I was. Totally focused on my own pitches. I'd reach into the bucket, pull out a ball, and fire it.

Those ten pitches were incredible. The ball seemed alive, that's how much it was moving. And it was late movement, the kind of movement that freezes hitters. Darting down and in, or down and away. I was unhittable. I could strike out the world.

I reached into the bucket for another ball, but it was empty. That's when I came out of it. I looked in to home plate, and I saw Reese. His face was blank. Behind him were all the baseballs. He hadn't managed so much as a foul tip.

He turned, started picking up the balls, and then tossed them to me. When they were all back in the bucket, he stepped back into the box. I throttled back, throwing him a batting practice fastball. He didn't even swing.

"Not like that," he said.

"Like what?"

"Don't cheat me, Shane."

So I focused on the plate, reached back for everything and something extra besides, and I let pitch after pitch fly. Knee-high, blazing fast, with movement. Nasty pitches. Nine straight swings. Nine straight misses.

"That's enough," Reese said after he'd waved weakly at the last ball.

I helped him put the balls back in the bucket. We walked to his car. He opened the trunk, stuck the bucket inside, then turned to me. "It's been good coming here, staying sharp. But this is it for me. I won't be coming anymore."

"You're not stopping because of today, are you?" I said. "One time doesn't prove anything. You'll catch up to good fastballs. You wait and see if you don't."

He slammed the trunk shut. "Sure I will," he said.

"Come on, Reese," I said. "Don't quit on me."

"I'm not quitting," he said, angry. "I'll play this year, but get the Hollywood ending out of your head, Shane, because it's not happening. Not for me, it isn't."

"But we could still—"

"We could still what?" he interrupted. "The season starts next week. It was a good try, but time's up."

I stood there, not knowing what to say.

"You want a ride home?" he said.

"No. I feel like walking."

"All right then. See you around."

"Yeah. See you around."

PART FOUR

CHAPTER 1 Ten days later, on a crisp February day, tryouts began. I stretched on the outfield grass, looking up at the big, puffy clouds flying across the sky. The grass was a solid green, with the smell of earth just below it. The players around me were talking of games yet to be played, while in the distance I could hear the clatter of bats as Grandison unloaded his van. I'd been crazy to think I could ever quit baseball.

Kim Seung, the transfer Kurt Lind had claimed was so good, turned out to be a skinny guy who couldn't have stood more than five feet five. The first few times he stepped into the batter's box, he didn't seem like much. A lefty, he'd slap a ball down the third base line, hit a ground ball back up the middle, then pull something to right.

It was what he didn't do that made him good. He never swung and missed, never popped anything up. Everything was either a hard ground ball or a line drive. He could move down the first base line more quickly than anyone on the team. In our practice games, he stole second base every time, sometimes going in standing up, which drove Benny Gold crazy. He played center field, and he ran down every fly ball that was near him. Try to take an extra base on him and he'd throw you out. I kept waiting to spot some flaw in his game, or at least something ordinary, but I never did.

Kim was so good the McDermott twins nearly got lost, but they were solid players too. They both had compact swings, yet still generated enough power to drive the ball into the alleys. And they ran well, too. Grandison put them in left and right field, and whatever fly balls Kim didn't catch, one of them did. As a pitcher, you see outfielders cover ground like that, and you know that if you get behind in the count, you can just fire the ball down the middle because even if the batter hits the ball hard, there's a good chance it will be caught.

Those three guys were impact players, starters anywhere, but a couple of other guys from the football team, Dirk Becker and Jason Crandle, were in the mix too. Both were black guys, seniors who had nothing to do, since they didn't have spring football. Grandison had collared them one day after school. "No more excuses," he'd said. "I want both of you on my baseball team."

They showed up, but I could tell they were feeling out of place. And with their muscles bulging, they *looked* out of place too. "What position do you want to play?" Grandison asked them. Becker looked at Crandle; Crandle looked at Becker.

"What's open?" Becker finally answered, bringing a laugh from everybody.

But nobody laughed when the two of them took batting practice. There were more than a few swings and misses, but there were also some long home runs. There was a fearlessness about them, too. They didn't care how bad they looked when they swung, and it made them doubly dangerous. Grandison ended up sticking Becker at third base. He was no Scott Rolen, but he made the routine plays. Crandle was terrible as a fielder, so Grandison made him our designated hitter.

On the last day of tryouts we played a simulated game. I pitched two innings, and I blew the first five hitters away. With two outs in my last inning, Kim came up. I got a quick first strike on him too, but on the next pitch he laid down a bunt. I charged off and fielded the ball between third and home. I should have just held the ball, but I wanted a perfect outing. I turned and threw to first . . . wildly. By the time Jim McDermott ran the ball down, Kim was standing at third. On my next pitch he faked down the line as if he were going to steal home. My concentration broken, I bounced the ball about ten feet in front of the plate. It skipped past Gold, and Kim trotted in. I did a slow burn, then struck out Crandle to end the inning. It wasn't until I was back on the bench that it occurred to me that Kim would be doing to other teams what he'd just done to me—creating a run out of thin air.

At the end of tryouts Grandison had to cut a half dozen players. It killed him to do it. He went on and on about how he wished there were more uniforms or that there was a junior varsity team. He told the guys he'd cut that they could be equipment managers or scorekeepers if they wanted.

I felt for them, but they'd never really worked at baseball. Besides, getting cut happens to everyone sometime. Even major leaguers reach a point when the competition is too tough and they have to hang them up.

The guys who were left were solid. We had speed and power. Pedro Hernandez had batted cleanup the year before. Now he'd probably bat sixth or seventh. Cory Minton was back, and he'd be our top starter. Hank Fowler had graduated, but Miguel was as good as Fowler had been. Top to bottom, we were deeper and stronger. If I could close out the games and keep the starters fresh, we'd be good.

The team picnic was on a Saturday. Gray skies, a chill wind, and drizzle—but every single player showed up. I brought Marian with me. "I have heard about you many times," Grandison said, his eyes on me as he shook her hand. "It's nice to finally meet you."

Perplexed, Marian turned to me. I looked away.

That was the first time I'd gotten a good look at Grandison's daughter. She had glowing skin and friendly eyes, and she wore her hair in cornrows. I smiled at her, and she smiled back, a bright smile. Since my father's death, I hadn't thought about dating. I noticed girls all the time, but I didn't have the energy to get anything going. I thought about talking to her. While I was working up my courage, Kim tossed a Frisbee in her direction. She caught it, then gave him a smile. "You must be Kim Seung," she said. He made a little bow. She threw the Frisbee back. So much for my chances.

Gold, who usually kept to himself, came over. "He was player of the year in Portland last year."

"What?"

"Kim. He was player of the year. I was at a minimart on Aurora and saw a newspaper clipping of him on the wall."

"What was a picture of him doing on the wall of a minimart?"

"I don't know. Maybe his parents own it. Anyway, he hit way over .400 and led the league in runs scored and stolen bases."

Marian came up to me, Frisbee in hand. "Will you play with me?"

"Sure," I said. "Why not?"

CHAPTER 2 High school baseball games don't get the attention of football or basketball, but there's a certain electricity that comes with every opening day, even if the bleachers are half empty. Everybody's even—anything can happen. We opened on the road, playing Bellarmine High of Tacoma. They were a big, Catholic powerhouse school, always near the top in their league.

Kim Seung led off. He took a couple of pitches, then smacked a routine two hopper to short. Bellarmine's shortstop stayed back on the ball and took his time with the throw. Kim was safe by two steps. From our bench we could see the Bellarmine infielders' shocked eyes.

Kim wasn't done. On the first pitch to Kurt Lind, he took off for second. He had such a huge jump that their catcher didn't bother to throw. Two pitches later Lind poked a grounder to the first baseman, moving Kim to third. Tim McDermott

then lifted a little pop into short right field. I thought Kim would bluff down the line, but he tagged up and then came flying toward home plate, challenging Bellarmine's right fielder to throw him out. The right fielder's throw was twenty feet over the catcher's head, and Kim scored standing up. We all high-fived him, but he acted as if it were routine. As we sat back down, Benny Gold nudged me. "You think anybody's ever been player of the year in two years in two different cities?"

The score was still 1–0 in the bottom of the second inning when with one on and one out, Bellarmine's catcher belted a deep drive into the alley in right center. The runner on first, certain it was a hit, was rounding second on his way to third when Jim McDermott stretched out to make a beautiful running catch. McDermott turned, fired the ball to Lind, who fired it to Pedro Hernandez for the inning-ending double play. *Pitching and defense win games.* My father had said that many times.

On the bench, guys were still buzzing about McDermott's catch as Kim came up for his second at bat. He faked a bunt on the first pitch, forcing the first baseman to creep forward a few yards. On the next pitch, Kim smacked a line drive right over the first baseman's head. By the time the right fielder tracked it down in the corner and threw it into the infield, Kim was sliding into third. "Did you see that?" Miguel said, looking up and down the bench. "You don't think he had that all planned, do you? The guy can't be that good, can he?"

Lind brought Kim home with a soft liner into short right that fell for a base hit. We scored again in the fourth, and then Jason Crandle smacked a two-run double in the top of the seventh. That's how I came to be standing on the mound with a 5–0 lead in the bottom of the seventh.

Gold put down one finger for a fastball; I nodded and went into my motion. My release was fluid, and the ball exploded out of my hand. It dipped a little to the right as it neared the plate, but the batter was so late with his swing that he wouldn't have hit my pitch had it been dead straight.

Gold put down one finger again; again I rocked and threw. Another late swing. Strike two. Gold tossed the ball back, then called for a changeup. I almost nodded, but I stopped. This guy couldn't hit my fastball, so why mess around? I shook Gold off. He put down one finger again, and a few seconds later the Bellarmine batter was headed to the bench, dragging his bat behind him.

The next guy was craftier. He didn't swing at the first pitch, and it dipped out of the strike zone for a ball. The second pitch did the same thing. With a 2–0 count, I stepped off the rubber and looked back at my fielders, poised and ready.

I stepped back up onto the rubber and delivered another fastball, only this time I took something off to make sure it was a strike. The Bellarmine hitter swung and sent a high fly to right center. He'd hit it well, but not well enough. Jim McDermott was off with the crack of the bat and ran it down easily for the second out.

The third batter was Bellarmine's best hitter, and he was up there swinging. Again I threw a fastball. Not my best, but a decent pitch. It tied him up, and all he managed was a ground ball to Lind. Lind pounced on it and fired to first; we were high-fiving one another on the infield while the Bellarmine guys packed their gear and headed to their waiting cars.

On the ride home, I kept waiting for Grandison to tell me how well I'd done. But he tuned the radio to a jazz station and tapped the wheel as the miles clicked away. finally, he pulled up in front of my house. "Thanks for the ride," I said as I opened the door.

"Sure. See you at practice. Oh, and nice game."

CHAPTER 3 Our next game was against Eastgate, at their field on the east side of Lake Washington. Grandison took me, Miguel, and the McDermott twins.

None of us could believe how big the campus was. We saw the sign for the school and then drove and drove. The baseball diamonds were behind the soccer fields, which were behind the football fields, which were behind the gym. All of Whitman could have fit in one corner of Eastgate.

Before most baseball games, you at least exchange glances with the other team, maybe even wish some of them luck if you come near them. But the Eastgate guys never once looked at us. They acted as if playing us was a nuisance, like taking care of your little brother.

Grandison noticed their attitude. Before the game started he called us together. "Listen, gentlemen," he said. "Their coach was just asking me how bad the score has to be before we stop playing. He seems to think we're some sort of JV team." He paused. "Let's beat 'em."

Miguel started, and he was wild in the first, walking the first two batters. But Benny Gold threw out a runner trying to steal third, and Kim Seung made a nice catch in the outfield to end the inning and save two runs.

After that, Miguel settled down, shutting down Eastgate with only a scratch hit here and there. But the Eastgate pitcher was tough, too. Tim McDermott got a hit in the second but was stranded at first. Pedro Hernandez hit a double in the fifth, but he didn't get past third. Heading into the top of the sixth, those two hits were all we'd managed.

Kim led off. He looked at a ball, then another one. "Take a pitch," I whispered, hoping that he could work a walk. The Eastgate pitcher went into his motion and fired. Kim wasn't taking. Instead, he turned on the pitch, something I'd seen him do only a couple of times. He caught the ball solid, sending a line shot down the right field line. We jumped to our feet and watched, amazed, as the ball rose against the sky. "Be fair!" I shouted, and a second later the ball landed over the fence just to the left of the foul pole. The umpire immediately started twirling his hand in the air. "Home run!"

On the bench we were jumping up and shouting, high-fiving each other. But I couldn't celebrate for long. "Hunter!" Grandison called out. "Can you go two innings?"

I hustled out and started warming up. My arm felt strong. Alex Knapp, a sophomore and our second-string catcher, noticed. "You've got it today, Shane."

I didn't say anything. Too many times last year I'd been great on the sidelines but then couldn't cut loose in the game. When I took the mound for my final warm-ups, it was eerie. I felt as if I were barely holding the ball, yet I could pinpoint exactly where I was going to throw it.

"Batter up!" the umpire yelled, and the game was on.

For the next two innings, all I saw was Gold's glove. I didn't look at any of the batters; I didn't care about any of the calls. I threw the ball, let it move, and dared any of them to hit it. And they couldn't. I don't remember the individual outs, don't remember coming in at the end of the bottom of the sixth or going out to pitch the seventh. It was just one pitch and then the next.

I do remember coming out of it when Benny Gold hopped out of his crouch and charged the mound, his arms wide, a huge grin on his face. Seconds later my teammates were slapping me on the back and high-fiving one another. In the van, Grandison looked over at me. "You were good." Only then did he turn on the radio.

It was a Monday, so Mom didn't have to work. When I opened the door and stepped inside the duplex, she asked about the game. Usually I don't say much, but this time, once I got started, I couldn't stop. And now, strangely, I could see every hitter as if I were back on the mound again, facing them down. As I talked, Marian came out to listen. When I was finished, she started talking about a poster she'd drawn in Mr. Coleman's class and how much fun it had been. Mom asked her to describe it, and she told us how she and Kaitlin had drawn a sea serpent around the border and had used black gel pens for the writing. When she stopped talking, we looked at one another, and I think we realized at that moment that we were happy—all of us at once. Simply happy.

I went upstairs, did some schoolwork, and read until the

people we shared the duplex with came in. They were new neighbors, and the man shouted all the time, mostly about stuff he'd lost. If it wasn't his watch, it was his wallet. If it wasn't his wallet, it was his keys. This time he was hollering about the mail. He'd put it down somewhere and couldn't find it, and there was a bill he just had to pay. I don't know how his wife put up with him.

CHAPTER 4 Those first two wins set the tone for our practices. Guys arrived early and stayed late. The things players usually dog—the stretches, the outfield running, the base-running drills—everyone took seriously. When Grandison told us the weight room would be open in the mornings, we showed up.

Thursday we had a game against Washington High School, way out by Enumclaw, more than an hour from Seattle. Mount Rainier loomed behind it, and the beauty of the mountain made the city—if you could call Enumclaw a city—seem more grim than it probably was. The high school was outside of town. It was another big, sprawling campus, but this one wasn't rich like Eastgate. There was something beaten down about the buildings, the field, the bleachers, everything. And there was a glare in the eyes of the guys on the Washington team. We were city kids, and they didn't like us.

Cory Minton started. His fastball wasn't all that fast, and his curve ball didn't curve much, but our defense came through for him. Everything the Washington players hit, somebody caught. You make plays in the field, and you come into the bench ready to hit.

Kim Seung led off the third with a bloop double into short right. The Washington pitcher didn't look back at Kim, so on the first pitch to Kurt Lind, he stole third base. Lind ended up striking out, but Tim McDermott singled Kim home. His brother, batting cleanup, walked, bringing up Jason Crandle.

Crandle had been swinging terribly in batting practice, so I wasn't surprised when he swung and missed on the first two pitches. The Washington pitcher nearly struck him out on the third pitch. Crandle got the tiniest piece of it, and the ball popped out of the catcher's glove. Crandle fouled the next two pitches straight back, and his swing suddenly looked fluid. On the bench, everybody leaned forward, tense.

Had I been pitching, I would have gone to my changeup and not risked another fastball. But the Washington guy reared back and fired. Crandle's bat flashed forward, and the ball rocketed high and deep against the blue sky. Washington's left fielder backed up, then turned and watched the ball sail over the fence. We jumped around on the bench, pounding each other on the back and pounding Crandle when he finished his home-run trot.

Grandison would have thrown a fit if he'd known that any of us were thinking it, but that was the game. There was no way any team was coming back against us, not with me in the bullpen.

I pitched the seventh. By then the score was 8–2. My arm felt as strong as iron, and when I rocked and fired, it was pure smoke. I struck out the first two guys, and the last hitter—

their star—rolled a soft grounder to first base.

When the game ended, we high-fived each other, but there was more quiet confidence in those high-fives than there was triumph. We'd done what we'd expected to do—no reason to get excited.

Miguel and I loaded up the school van. Usually Grandison was in a hurry to get home, but this time he stood for five minutes in front of the truck talking with a man I'd never seen before.

It was a long ride back to Seattle. I fell asleep and didn't wake up until the van pulled to a stop in front of Miguel's apartment building. Miguel hopped out. "See you tomorrow," he said.

Grandison backed out of the driveway, then looked over his shoulder at me. "You awake?"

"Yeah."

"Did you see that man I was talking to after the game?"

It took me a second to remember, but then I got a clear picture. Gray hair, gray beard, thin. "What about him?"

"His name is Dave Wood. He's an assistant baseball coach at the University of Portland. He's here to take a look at Kim Seung." I hadn't really thought about college recruiters, but it made sense that they'd be looking at a player as good as Kim. "There'll be lots of college coaches around to see Kim," Grandison went on. "And major league scouts, too, though I think Kim's family is set on him going to college."

"Good for him," I said.

"You bet it's good for him. And it's good for you, too."

"What do you mean?"

"I mean they'll see you, too. Take Wood tonight. He asked a lot of questions about Kim, but he also asked a couple about you."

"About me?"

"He wanted to know the pitches you throw, the kind of kid you are."

"What did you tell him?"

"That you've got a great fastball, a good changeup, no curve, and that you're a good kid."

Whenever my dad had said something good about me, my face flushed and my throat tightened. That's what happened to me now. I turned away and looked out the window, afraid Grandison might notice. Neither of us spoke as the van rattled up Greenwood Avenue. Finally he turned onto my block.

"Do you really think I have a chance at a baseball scholarship?" I asked as my house came into sight.

Grandison pulled up to the curb. "You'll have to pitch lights out all season, but you've got a shot. A ninety-mile-an-hour fastball is a rare thing."

I grabbed my equipment bag and stepped out. But before I closed the door, I had one more question. "Coach, does Mr. Wood know about . . ." I stopped, unable to finish my sentence.

Grandison looked at me. "About what?"

"Nothing," I said.

CHAPTER 5 I thought about telling Mom. I knew how worried she was about money for college, not just for me, but for Marian too. A baseball scholarship would solve everything. But if I didn't get a scholarship, I'd feel as if I'd let her down. So in the end I kept my mouth shut.

It was hard to keep quiet. For the next few weeks, it seemed as if every day she was either on the phone asking about college loans or sitting at the kitchen table filling out forms. As far as she was concerned, I was headed to Western Washington University. She kept reminding me how great the school looked. I guess my replies didn't sound enthusiastic. "You still want to go there, don't you?" she finally asked.

"Oh, yeah," I said. "You bet I do."

All through those weeks, we kept winning, and I kept pitching well. During the games, I'd watch the other team, looking for any edge I might have with any hitter. I kept imagining the reports Grandison was sending down to Portland about me. I had to make sure there could be nothing but good stuff in them. Every day I wanted to ask Grandison whether he'd heard anything more, but I knew he'd tell me if anything broke.

On Tuesday night I pitched a scoreless seventh against Ingraham, and we won 7–4. After the game, Grandison asked me to meet him at the coaches' office in the gym before school on Wednesday. He was rarely there in the mornings. "What's up?" I asked.

"Just be there."

The next morning, as soon as the bus let me off, I hustled to the gym. The hallway was dark, but I saw light leaking from under Grandison's door and heard voices inside. I tapped on the door. "It's open," Grandison's voice barked. "Come right in."

I opened the door, stuck my head in. "You wanted to see me, Coach?"

"Yes, I did. There's someone here to meet you. Shane, this is Coach Dravus from the University of Portland."

My body froze. Coach Dravus, a big man with dark hair and bushy eyebrows, stuck his hand out and shook mine. "Good to meet you, Shane."

"Good to meet you, sir."

Grandison looked from me to Coach Dravus and back to me again. "Well, I'll leave you two to talk things over." And with that, he was gone.

Coach Dravus sat down in the chair behind Grandison's desk. I sat in a blue plastic chair across from him. For about five minutes, Dravus asked me about school and my grades. He was trying to get me to relax, but my mouth was so dry I could hardly talk. "Let's talk baseball," he said at last. He picked up a sheet of paper. "Coach Wood liked what he saw when he was up here earlier. And Mr. Grandison has been keeping me posted on your year. Very impressive numbers."

"I've got a great defensive team behind me. They catch everything."

He tapped the desk with his fingertips for a while, his eyes on the papers in front of him. "You quit pitching last year, didn't you? Why was that?"

I felt cold suddenly. "I don't know. I just lost my confidence. I couldn't throw strikes; I couldn't get anybody out. It seemed like the only thing to do."

He frowned. "I'm not here to play games. And I don't

want to bring up ghosts from the past. But you hit a boy in the head last year, didn't you? Sent him to the hospital. Is that what unnerved you?"

I saw Reese on the ground, his legs twitching, his helmet off to the side, the medics huddled around him.

"Yes, sir," I said. "It was."

"Hitting someone like that is a frightening thing. It takes time to get over it. And you were having a rough go of it anyway, weren't you?"

I nodded, not knowing how much he knew about me.

"But you're throwing free and easy now? No demons?"

"No demons."

His eyes honed in on me. "Do you throw to the inside part of the plate?"

I paused, not sure what to say. Then I shook my head. "No, I don't pitch inside, at least not on purpose. Basically I just aim down the middle and hope the ball moves some. Most of the time it does."

He leaned back. "You know what I like about the speed gun, Shane? It doesn't lie. I'm going to be straight with you. You've got the physical ability to pitch at the college level. No doubt about it. It's not your arm that worries me, it's your head. Nearly every player who gets a scholarship to Portland, or to any college for that matter, has at least two excellent— and I mean *excellent*—years of high school baseball behind him. Most have three or four. Plus summer league experience. All you've got is half a season. You're a risk. But I like the way you've fought back, and my baseball team needs a closer. So I'm going to give your mom a call and introduce myself, explain who I am. And I'm going to watch you pitch Saturday.

If everything works out, this time next year you'll be playing baseball for the University of Portland Pilots." He stopped and smiled. "That is, if you're interested."

"I'm interested," I said quickly.

He slid a thick manila envelope over to me. "There's an application in there, and some information about the school. fill out the forms and mail them to the registrar. I'll be in touch. And keep your grades up."

For the rest of the school day I felt as if I might float off into space. A full scholarship . . . pitching at the college level—it was too good to be true.

When school ended I headed to the baseball field. That's when the nerves hit. As I was lacing up my cleats, my hands started shaking. So much was on the line. I wanted the scholarship for me, but I wanted it for Mom too. *If everything works out.* That's what Coach Dravus had said. My numbers had to stay good for the rest of the season.

That afternoon the ball felt strange in my hand. I couldn't focus on home plate, couldn't get comfortable on the mound. My pitches were wild, and they had no movement. Grandison noticed and came over. "Your arm okay?"

"It's fine."

"If something hurts, you tell me."

"Really, I'm fine."

"Well, go easy. Dravus will be at Saturday's game. You'll want to be sharp then. I promised him I'd give you two innings."

I dreaded going home after practice. Coach Dravus would have called. Mom would be excited, and I didn't know how to explain to her that if I pitched badly, I'd blow it all.

I hoped she'd left for work, but when I opened the door to the duplex, she was sitting next to Marian on the sofa, her eyes shining. "So tell us all about it," she said excitedly.

"There's nothing much to tell," I said. "They're just looking at me. I'm sure they look at lots of guys. Coach Dravus didn't promise anything."

"But did you like him?" Mom asked. "Does it seem like something you'd want to try?"

"Yeah. I guess. I talked to him for only a few minutes."

"Maybe someday you'll be a major leaguer," Marian chimed in.

"Don't be stupid. I'm never going to be a major leaguer."

"Your sister is just excited for you, Shane. Don't bite her head off."

"I'm sorry. Neither of you seems to understand. They're only looking at me. They look at lots of players. I pitch lousy once, and that's that."

Mom's voice changed. "Shane, whether you get the scholarship or not, that a college coach would consider you is an honor, and you should be proud of yourself, just as we're proud of you."

I stood facing her and Marian, feeling awkward, not knowing what to say. At last Mom glanced at her watch. "I have to go to work. There's an enchilada dinner in the microwave. Three minutes, then turn it and cook it another two." She kissed me on the cheek and went out.

"What's your problem?" Marian asked as soon as Mom had left.

"Nothing. Only don't ask me any more questions. Okay?"

"Don't worry. I won't."

I microwaved the enchilada dinner and ate it at the kitchen table. After that I did my homework. I was finished by eight. I put on my coat and went downstairs. "I'm going to the library," I said to Marian. She looked up at me. I knew she wanted to come along. "You can come if you want."

It was a clear, starry night—unusual for Seattle. I'd felt stifled and hot for hours. The cold air was calming. "I'm sorry I was mean to you," I said.

She looked over. "Why were you so mad?"

"I wasn't mad. I just want this scholarship so much. It would make everything easier, and I have a feeling I'm not going to get it."

"Why not?"

"I don't know. I just feel like I'm going to blow it."

"You won't, Shane. You'll do great." She paused. "Mom says that she'll try to go to some of your games. I'm going too."

I groaned. "Mom gets bored when I'm not playing, and she can't watch when I am. And you don't like the games either. You know it."

Marian shrugged. "She only said she was going to try. She'll probably never do it. You know how much she works."

We'd reached the library. For once it wasn't crowded, so I didn't have to wait for a computer. I typed in Shorelake Academy's website address, and after a couple of clicks I was on the baseball team's homepage.

I was hoping for individual statistics, but the website was nothing more than a list of the games Shorelake had played and the games still to come. I couldn't tell anything at all about Reese. Discouraged, I was about to log off when my eye happened to fall on their schedule. Shorelake had a game against O'Dea on Friday night on field one at Woodland Park. Our game wasn't until Saturday.

I logged off, waited while Marian checked out three books, and then started for home. The sky had become even clearer, the night air colder.

"Look at all the stars," Marian said. "There must be thousands of them."

I looked up. "There are millions more we can't see."

She stopped, and so did I. "Remember that time Dad took us camping at Diablo Lake?" she said. "When he woke us up in the middle of the night and made us get out of the tent and look at the stars?"

I smiled. "Sure, I remember. I was mad at him for waking me, but that sky was unbelievable, wasn't it? Way more stars than tonight even."

"A hundred times more, I bet. And shooting stars too." She paused. "Remember how he bought those glow sticks and then passed them out to all the kids at the campground so we could play tag late?"

"That was fun." I paused. "I wish we'd gone camping with him more."

"Still, we went every summer," Marian said. "Laura's dad has never taken her camping. He always says he's going to, but then he doesn't. It makes her mad."

CHAPTER 6 Woodland Park: I didn't think about it being the field where I'd hit Reese until I got there. It had been a full year, but when I saw the field, my stomach started churning, and I thought I might throw up. Then the nausea passed, and afterward came an odd sort of exhilaration. Maybe everything could still turn out all right. Maybe, on this night and on this field, I'd see that Reese was on his way back.

I didn't sit in the bleachers. I couldn't sit on the Shorelake side, not with Greg's, Cody's, and Reese's parents. And I couldn't sit on the O'Dea side. So I watched the pregame warm-ups from a spot near the bike jumps. Reese was out in center field running down fly balls. I'd been watching Kim Seung for months, and I'd thought he was the best. But good as he was, Reese was better. He didn't so much sprint after a fly ball as glide. It was beautiful. That's the only word to describe it.

After the outfield warm-ups, Shorelake took batting practice. Reese had only five swings, and the pitches were grooved. Still, he stung the ball three times, and he didn't look like a player who was afraid. Finally it was game time.

I figured Reese would be batting in the middle of the lineup. Fourth or fifth, probably, but no lower than sixth. That meant that at most I'd have to wait until the second inning to see him bat. And if Shorelake got something going early, I might see him at the plate in the first inning.

O'Dea's pitcher was a big left-hander. It was fastballs all the time, most of them right down the middle, though now and then he let fly with something wild. He was the kind of pitcher Reese used to feast on. In the first, he powered through Shorelake's lineup, three up and three down. But that was okay.

Reese had gotten a good look at him. He'd know what to expect when he got up there in the second inning. He'd be ready.

But Reese didn't bat cleanup, and he didn't bat fifth or sixth or seventh. I had to wait until the third inning before he finally stepped up to the plate. He was batting ninth.

Reese Robertson.

Ninth.

As he stood in, I remembered the confidence that had been in his eyes, in his stride, in the way he'd dug in to hit. All of it was gone. Now he looked worse than he'd looked in the summer. Worse than he'd looked in December, January, and February.

If I saw it from three hundred feet away, the O'Dea pitcher had to see it from sixty feet six inches. "Come on, Reese," somebody yelled from the bleachers.

The left-hander got the sign, then delivered. A fastball, on the inside part of the plate. Reese jumped out of the box as if it were going to hit him. "Strike one!" the umpire called. "Hang in there, Reese," a voice called out, and I knew it was Reese's dad.

The O'Dea pitcher came right back to the inside half of the plate. Again Reese jumped out. "Strike two!" the umpire yelled. Reese pounded his bat on home plate, trying to look determined, trying to look like a hitter. The next pitch was probably a foot outside. Reese stepped toward third base, reaching with his arms and waving feebly at the ball. "Strike three!" the umpire yelled.

Reese's second at bat came in the fifth inning. The O'Dea pitcher was wearing down, and Shorelake was coming back. There were runners on first and second with nobody out. This was when Reese had been his most dangerous. A pitcher reeling, teammates dancing off the bases. This had been his time. "Come on, Reese," I whispered. "Do it."

O'Dea's pitcher went into the stretch, delivered. Reese squared around and laid down a sacrifice bunt. It was a good bunt. The pitcher fielded it, and his only play was to first. Both runners moved into scoring position. But it was a bunt.

As Reese returned to the bench, his teammates surrounded him, clapping him on the back and high-fiving him as if he'd hit a home run. In the bleachers parents were up on their feet, giving him a standing ovation. He'd become a charity case: the scrub who tries so hard everybody roots for him. If I had been him, I'd have quit. I couldn't have taken it.

But he high-fived everyone, then picked up his outfielder's glove and sat down by himself at the end of the bench. He was playing it out, just like he told me he would. I left a couple of minutes later. I'd seen enough.

CHAPTER 7 On Saturday afternoon Coach Dravus came to our house for lunch. Mom took the day off and spent an hour cleaning. On the kitchen table she put out a bouquet of flowers she'd bought at Safeway. "He's just a baseball coach," I said to her. "He's not the president."

But in the hour before he came, I kept looking out the window for his car. And when he was five minutes late, I started worrying he wouldn't come. Finally the car pulled up, and a minute later he was sitting on the sofa, a cup of coffee in his big hands.

It was awkward at first; nobody seemed to know what to say. But then Coach Dravus noticed one of my mom's books on the coffee table. "Do you like mysteries?" he asked, picking it up.

"Oh, yes," my mother replied. "Very much."

"So do I," he said, and then they were off, talking about different authors and books. Marian and I just sat looking at each other. Mom had made ham sandwiches for lunch. I could hardly eat, and Mom was the same. But both Marian and Coach Dravus made up for us.

After lunch we went back to the front room, and he started talking about the university. It turns out it's a Catholic school, which I hadn't known, and neither had Mom. "We're not Catholics," she said.

"That's not usually a problem," he said. "There are some religion classes that Shane would be required to take. Mainly the history of religion. So unless you object to Christianity . . ."

Mom flushed. "Oh, no, nothing like that. I was raised a Lutheran. I always intended to have Shane and Marian go to church, but somehow there just never seemed to be time."

He nodded. "Mrs. Hunter, I wish I could promise Shane a scholarship this very minute. But I can't. At this point all I can tell you is that if you're interested, we're interested. Time will tell if it can all be worked out."

I knew what that meant. I had to keep pitching the way I had been pitching.

The drive down to West Seattle was awkward. I was used to sitting in Grandison's van with Miguel, joking with him to cut the nervousness. Now I was by myself, looking out the window while Mom and Coach Dravus talked about the beauty of Puget Sound and how nice it was to live near water.

It was a relief to reach the field, find Miguel, and start loosening up with him. He asked me a bunch of questions about the visit by Coach Dravus, but I barely answered.

Dravus was up in the stands sitting next to my mother. She was looking at me, but his eyes were fixed on Kim Seung, who was running down fly balls in the outfield. Kim knew he was being watched, because he went after everything as if it were the World Series. finally Dravus's eyes shifted to me.

Immediately my palms became sweaty. My next throw to Miguel was probably twenty miles an hour faster than the throw before. "Ow!" he said, but then he spotted Dravus watching me, and he smiled. I fired the next five or six pitches at him, and he didn't complain.

West Seattle was like us—a team on the rise. Their school had been rebuilt, and they had some dynamo principal whom everybody loved. The baseball field where they played had been remodeled, and the stands had a fair number of adults and kids.

Right from the start the game was close. Miguel was sharp, striking out half the guys he faced. The only hits West Seattle had were little infield squibbers that nobody could get to and a two-out double. After four innings, they didn't even have a base runner reach third.

West Seattle's starter was matching Miguel. Only Kim hit him hard. He'd lined a single to center his first time up and his next time up had crushed another line drive right past the third baseman for a double.

In the top of the sixth, the West Seattle pitcher struck Jason Crandle out on three pitches, and then got Dirk Becker to pop up. Two outs, nobody on—it looked like another dead inning. But then Pedro Hernandez smacked a fastball right back up the middle and into center field for a single. Benny Gold followed with another hard-hit ground ball, this one past the first baseman and into the right field corner, an easy double. If I'd been coaching at third, I'd have sent Hernandez to the plate. Grandison held him up, though, and it turned out to be the smart play. The throw from right field hit the cutoff man perfectly, and he fired a strike to the plate. Hernandez would have been out by twenty feet.

Two outs, runners on second and third, and Brian Fletcher—our number-nine hitter—stepped to the plate. From the bench we shouted encouragement, but Fletcher had never come through with a clutch hit in a close game.

The West Seattle pitcher bounced his first pitch up to the plate, and only a good block by the catcher prevented Hernandez from scoring. I knew the next pitch would be right down the middle. I hoped Fletcher knew it too and that he'd take a swing at it.

The pitcher checked the runners, then delivered. A fastball, right down the middle. Fletcher's bat whipped through the hitting zone and caught the pitch solid, sending a line shot to right center. For a split second I thought he'd hit it too hard, that it would hold up for the right fielder to catch. But then I saw the fielder pull up. The ball bounced once, and Fletcher was standing at first with two RBI and a huge grin on his face. A second later I heard the magic words from Grandison. "Hunter, get loose."

At least Kim gave me time to get warm. He fouled off

about a half dozen pitches before finally lining out to deep center field—another great at bat, even if he did make an out. He had to have impressed Dravus.

I trotted out to the mound, bent over to stretch out my back, then made my final warm-up tosses to Gold. I stepped off the mound and rubbed up the baseball. This was it. This was my chance.

I climbed back onto the mound. The batter took a couple of practice swings, then stepped in. The umpire motioned for me to pitch. "Batter up," he called, and the game was on.

I knew the hitter. Miguel had handled him easily. He had a long swing that made it impossible for him to get around on a fastball like mine. Gold put down one finger. I nodded, went into my wind-up, and delivered. But instead of my good fastball, what came from my hand was a nothing pitch, a batting-practice fastball. The batter was all over it, sending a line shot whistling past my ear into center field.

I had to bear down.

The next hitter was a little guy, no more than five four or five five. He crouched at the plate, too, making his strike zone minute. I should have ignored him and thrown right at Gold's glove. Instead, I let his size get into my mind, and four pitches later he trotted to first base with a walk. Two on, nobody out. I looked up into the bleachers. Coach Dravus was leaning forward, elbows on his knees, chin in his hands.

I felt it then, the same dizziness that had come over me the year before, that same roaring in my head. It was as if I were about to topple into a huge hole. Grandison called time and trotted out. "You sick? Because if you are, tell me and I'll get you out of here."

"I'm fine."

"You don't look fine."

"I'm fine," I repeated.

"All right. Now listen. The next hitter is a lefty who likes the ball low and inside. So you keep it chest high and you keep it outside. Understand? He's not fast, so if you can get him to hit a grounder, we'll double him up."

I nodded. Grandison trotted off; Gold crouched down. I saw myself throwing the perfect pitch, the high strike on the outside corner. I knew I could do it. I checked both runners, but as I made my move to home plate, the roaring came back. Instead of finding the outside corner, I threw right into the hitter's wheelhouse, to the very spot Grandison had told me to stay away from. The batter took what looked like a golf swing at the ball, but he caught it solid. The ball rocketed down the right field line, high and deep, but hooking toward foul territory.

I looked to the umpire. No one breathed. Then came the call. "Fair ball!" He twirled his index finger to indicate a home run. Just like that, West Seattle was ahead 3–2.

I don't remember the rest of the inning. I got through it somehow, though West Seattle did score another run. We went down in order in the top of the seventh. The final score was 4–2.

I'd blown the game, blown my chance for a scholarship, blown everything.

As I stuffed my gear into my warm-up bag, one teammate after another came by. "It happens. . . . Next time. . . . Forget about it. . . . Lucky swing."

I felt weak in the legs. I wanted to bury my head in my

hands, but I forced myself to look them in the eye, to say something.

"You've got a nice, smooth delivery," Coach Dravus said in the car as we drove home. "I like the way you use your legs. You'll avoid injury that way."

"Thanks," I said, then I looked out the window. After that no one spoke.

When we reached our house, Mom invited him in. "I'd better get on the road," he said. "I'm driving back to Portland tonight."

"Can I at least make you a cup of coffee?"

"No, but thank you. The sooner I'm off, the sooner I'll be home." Then he turned to me. "Keep your chin up. Even the best closers blow a save now and then."

Inside the house I dropped onto the sofa. "I blew it. I'm sorry."

"You did your best," Mom said. "You can't do any more than that."

"That's just it. I didn't do my best. I choked."

I sat for a few minutes feeling sorry for myself. "I'm going to take a shower," I said and headed for the stairs.

"Wait a minute, Shane," Mom said. "There's something I want to say."

I turned back. "What?"

She paused. "Maybe you did lose your chance at a scholarship today. I don't really know. What I do know is that I saw something today that matters more than any scholarship. You're growing up, Shane. And I like the young man you're becoming, much more than I liked the boy you were."

I looked at her, confused. "What was wrong with me?"

"Nothing was wrong with you."

"Something must have been, or you wouldn't have said what you just said."

She paused. "Promise not to be hurt."

"I promise. Just tell me."

"Okay then. Until this year, I never liked the way you talked about your teammates. It was as if they were just sort of *there* as a backdrop for you and all the great pitches you made. Today I could see that those are your friends, that you care about them, and that they care about you. I liked seeing that."

CHAPTER 8 At the next practice, Miguel pulled me aside. "We need you to hang in there. There are still lots of games left."

For a while I was perplexed. What was he worried about? Then I knew. "Don't worry, Miguel. I won't quit. You might want me to, if I keep stinking it up, but I'll keep trying."

"You won't stink it up."

Grandison was worried too. He had me throw twenty-five pitches, at full speed. I smacked Benny Gold's glove with throw after throw, and a thin smile came to Grandison's face. "Looks good," he said. But he knew what I knew. The problem wasn't my arm.

Our next game was against Nathan Hale. Hale was a decent team, 5–5 or something like that. They came out swinging, scoring twice off Cory Minton in the first inning, and they kept that two-run lead through the first four innings. But in the fifth their shortstop booted two ground balls in a row, and we jumped on them. Gold smacked a long double to tie the game, and he scored the lead run on a single by Jeff Walton.

In the sixth Grandison sidled over to me. "Minton can't make it, Shane."

"I can close it out," I said, hoping it was true. "Just give me the ball."

Warming up along the sidelines, I felt incredibly nervous. But was it the good nervousness, the nervousness that meant I'd be sharp? Or was it the first sign of disaster?

We went down in order in the top of the seventh. Grandison, trotting in from his third-base coach spot, pointed toward me. I nodded, then hustled to the mound.

Gold came out and handed me the ball. "Let's win this thing," he said. Then he returned behind the plate. As I took my warm-up tosses, waves of heat and cold took turns rolling through my body. The umpire called out: "One more." I threw a final pitch to Gold, who fired it down to second. The ball went around the infield, then came back to me.

Nathan Hale's batter stepped in. I stared at Gold's glove, then went into my wind-up. This was it. I rocked back, and suddenly all the tightness seemed to go away. My arm felt loose as a whip, and the ball came out of my hand with speed and accuracy.

Then something I wasn't ready for happened. The batter swung, sending a dribbler out in front of home plate. Instead of pouncing on the ball and firing to first, I stared at it as if it were a hand grenade. I'd been so focused on my pitch that I'd forgotten everything else. finally I broke for the ball. Picking it up on the run, I made an awkward throw toward first. The ball skipped wildly past Pedro Hernandez, and the runner cruised into second.

I looked at Grandison, at my infielders. They thought I was going to choke away another game. I rubbed up the baseball as the next batter adjusted his batting gloves and then stepped in. He was a little guy with a bit of a gut. I'd watched him take his cuts against Minton. His bat was slow; I could blow the ball right by him.

And that's what I did. He never even managed to swing at any of my pitches. But my fastball had so much movement that I ended up walking him on a 3–2 pitch that barely dipped outside.

I stepped off the mound and rubbed up the baseball. For a second I held the ball in my fingertips. My arm still felt loose. I climbed back onto the mound.

Behind me, the infielders were quiet, too tight to chirp at the batter. Gold put down one finger, then pointed to the ground. The low fastball. I nodded, checked both runners, and fired. I took something off it, hoping to get the batter to swing.

It worked. He went after the pitch, catching the top half of the ball and sending an easy two hopper to short. Brian Fletcher fielded it, tossed to second for the force. The relay back to first was in plenty of time to complete the double play.

From the bench Grandison called out, "That's it, Shane. Just like that." Behind me voices came alive. "You're the man, Shane."

All we needed was one more out.

I looked at the runner dancing off third, but that was only a habit. All my attention was on the hitter. Pure heat. That's all he was getting. I wasn't taking anything off my pitches.

"Strike one!" the umpire yelled as the first pitch blew past him. "Strike two!" he yelled when the second did the same. The batter stepped out and took two vicious practice swings as if there was no way in the world he was going to watch a third strike go by. But my third pitch was the fastest. The bat stayed glued to his shoulder. "Strike three!" the umpire yelled, and he peeled off his mask and headed off the field as my teammates rushed the mound.

CHAPTER 9 Before the next practice Coach Grandison called the team together. "I've got some good news. Kim Seung has accepted a scholarship to play baseball for the University of Southern California."

Immediately we let out a cheer, then crowded around Kim, patting him on the back, tousling his hair, and congratulating him. "Those USC pitchers are going to love having you in center field," I said when it was my turn. "You've made me look good." Kim, normally so stone-faced, couldn't keep from smiling.

After I did my usual throwing along the sidelines, I went to the outfield and ran and ran and ran, my mind churning. It was all over. With Kim committed to USC, no college coaches would bother with our games. I hadn't known I was still hoping for a scholarship until there was no hope.

After that, Kim was loose and happy, laughing all the time. It turned out that he knew more English than he'd let on. "Talk about pressure," Kurt Lind told me at one practice as we tossed the ball around. "His whole family was watching him. Aunts, uncles, sisters, brothers, grandparents. They were all waiting for that scholarship. Even his relatives in Korea were waiting. He must feel a hundred pounds lighter now."

In a different way, Kim's scholarship took the pressure off me, too. I stopped peeking up into the stands to see if college recruiters were there. I just played.

And the team went on a roll. We steamrolled Redmond, Cleveland, and Eastside Catholic. We lost to Roosevelt when Miguel couldn't find the plate and walked seven batters in the first two innings, but then we got right back on track with two straight wins over Garfield to end the regular season. Whitman High hadn't won the Metro title in twenty-two years, but we won that year, and we won it easily.

"We're in the district tournament," Grandison said when he called us together. "I don't know how we'll do. Maybe we'll win the thing and make it into state. Maybe we'll lose two straight and go home. The main thing is, we're going."

The McDermott twins had filled a cooler with ice water. As Grandison was talking, they sneaked around behind him, each holding one end of the cooler. Benny Gold grinned. The idea was to dump the water over Grandison's head, but Gold's grin alerted him. Grandison turned to see what was going on behind him just as the McDermotts let the ice water fly. Instead of getting it over his back and neck, he took it right in the face. For a second, you could see his body tense with anger. But just for a second. When he turned back to the rest of us, a smile was on his face. Somebody started singing "For He's a Jolly Good Fellow." It's got to be the world's dumbest song, but we all joined in at the top of our lungs.

CHAPTER 10 There was a buzz around school, but nobody expected us to go far in the tournament. The suburban schools and the private schools always crush the city teams. Still, you never know. After practice on Monday, Grandison led us into a meeting room in the gym. Posted on the wall was a chart of the tournament. At the far left were lots of lines with high schools' names on them. Explorer . . . Juanita . . . Overlake . . . Kentridge . . . Shorelake. I spotted our name about three-fourths of the way down. As games were played, teams would lose and be eliminated. At the far right of the chart there was only one line with room for the name of only one team. Underneath that line were the magic words "District Champion—to State Tournament." Grandison stood in front of the chart. He was barking at us. "Take it one game at a time, or you'll get your heads handed to you on a plate." But he couldn't keep us from dreaming.

When he finished explaining how the tournament worked, he dismissed us. I was almost out the door when he called my name. "Shane, stay here a minute."

Something in his voice made me nervous, and I grew more nervous when he closed the door behind the last guy to leave the room. Miguel looked back through the window at me. I shrugged.

Grandison sat in one of the blue plastic chairs. I did the same. "Coach Dravus is coming to Saturday's game."

"To see me?"

"Well, he's not coming to see *me*. I've been sending him regular reports on you. Strikes, balls, hits, runs, all that sort of stuff. His team is up here for games against UW this weekend." I must have gone pale. "You just keep pitching like you've been pitching, and everything will be fine. Okay?"

"Okay."

He looked at the clock. "Now get out of here. I've got things to do."

CHAPTER 11 Our first tournament game was on Monday, against Woodinville at their field. The school sat on a hill, with the playing fields spread out below. It looked more like a college than a high school.

Miguel had been our best pitcher for weeks, so Grandison had everybody shaking their heads when he picked Cory Minton to start. It made no sense. Then, watching Minton warm up just before game time, I understood. Cory was a three-year letterman. He'd stuck with the team through tough times. He deserved the start, and Grandison was right to give it to him.

On the bench before the game, we were tight. If we could just get a run in the top of the first, everybody would relax. And it looked as if we would, too. Kim Seung hit the first pitch into right field, a sinking liner that seemed like a cinch base hit, maybe even a double. But Woodinville's right fielder made a sliding one-handed catch that brought their fans to their feet. After that, Kurt Lind and Tim McDermott went down on easy groundouts.

Minton took the mound. I watched his final warm-up tosses, but you can't really tell anything from warm-ups. I clapped my hands. "One, two, three," I shouted.

The Woodinville batter stepped in, a lefty with a short stroke. Minton threw a ball, then a strike. With the count 1–1, the hitter laid down a perfect drag bunt. Startled, Minton got a late break on the ball, and our second baseman was way too deep to come in and make the play. The Woodinville guy flew down the line, safe at first.

That bunt single rattled Minton. The next hitter was trying to bunt the runner to second, but Minton was so wild he couldn't do it. Four straight balls, none of them close, put runners at first and second.

Brian Fletcher did the right thing. He trotted in to talk to Minton. I could read his lips. "Keep the ball down," he was saying. "A ground ball, and we'll turn a double play and get out of this."

I leaned forward, hoping for just that. Minton stretched, checked the runner, delivered. A fastball, right down the middle, belt high. The Woodinville hitter swung so hard he almost came out of his shoes. The ball, hit solidly, rose in a high arc against the sky. When it came down, we were three runs behind.

It got worse. A walk, a stolen base, and a single to center brought home a fourth run. Minton struck out the next hitter for the first out of the inning, and the batter after that lined out to third. But the following hitter blooped a double down the first base line. The runner, off on contact, scored the fifth run of the inning when Benny Gold couldn't handle the throw from the outfield. When the third out was finally made—on a comebacker—the guys trudged in, heads down.

Grandison walked up and down the bench, clapping his hands. "We've got six more innings to play, gentlemen."

Right on cue, Jim McDermott took the first pitch he saw and whistled a line drive past the pitcher's ear and into center field for a single. On the very next pitch, he took off for second. It's usually bad baseball to try to steal when you're down a bunch of runs. Get thrown out, and you look like an idiot. But even though the Woodinville catcher threw a strike, McDermott beat the throw with a headfirst slide. He made third on a groundout and scored a run on a sacrifice fly. The score was 5–1 as we took the field for the bottom of the second, but at least we'd started on the road back.

And we kept coming back. Minton settled down and retired Woodinville in order in their half of the second inning. In the third, Gold walked, took second on an infield out, and scored on Kim's double: 5–2. In the fifth Pedro Hernandez took a 2–0 pitch over the fence down the line in left: 5–3. Grandison had me warm up during our half of the sixth. "If you can hold them," he said to me, "we'll win. I can feel it."

I could too. We all could. It was a strange thing to be down two runs with one at bat left and still feel confident, but we did. Minton had held Woodinville in check with an assortment of junk pitches. Curve balls, changeups, the occasional fastball. I came in and threw nothing but heat, and they weren't ready for it. It didn't hurt that the umpire suddenly seemed to be in a hurry to go home. Every close call went my way. I struck out the side, throwing a total of twelve pitches. When we came in for our last at bat, guys were whooping as if we were ahead.

Fletcher was first to bat. He worked the count to 2–2, then took a good swing at a fastball right down the middle. Had he hit it solidly, the ball would have gone sixty miles. But he was just a tad under it, sending a sky-high pop-up into short center. Woodinville's center fielder had to play the wind, but he stayed with it and made the putout. On the bench, guys went quiet.

But they didn't stay quiet, because on the first pitch he saw, Kim smacked a single into right. Lind followed that with another single back up the middle. The two of them then pulled off a double steal, putting the tying runs in scoring position. The game was right there, waiting for us to grab it.

Tim McDermott was at the plate. The pitcher took his time, working inside and out, until the count reached 3–2. I remembered how big the umpire's strike zone had been for me. "Be a hitter!" I screamed out, but McDermott took the pitch. "Strike three!" the umpire yelled, and we all groaned.

We were down to our last out. Woodinville's coach called time and ran out to talk with his pitcher. The guy was just about done. Drops of sweat were rolling down his face. He nodded his head up and down way too fast. Miguel punched my arm. "Shane, we're going to win this game. I can feel it."

"Play ball," the umpire called out. Woodinville's coach trotted off the field. Jim McDermott stepped in.

He was looking for a first-pitch fastball, and he got it. His swing was fast and fluid, and at the crack of the bat we all started screaming. The ball rose high and deep in the air to straightaway center. The outfielder turned and went back on the ball, to the warning track. He stopped at the fence and leaped. A second later he was running toward the infield, holding the ball aloft, a huge smile on his face. The Woodinville players surrounded him, grabbing at his hat and jersey, delirious with joy.

CHAPTER 12 It's hard to get up for practice so late in the season, especially after a loss. You've done drills so many times that they're a bore. So I wasn't looking forward to Tuesday's workout.

We stretched as usual, but instead of having us break off into our different groups, Coach Grandison called us together. "I liked the way you fought back yesterday. I was proud of you, and you should be proud of yourselves. So I don't want to see anybody with his head down. You hear me?"

We all nodded.

A smile formed on his lips. "We're going to do things differently today. Change things up. Instead of regular drills, we're going to play a game I like to call Maniac."

I can't begin to describe how the game works. All I can say is that Maniac is the right name for it, because that's what you needed to be in order to win. Grandison pulled out about two dozen rag baseballs, the kind they use with little kids. There were two teams. The guys on one team would stand in the vicinity of home plate and hammer ground balls as fast as they could at the guys on the other team, who were all playing different infield positions. The idea was to field as many as possible and throw to the first baseman. But with so many balls flying around the infield all at once, it was total chaos.

After Maniac, we played Demon. At first this game didn't seem quite as crazy because the balls were thrown, not batted. But after a couple of minutes, balls were coming at you from two or three directions, and if you weren't looking, you'd get beaned.

Grandison kept the games going fast and furious all through the practice. The two hours flew by. Later, in the locker room, we were still laughing about balls that had bounced off somebody's head or butt.

Before heading to the bus stop, I slipped into the room with the big tournament chart hanging on the wall. Grandison had filled in the results. I saw our name in the losers' bracket. It would be a tough road from down there to make it to state.

I was about to leave when something caught my eye. I looked back and saw that Shorelake had also fallen into the losers' bracket. Kamiak had nipped them 4–3. Their name was just a couple of slots above ours. I followed the little lines as they moved to the right. Then I followed them again. I started to do it a third time but stopped myself. It was clear. If they won, and if we won, we'd play each other on Saturday.

After school on Wednesday, Coach Grandison met Miguel and me and a couple of other guys. We were playing in Marysville, and he was worried about traffic on I-5. "I don't want to forfeit," he said, "so be ready to go." As it turned out, we made it to the field with an hour to spare.

All through warm-ups Miguel talked loudly to anyone who would listen, a smile on his face. He did the same in the top of the first as our guys batted. But when Tim McDermott popped up to end the inning, Miguel grabbed his glove, then turned to me. "I don't think I can do this."

"You can do it, Miguel," I said. "You can do it."

As he warmed up, Grandison came and stood by me. "He's going to do great, Coach," I said. "Don't worry."

Grandison looked at me. "You sure?"

I shook my head. "No."

He smiled. "I guess that's why we play these games, isn't it?"

"Play ball!" the umpire yelled, and the Marysville batter stepped up to the plate. He tugged on his gloves, his pants, his gloves again. He took a practice swing, then another. finally, he stepped in. Miguel looked at Benny Gold, nodded, went into his wind-up, and fired. "Strike one!" the ump called, and some of the tightness went out of Miguel's face.

He struck the first batter out, getting him to swing at a two-strike pitch in the dirt. The next two hitters went down on a pop-up and a groundout. Just like that, the first inning was over, and instead of being down a bunch of runs, we were knotted in a scoreless tie.

Rather than squeeze the bat to death, guys stayed loose. And loose muscles are quick muscles. A one-out single, followed by a walk, an error, and another single brought two runs across. For the first time in the tournament, we had a lead.

Miguel shut Marysville down in the second and third, working out of trouble in both innings. In our half of the

251

fourth, Pedro Hernandez lifted a leadoff fly ball to right center. Both the right fielder and the center fielder broke on the ball. It should have been the center fielder's ball. I don't know if he called for it or not, but the right fielder kept coming. They collided, and both of them went down as if they'd been shot. The ball dropped between them. Hernandez lumbered around the bases as fast as he could. By the time the second baseman had retrieved the ball, Hernandez was almost to third. Grandison waved him home. The relay throw was high and wild, and we had our third run.

As soon as Hernandez scored, the umpire called time out. The Marysville coach ran out to check on his players. The right fielder was up, but the center fielder stayed down, his legs swinging side to side. They had him lie there for a good five minutes. finally he stood up and, with everyone clapping for him, walked off the field.

I looked over to Miguel, and our eyes met. You never want to see an opponent hurt. Still, the center fielder had been their cleanup hitter, strong with speed. Now he was out of the lineup.

Miguel struggled again in the fourth. The Marysville hitters were working the count, taking as many pitches as they could. And the umpire's strike zone seemed to shrink. A single and a couple of walks loaded the bases with two outs. The number-three hitter then smacked a grounder up the middle and into center field, making the score 3–2. Miguel's eyes had a wild, scared look in them.

The four spot was up, the spot that should have been filled by Marysville's center fielder. Instead, his replacement stepped to the plate. Miguel's first pitch was over the batter's head, but he was so nervous he swung anyway. The scared look went out of Miguel's eyes; he knew he could get him.

He burned the heart of the plate for strike two, then fanned the hitter when he swung at another pitch up in his eyes. I was clapping for Miguel as he came to the bench, but his eyes went right past me. "Coach, I'm done."

Grandison turned to me. "Can you go three innings?"

As I took the mound for the bottom of the fifth, I knew I'd have to pace myself. If I went for strikeouts now, I'd be out of gas by the seventh inning. My pitches would come up in the strike zone, and the Marysville hitters would have a field day. I had to concentrate on location, not velocity. "Keep the ball down," I told myself.

My first pitch was so low it bounced up to the plate. I half smiled but then came back with a changeup about eight inches off the ground. The hitter beat it into the dirt toward third for an easy out. The next guy looped a single to right, but the batter after that bounced a one hopper back to me. I fired to second for the force-out, and the return throw was in plenty of time for the double play. I was out of the inning, and I hadn't thrown ten pitches.

"Let's get some runs," Grandison shouted as I jogged back to the bench, but we didn't manage so much as a hit.

As I trotted out for the sixth, I was tempted to bring out my fastball and try to power my way through two innings. But I had to keep pacing myself until I could see the end of the game. Only then could I cut loose.

The Marysville batters must have gotten some coaching. In the fifth they'd been up there swinging, making things easy for me. In the sixth, the first batter took a fastball that couldn't have been more than two inches outside for ball one; then he took another that I swear was a strike but that the umpire called ball two.

I stepped off the mound and rubbed up the baseball. If the hitter was taking, that meant I could split the heart of the plate and he wouldn't swing. Gold called for a fastball, and I threw a nothing pitch, a batting-practice fastball, right down the middle. The hitter's eyes lit up, but he let it go. "Strike one!" the ump yelled.

That was when he dug in. But he wasn't getting any more fat pitches. I threw him a hard fastball, low and outside. This time he swung, sending a sharp grounder right to first base. Hernandez fielded it and stepped on the bag. One out.

The next batter stepped in. As I started my wind-up, he went into that fake bunt routine that is supposed to distract pitchers. I put a belt-high fastball over the plate, and he was too off-balance to swing. Strike one.

Gold signaled for a changeup. *Why not?* I thought. I choked the ball in my hand and let it fly. The ball must have looked as big as the moon. The batter swung but was way out in front, sending a soft roller toward short. Brian Fletcher charged but tried to throw before he really had the ball. It rolled up his arm, then bounced off his belly. The tying run was on base. Fletcher picked up the ball. Head down, he walked over to me. "Sorry, Shane," he said.

"Forget that one," I said. "Because the next one's coming to you."

And it did. A two hopper that drew Fletcher toward second base. He fielded it on the run, stepped on the bag, and fired to first for another inning-ending double play.

"How do you feel?" Grandison said as I took my spot on the bench. "I could put Minton in if you're tired."

"I feel great."

We didn't score in our half of the seventh, so it was up to me to get the final three outs, with only one run to work with, which is the way I wanted it.

Based on how I'd pitched, the Marysville players must have thought I was a control pitcher, that my game was working the corners and keeping the ball down. Well, they'd find out differently. They were going to see three pitches from me: fast, faster, fastest.

The first batter, a guy with thick arms, had a long swing with a hitch in it. Gold gave me a target on the outside corner. I missed with my first pitch, but I didn't miss after that. The hitter swung so hard that he would have hit the ball into outer space if he'd connected. On strike three, he corkscrewed himself into the ground and then glared at me as he walked back to the bench.

Two outs to go.

I stepped off the mound to rub up the ball. My jersey was drenched in sweat, and sweat was rolling down my forehead. The next batter, a little guy who choked up on the bat, stepped in. My arm suddenly felt tired. But I wasn't going to give in to it. If Marysville was going to beat me, they were going to have to hit my fastball. I reared back and fired pitch after pitch.

They were strikes too. One after the other. The batter just poked at them, slapping foul ball after foul ball down the first base line, spoiling pitch after pitch. He worked the count to 1–2, then 2–2, finally 3–2. Grandison called time and came out to the mound. Gold trotted out to listen. "How about a changeup, Shane?" Grandison said. "He'd be way out in front."

I shook my head. "I'm not giving in."

"Your arm is going to fall off."

"My arm is fine. I don't want to walk this guy, Coach. I'm not sure I could throw a changeup for a strike. Not now, anyway."

"Okay, Shane. It's your game."

Gold went back behind the plate. I looked in for the sign. He showed one finger for fastball. I shook him off. He showed a fist for the changeup. I shook him off. The batter stepped out, confused, which is exactly what I wanted. When he stepped back in, Gold put down one finger again. This time I nodded.

I slowed my wind-up just a hair, but when I came over the top, I put every ounce of energy I had into the pitch. I think he must have been expecting a changeup, because he started after the pitch, then stopped. "Strike three!" the umpire yelled. My teammates on the bench were up, screaming. One more out.

Only I was done. My arm felt so tired I could barely lift it. And stepping to the plate was their number-three hitter. I don't usually take much time between pitches, but I did then. I had to.

Finally I stepped back onto the mound and looked in for the sign. Gold held down a fist for the changeup. I almost shook him off, but then I thought, *Why not?* The batter had to be expecting the fastball. How would he know I didn't have another fastball in me?

I gathered my strength and delivered. The ball went right down the middle, but he was out in front. He tried to hold back but couldn't. The bat caught the ball, sending a lazy pop fly in foul territory down the first base side.

There was no way Jim McDermott could reach it, but he took off anyway. I half watched as he raced into foul territory. But when he dived for the ball, I was more than half watching. He was going to come up short, I was sure, and when he didn't I was certain the ball would pop out of his glove. In spite of the impact from his dive, it didn't. It stuck out of the webbing of his glove like a snowball. The umpire's thumb went up into the air.

McDermott jumped to his feet, took the ball out of his glove, and, with his arms widespread and a huge grin on his face, raced toward the infield. We met him just behind first base, clapping him on the back and shaking him so hard his cap fell off.

CHAPTER 13 As soon as school ended on Thursday afternoon, I hustled over to the gym. I was the first player there. In the locker room I spotted Grandison. He was in the meeting room, a permanent marker in his hand, and was filling in the names of the teams that had advanced. When he saw me, he stopped.

"Is it Shorelake?" I asked.

"Yeah, Shane. It's Shorelake."

I wanted a tough workout at practice, but Grandison wouldn't let me pitch at all, and he stopped me when I started running hard in the outfield. "You need to be strong on Saturday. What you need is rest." He was right, if he was talking about what my body needed. But it wasn't my body I was trying to wear out.

When I opened the door to the duplex that night, Marian was on the sofa. She didn't have a book open, which was odd. She was just sitting there. "Mom at work already?" I asked.

She nodded. "How was practice?" she asked.

"It was okay."

On any other day I'd have gone into the kitchen and eaten dinner. But something made me sit down in the chair across from her. For a time she looked out the window. I didn't say anything. I just waited. Finally she looked back to me. "Do you think about Dad anymore?" she asked.

I felt my face go red. "Yeah. Sure I do." I paused. "Maybe not as much as I used to, but I think about him. How about you?"

She shrugged. "Not too much. But once in a while, when Mom's gone and you're gone, I'll pretend he's upstairs in his study like he used to be. There's nothing I really want to say to him. I just pretend he's up there with the door closed." She paused. "It makes me feel better for a while, and then I feel worse."

I picked a rubber band from the floor and played with it. "Stuff like that happens to me, too," I said at last. "As I was heading to the parking lot after our last game, one of the men

258

said: 'Way to go, son.' I knew he wasn't talking to me, but I still turned around."

Marian looked at me for a while, then stared out the window. "You don't think Dad was a criminal, do you?"

"I don't know, Marian. Maybe he was, maybe he wasn't."

"I don't think he was," she said.

We sat still for a while, then she reached for a book. "Mom will be mad if you don't eat the food she left for you."

CHAPTER 14 May weather in Seattle is hard to figure out. One day it can be as bright and sunny as a day in July, and the very next day it can be as cold and rainy as the worst days of January. Before I went to bed Friday night, I stepped outside and looked at the sky. I could pick out a few stars, which meant the clouds weren't thick. The last thing I wanted was a rainout.

Saturday morning broke cloudy and cool, but by noon the sun was peeking out. The Mariners game was on TV, which was perfect. For three hours I just stared at the tube. When the game ended, I ate half a hamburger and some fries Mom had bought at Zesto's.

Game time was six o'clock. At four-thirty we all piled into the car for the drive to West Seattle. Mom had arranged to take the night off. "I'd be thinking about you, and not the orders anyway. I won't make you more nervous, will I?"

I shook my head. "Nothing could make me more nervous."

"I think I'll take Marian to Starbucks," Mom said when

she pulled into the parking lot and let me out of the car. "But we'll be back for the game."

She drove off, and I headed to our bench. As I neared it, I spotted Coach Dravus talking with Grandison. They stopped talking when I approached.

"Good to see you again, Shane," Coach Dravus said as he shook my hand.

"Good to see you, too," I answered.

Grandison moved off to talk with Benny Gold.

"How do you feel?" Coach Dravus asked me.

"I'm nervous, but my arm feels really good."

Dravus looked toward the Shorelake players, who were beginning to warm up. "This is going to be a tough game for you. It's difficult to pitch against your former teammates."

I shrugged. "I know some of those guys, but it's been two years. Lots of them I don't know at all."

We both watched in silence for a minute. "Which one is the boy you hit?"

My throat tightened. "Number forty-four. He's warming up over by third base."

Dravus's eyes shifted in that direction. "How's he been doing?"

"Okay, I guess. But I don't think he's much of a hitter anymore."

Dravus nodded. "It takes time to come back from something like that. Well, I'll go find myself a seat in the bleachers and leave you to your game. Good luck."

Once Dravus was gone, Grandison returned. "What did he say to you?"

"Nothing, really."

"How's your arm?"

"Fine. I could pitch two innings, easy."

Grandison shook his head. "Forget it. You'll pitch the seventh, but no more. The last thing Coach Dravus wants me to do is blow your arm out. Now get out there and play catch with Miguel."

As Miguel and I tossed the ball back and forth, I peeked at the bleachers behind Shorelake's bench. I spotted Greg's parents, and Cody's. I saw a few girls I'd known, only they looked more grown up. Reese's parents were in the middle of the bleachers, surrounded by other parents I half recognized. I wondered if any of them were sneaking peeks at me, pointing me out, saying, "That's Shane Hunter, the kid whose father killed himself, the one who hit Reese." Waves of heat rolled through me. My face and ears reddened, and a few seconds later I felt as if the blood were draining out of me, and I was cold as ice.

At last it was game time. Grandison called us in, and we formed a circle around him. "Just play your game. That's all." He paused. "Let's do it!" We let out a roar, and the starters raced to their positions on the field.

What we needed was a clean top of the first. Guys who'd played against Shorelake the year before remembered how they'd crushed us, and the new players had heard about it. Besides, the name *Shorelake* was just plain intimidating— you're playing both the team and the tradition behind it.

I'd vowed to stay relaxed, but after the first pitch I was up on my feet, my fingers gripping the chainlink fence. "He's nothing," I shouted to Cory Minton. "Strike him out!"

Instead of striking out the leadoff batter, Minton walked him. Then he walked the batter after him. With two on and nobody out, he grooved a first-pitch fastball that was drilled into right center for a run-scoring double. The next hitter smacked a curve ball up the middle for a two-run single. The game wasn't five minutes old, and we were down 3–0. It was going to be just like last year. They were better than us. Plain-and-simple better. And they were going to crush us.

Grandison clapped his hands together. "Hang in there, Cory."

Greg Taylor was at the plate. He looked bigger and stronger than I remembered. Minton checked the runner, delivered. Again it was a nothing fastball, and again it was smacked, this time into right center. The runner on first took off, certain it was over Kim Seung's head.

But Kim had gotten a great jump, and the ball seemed to hold up in the wind. At the last second he stretched out, making a great running catch. Immediately he spun around and fired a two-hop strike to first base to double up the runner. The parents behind our bench rose and cheered, and they cheered again when Minton struck out Cody Miller to end the first.

Three runs.

It was bad, but not as bad as it could have been.

"Come on," I shouted as my teammates raced in. "Let's get some hits!"

I didn't know the Shorelake pitcher. He was no freshman

or sophomore, though, so he must have been a transfer. He had the stubble of a guy who needs to shave every day but hadn't for a week. He wore number thirteen, and he pulled his cap so far down that his dark eyes, hidden under the bill, were menacing. His first pitch to Kim was a fastball a foot inside. Kim jumped out of the way and then looked out. The pitcher scowled at him.

Kim stepped back in, then took a weak swing at the next pitch and sent a two hopper right to the bag at first. Kurt Lind tapped back to the mound for the second out, and Tim Mc-Dermott popped up to second to end the inning.

Minton started the second as badly as he'd pitched the first, walking the leadoff guy on four pitches. Next up was Brad Post, the player who'd taken Reese's spot in center field. I looked over to Reese. The guys around him were clapping their hands, calling out encouragement, but Reese just sat and watched.

Post was a big kid with a big swing—a pure fastball hitter. Minton threw him nothing but off-speed pitches, and Post finally struck out on a curve in the dirt. He swung so hard he nearly toppled over. That strikeout seemed to settle Minton. He went through the second inning without giving up a hit, and he gave up nothing in the third or fourth either.

If we could have scratched out a run or two, we'd have been right back in the game, but number thirteen just blew through our order. From where I sat, his pitches didn't look that fast. I thought he was as much bluff as anything, but I wasn't up there hitting against him.

Minton started the fifth strong, getting the first two batters easily, but the third hitter smacked a grounder right back up the middle and into center field. That brought up Post again.

All Minton had to do was throw off-speed stuff, little curves and changeups, and Post would get himself out. Instead Minton tried to sneak a first-pitch fastball by him. Post took that huge swing of his and connected, sending a deep drive into left center. For a second I thought the wind would hold it in the park, but then Tim McDermott looked up, the Shorelake fans screamed with joy, and we were behind 5–0.

The guys around me were pawing the ground with their cleats. We'd worked for months, won a bunch of games, and made the tournament. If we had to go out, at least we wanted to go out fighting. But this game was slipping away from us.

When the Shorelake players took their defensive positions for the bottom of the fifth, Post was on the bench and Reese out in center field. It didn't take long before he got into the action. With one out, Kim laced a line drive into center. If Post had still been out there, it would have dropped for a hit, but Reese raced in and made a beautiful shoestring catch. As he tossed the ball back to the infield, fans on both sides gave him an ovation.

That play mattered, too, because Lind doubled on the next pitch, and McDermott followed that with another single, bringing across our first run. All the guys were up and cheering, but the rally ended on a deep fly to right. "It's okay," Grandison called out as the inning ended. "We got one back. We'll get more."

Miguel pitched the top of the sixth. He was fresh, and the Shorelake batters were up there swinging, so he breezed through them one, two, three. I didn't know whether I was imagining it, but as the guys came in for the bottom of the sixth, there seemed to be a little hop in their step, a little fire in their eyes.

The top of the seventh was mine. As I headed out to warm up along the sideline, I glanced at number thirteen on the mound. His cap wasn't pulled down so far over his eyes; the scowl wasn't so set on his face. I looked at the Shorelake bench. Coach Levine was pacing back and forth in the dugout, but he had no relief pitcher up and throwing.

Pedro Hernandez stepped to the plate. Like all tired pitchers, number thirteen wanted to get ahead in the count. He started with a fastball, hoping Hernandez was taking, but Hernandez ripped it into left center for a standup double. I looked over to the Shorelake side. Still no sign of a relief pitcher.

Benny Gold was our next hitter. In his earlier at bats, he'd been overmatched. But not now, not with a tired pitcher on the mound and a runner leading off second base. Gold took a ball, then another, then lined a single into right field. Hernandez scored easily, and we were down three.

Dirk Becker batted next. He hit a sizzling ground ball down the first base line. I was sure it would skip into right field for another double, but the first baseman made a backhand stab and beat him to the bag for the first out. The Shorelake fans cheered, and our bench went quiet. But only for a moment, because Jason Crandle laced a 2–2 pitch into right field for an RBI single. Now the sweat was pouring down number thirteen's face.

I stopped throwing to watch Fletcher's at bat. If he made

an out, then the Shorelake pitcher might just be able to suck it up and finish off the inning. But if Fletcher reached base, we'd have Kim at the plate representing the winning run.

Thirteen checked on Crandle, then delivered. Ball one. The crowd quieted. Another pitch . . . another ball. "Get a walk," I whispered. Number thirteen took his stretch, came to the plate. Fletcher ran up on the ball and laid down a beautiful drag bunt. It dribbled past the pitcher, toward the second baseman. He raced in, but by the time he reached the ball, Fletcher was flying across first, Crandle was standing safely at second, and Kim was knocking the dirt out of his shoes on his way toward the plate.

"Strike him out!" someone shouted from the Shorelake side. I nearly laughed out loud. You never know what's going to happen in baseball. You can cream the ball and hit it right at somebody for an out. But I knew one thing wasn't going to happen—Kim wouldn't strike out.

He looked totally in control, even after he fouled off the first two pitches. It was as if he was waiting for *his* pitch, and on the 1–2 count he got it: a fastball, off the plate about three inches. Kim reached out and slapped it over the third baseman's head into the left field corner. Two runs scored easily, and Kim slid into third headfirst with a triple.

The game was tied.

Everybody was up on both benches as Lind stepped to the plate. Number thirteen's arm must have seemed as if it weighed one hundred pounds. He checked Kim dancing down third, delivered.

Lind should have been taking. He should have made the

guy pitch and pitch. Instead, he swung and lifted an easy pop-up to first for the second out.

Coach Levine called time and ran out to talk to his pitcher. He was buying him time, trying to get him a few minutes of rest so he could get that one final out. At last the umpire had had enough. "Let's play ball," he shouted, and Levine walked slowly back to the bench.

"Come on, McDermott!" I yelled. "Get a hit!"

The rest seemed to help number thirteen. He threw a fastball right down the middle that had some zip to it. "Strike one!" the ump yelled. McDermott backed out, then stepped back in. Another good fastball. "Strike two!" This time McDermott didn't back out. Number thirteen went into his wind-up. He came straight over the top with all he had.

Only it was too much. He overthrew the fastball, bouncing it about three feet in front of the plate. It skipped past the catcher and all the way to the screen. Kim flew down the base line and slid across home plate. We were ahead 6–5. On the next pitch, McDermott struck out swinging to end the inning. I threw a final warm-up pitch along the sideline and headed to the mound.

CHAPTER 15 Every coach will tell you that with the game on the line, you've got to block everything out and concentrate on what you're trying to do. But there was too much for me to block out. So I gave up and let it all in. My dad . . . my mom . . . Grandison . . . Kraybill . . . Dravus. Somehow I was aware of all of them. But most of all I felt Reese, down at the end of the Shorelake bench, a bat in his hand, staring at me. I made my last warm-up toss from the mound; the Shorelake batter stepped in.

This was it.

I blew out some air and got the sign from Gold. Changeup. Not a bad call to start a big inning. The hitter would be expecting a fastball, and the Shorelake team knew I had a good one. I nodded, then came to the plate. The ball must have looked like a watermelon to the batter. His eyes were as big as saucers, and he swung from the heels. Only he was way out in front. He tried to hold back but the ball squibbed out between the mound and third base. Becker charged in, trying to bare hand the ball and throw to first all in one motion. He almost pulled it off, but his throw sailed just over the top of Hernandez's outstretched glove and down the line into right field. The hitter hustled safely into second base before Jim McDermott could get the ball back to the infield. One pitch into the inning, and Shorelake had the tying run in scoring position.

Greg Taylor was up next. As he left the on-deck circle, he nodded to me, and I nodded back, and that was that. Once he stepped into the batter's box, he had one job: moving the runner to third base. I had one job: stopping him.

Greg was a decent hitter, but it had always seemed to me that he was overanxious. I threw him a fastball that was at least a foot outside, but he swung at it anyway, just like I thought he might. Gold, thinking along with me, put down the sign for a changeup. I nodded, then threw the best changeup of my life. Greg lifted a little pop-up toward third base. "I've got it," Becker called out. A second later he squeezed it for the first out of the inning.

Up next was a little guy I didn't know. He had an exaggerated crouch, choked way up on the bat, and waved it around slowly. It seemed as if his strike zone was about two inches by two inches. I was outside on the first pitch, high with the second, and then outside with the third and the fourth. He trotted down to first, and Shorelake had both the tying and winning runs on base.

"Throw strikes!" Grandison shouted.

I'd faced only three batters, but I was sweating as much as number thirteen had in six full innings.

Before stepping in, the next hitter took five vicious practice swings off to the side. I don't know what tipped me off. Maybe it was what Fletcher had done in the top of the inning or something in the way this batter held his bat; or maybe it was those exaggerated swings. But as soon as I delivered the pitch, I knew he was going to try to bunt his way to first.

It wasn't a bad bunt, but I pounced on it. I might have had a play at third, only I didn't want to risk making a bad throw, so I lobbed the ball to Hernandez at first.

Two outs . . . but now the tying run was at third—only ninety feet from home plate—and the winning run was standing at second.

It had been loud throughout the inning. Loud the way a baseball game is supposed to be loud. People screaming out advice and encouragement or just plain screaming. But as I walked back onto the mound, the cheering changed to a murmur, then a hush. I looked in at home plate and understood why.

Reese Robertson was walking toward home plate.

From our sideline I heard Grandison yell for time. A second later he trotted out to the mound. "Let's walk this guy," he said. "If we load the bases, we'll set up a force at every base. It's the smart play. Okay?"

He was trying to make it seem as if it was strictly baseball, as if he hadn't even noticed Reese. I wanted to nod and say, "Sure, Coach." But that would have been the coward's way.

I shook my head. "I have to pitch to him, Coach."

Grandison looked me in the eye. "All right. Then pitch to him." And with that, he trotted back to the bench. Reese took a final practice swing and stepped in.

Gold knew who was up. He called for a changeup on the outside part of the plate, but I shook him off. I had to go after Reese with my best fastball. That's what he'd want, so that's what I was going to do.

I checked the runners, paused, then fired. I was trying to put the fastball right down the middle of the plate, but the pitch sailed inside. Reese jumped back and out of the way, his helmet coming off in the process. "Ball one!" the umpire cried, and from the Shorelake side I heard a chorus of boos. "Watch your pitches, kid!" somebody yelled.

I took off my glove, rubbed up the baseball, and stepped back onto the pitching rubber. Gold put down one finger, but this time he set up on the outside corner. I stretched, my eyes focused on his glove, and I delivered. Reese let it go by. "Strike one!" the umpire yelled.

Gold tossed the ball back to me. I looked in for the next sign, but I also watched Reese's feet. He didn't move up in the batter's box. Gold called for another fastball on the outside corner. Again, I stretched, checked the runners, delivered. My arm felt strong; the ball rocketed to home plate. "Strike two!" the umpire called.

"That was outside!" some parent on the Shorelake side yelled.

"One more strike!" Grandison called.

Reese stepped out of the batter's box, adjusted his batting gloves, then stepped back in. Only this time, he moved closer to home plate.

I knew what was going through his mind. He was hoping I'd lay another fastball on the outside corner. If I did, he would try to poke it into right field.

I looked in for the sign. Gold called for another fastball. I nodded, but I wasn't going outside this time. I'd set him up for the fastball inside, set him up to strike him out. So that's what I had to do. I went into my stretch, checked the runners, and delivered. The ball flew out of my hand: a letter-high fastball that painted the inside corner. Reese jumped back as if it were close to hitting him. For a long second the umpire said nothing. At last, he brought up his right hand. "Strike three!"

A few seconds later guys were all around the mound, pounding me on the back and pumping my hand up and down. "Great game!" they said. "Way to go!" And I said the same things back to them. Grandison was in the middle of us, a huge smile on his face. I was turned this way and that, but I did manage to spot my mom by the fence waving excitedly, her eyes shining. Standing next to her was Coach Dravus.

After that we formed a line and shook hands with the Shorelake guys. They were classy, wishing us good luck in the tournament, telling us we could go all the way. When I reached Reese, I didn't know what to say. All I managed was "Good game."

"You too," he said.

I found my mother and started with her to the car. We were about halfway to the parking lot when Grandison's voice boomed across the field. "Whitman players, get back here!"

"What's he want?" Mom asked.

"I don't know," I said. "But he doesn't sound happy."

I put my equipment bag down and jogged back to the infield. Grandison was pointing to our bench area. "This is a mess," he said as a bunch of us approached. "I want you to clean up this garbage."

We'd been so excited about the victory that we'd left water bottles, towels, and half-eaten bags of sunflower seeds strewn around. In a few minutes we had cleaned it up. "All right," he said. "That's better. You can go now."

CHAPTER 16 On the ride home, Mom talked about how exciting the game had been and how well I'd pitched. I did my best to hold up my part, but I suddenly felt so tired and the game seemed so long ago that it was hard. I was glad to get home, head upstairs, and take a shower.

When I came out of the shower, Mom called me downstairs. Her eyes were beaming. "Coach Dravus called. He's coming over in a few minutes to talk to both of us. Shane, I think you're going to get that scholarship."

My stomach turned over. "It might not be that."

"You're going to get it," Marian said. "You know you are."

"It's not for sure," I snapped.

My mother put up her hands. "Stop it. Both of you. We should be happy, not bickering." She turned to me. "Why don't you go upstairs and read or something. It won't be long."

She was right. Within five minutes there was a knock. When I went downstairs, Coach Dravus was standing in the front room. "That was quite a game you pitched today," he said. "Lots of pressure, and you didn't back down. That last fastball was ninety-one miles an hour. Did you know that?"

"No," I said. "I didn't."

"I'm not going to beat around the bush, Shane. I'd like you to come to the University of Portland next year and pitch for us. I'm offering you a full scholarship."

Marian clapped her hands together. My mother smiled broadly.

"Would you like me to go over anything again before you decide?" Dravus asked.

I shook my head. "Not really. Can I just say yes?"

He laughed. "Yes, you can."

After that he took out a bunch of paperwork and went over it in the kitchen with Mom. I sat with them, looking at whatever he handed me, reading the rules and regulations that go along with a scholarship, or at least pretending to.

After a few minutes, the telephone rang. "I'll get it," I said, glad to have an excuse to get away.

It was Benny Gold. "Grandison just called me. He's got the back room at Zeek's reserved for us. A celebration, he said. What do you say?"

"I don't know if I can," I said. "Let me check."

I put my hand over the receiver and asked Mom. She turned to Coach Dravus. "Does Shane need to be here?"

He shook his head. "I think Shane should be with his teammates tonight."

I took my hand away from the receiver. "Yeah, Benny, I can come."

"Great. I'll pick you up in about five minutes. You're right on the way for me."

As I started upstairs to get my jacket, Mom came out of the kitchen. "Shane," she said, her voice low so that Coach Dravus couldn't hear. "Is something wrong?"

"No. Everything's fine."

She looked at me, unsure. "You don't seem very happy."

"I'm happy. Really, I am. I'm just in a state of shock."

"You want this, don't you?"

"Yes. Definitely."

CHAPTER 17 Benny's car pulled up a few minutes later. By the time we reached Zeek's, half of the team was already there. As soon as we walked in, we heard our names hollered from all around. The same happened whenever anybody new entered.

Grandison was way in the back. He had a huge slice of pizza in his hand, and he held it up to us and pointed to a table that had six different pizzas spread across it. I worked my way back to the food, loaded up my plate, then sat down in a booth near a table where Miguel and Pedro and three other guys were talking. Benny sat right across from me, which surprised me. Benny and I got along okay, but we'd never hung out together.

I ate a little, but mainly I listened to Miguel and the other guys. Their voices were loud, excited. All of the talk was about our season. "Remember that triple Kim hit against Bellarmine? . . . How about the catch McDermott made against Marysville? The one in foul territory. . . . That catch was great, but what about . . ." In the next hour, every key play in the season was relived.

I listened and smiled. If somebody asked me something, I answered. A couple of times I thought about telling everybody about the scholarship, but I didn't. I was glad Benny was sitting across from me. He was always a quiet guy, never saying much, never asking anything, and that suited me just fine.

At eleven Grandison tapped a spoon against his glass, then gave a speech full of the normal stuff. When he finished, everybody cheered. A couple of minutes later, Grandison left. Once he was gone, the guys started leaving too. At eleven-thirty Miguel reached over and shook my shoulder. "See you Monday," he said. A minute later, his table was empty.

The McDermott brothers were playing video games toward the front. Lind, Fletcher, and Crandle crowded around them, waiting for a turn. Only Benny and I remained in the back. For the first time all evening, it was quiet. Benny took a sip of his Coke, then looked at me. "It didn't feel right, did it?"

My stomach knotted. "What are you talking about?"

"Come on, Shane," he said, his voice soft. "You know what I'm talking about. I was the catcher, remember? He went down right in front of me. I can still hear the ball hitting him in the head. I can still see him lying on the ground, the blood pouring from his nose. And to win tonight by striking him out like that . . ."

He leaned forward, his voice still not much above a whisper. "You know what I was hoping when he stepped up to the plate? I was hoping he'd be the player he used to be. Imagine how incredible that would have been. You against him, with everything on the line. Even if he'd hit a home run and we'd lost, that still would have been something. You know what I mean?"

"Yeah," I said. "I know exactly what you mean." And I did.

The lights in the restaurant flicked on and off a few times. "That's it, boys," a voice called out. "We're closing."

We walked out to the parking lot and got into his car. Neither of us spoke as we drove up Greenwood, but at a red light Benny looked over. "Do you know where we play on Wednesday?"

"The rest of the playoffs are at UW."

"I've never played there. I hear it's great."

"That's what I've heard, too."

"And your arm's okay? Because we're going to need you."

"Don't worry about me, Benny. Whatever comes, I'll be ready."

We were silent the rest of the way to my house. He pulled into my driveway, and I got out. "Thanks for the ride," I said.

But before I could close the car door, Benny leaned across the seat toward me. "He could still come back, don't you think? If he works at it. Look at you. You struggled. You couldn't throw strikes; you couldn't throw hard. But you worked at it, and you made it back. You're the same player you were before you hit him. Right?"

I swallowed. "Yeah, Benny," I said. "I'm the same."

He nodded. I closed the car door and stood on the lawn as he backed out of the driveway and drove off into the night. Only then did I head up the walk to my home.

I hadn't lied to Benny. What I'd said was true. I was the same. Only I was different, too. Entirely different.

Date Due

SEP 1 0 2004		
SEP 2 7 2004		
MAR 2 2 2005		
APR 1 5 2005		
OCT 1 2 2006		
APR 1 7 2009		
JAN 0 5 2010		
MAR 2 2 2012		
SEP 2 4 2012		
SEP 2 7 2012		